Robbing the Pillars

by

Mike Breslin

Robbing the Pillars

FIRST SUNBURY PRESS EDITION
Printed in the United States of America
January 2011

ISBN 978-1-934597-30-9

Published by:
Sunbury Press
Lemoyne, PA
www.sunburypress.com

SUNBURY
PRESS

Lemoyne, Pennsylvania   USA

Foreword

This book has been in the works off and on for over ten years. During that time, my phenomenal wife Susan and my children, Erin and Michael, have offered encouragement and, more importantly, have generously given me the time alone to labor over it. For that I owe them an enormous thank you, and I dedicate this to them.

This is also a tribute to the miners who died in the anthracite coal fields of Pennsylvania. Official numbers say that some 31,000 men lost their lives in anthracite mines between the 1860's and 1950's. But there are many more who died in obscurity, their lungs filled with coal dust, their last years spent hacking their lives away in agony suffering from *pneumoconiosis*, known throughout the Coal Region simply as *Black Lung*.

I dedicate this book, too, to my parents. To John R. "Regis" Breslin, my Pop; the consummate story teller; the fabricator of 'factoids' that embellished his tales; the purveyor of his own weird brand of *Pop logic*.

One regret I have is that Pop never had the patience to teach me to shoot pool as well as he did, nor could he explain the intricacies of betting at craps. It was his prowess—ok, luck—with dice in an Oklahoma Army barracks that got him enough money to buy an engagement ring and a train ticket west for the love of his life—Lois Perrin.

To Lois, my Mom—well read, conversant, opinionated, and very outspoken. You never had to guess where Mom stood on an issue; she'd tell you straight out, whether you wanted to hear it or not.

Regis and Lois are both gone now, but I pray that they know about this book...and more so....that they approve of what I write.

Mom: I apologize, but there are a few cuss words thrown in to make the dialogue realistic. OK? Thanks. I know you'd understand.

Mike Breslin, 2010

Prelude

I smoke. Luckies, unfiltered. Stubby little things —white pack, red circle. That's the way they come now. The wrapper used to be green, you know. It was changed to white during the war so the military could use the green coloring to make other things that would kill people. The cigarette folks played up the change big time. "Luckies went off to war" was the spiel. I suspect they reaped a bunch a' goodwill with that. But to me and my buddies it didn't make any difference. They coulda' put the ciggies in pink packs, just as long as the Army kept doling them out like candy at Halloween.

Some fifty years into the habit I still savor the rush from my first morning smoke with a cup of coffee. After that, it's pure habit that has me lighting up one after another until by night my throat is raw. My addiction to them isn't something I'm particularly proud of, but I'm not about to lose any sleep over it if you don't approve.

Maybe you'll cut me a little slack if you hear how I got hooked on the wicked things in the first place.

I was nineteen years old, staring wide-eyed at the first human being I shot. It wasn't anything like standing over a downed buck in the woods. Back home I killed plenty of things: deer, pheasants, rabbits, even squirrels Did it since I was eight when the recoil from the hand-me-down single-shot twelve-gauge knocked me on my ass. I was putting food on the table—something to be proud of. Now I was a million miles from Pennsylvania outside some godforsaken village somewhere in France staring down at a dead man at my feet.

A few minutes earlier he was crouched behind a tree aiming a carbine at my chest. I guess it just wasn't my time to go. The cloud cover broke momentarily and I caught a reflection from a smear of grease on his weapon. I drew a quick bead and got my shot off before he did. One well-placed—call it lucky—shot just to the left center of his chest.

He didn't yell or thrash around like they do in the movies; he just flopped over dead. At least he didn't suffer. That's how I reconciled it. But how was I to know? That thought crossed my mind as I stared into the glazed-over lifeless eyes staring up at me. An empty, vacant stare. *You lucky son of a bitch* his eyes said.

A stubble-beard dirt-streaked sergeant walked up next to me and nudged me with his shoulder. I turned and saw his twisted grin. They called him Boss. I had never met him face-to-face but I knew him by reputation. Depending on whose story you believed, this guy had personally killed somewhere between eight and thirty-four krauts. When asked was the true count was, his reply was a shrug and a mumble, "Who gives a shit?"

"Good shot," Boss said, bending over to eye the neat round hole in the dead man's chest. With a mud-caked boot, he rolled the corpse over. Mushrooming inside the dead man's chest the peanut-size bullet from my rifle came out his back the size of a softball, creating a gaping raw crater and a pool of congealing blood on the ground. I sucked in air and swallowed the foul bile that rose in my throat.

"Held your sights on him till you were sure he was dead? Before you walked up this close...with your weapon tucked away like that?" Boss added, glaring at the rifle slung over my shoulder.

"Yeah, I guess so."

"Never guess and never park your weapon that way, you stupid..." Boss barked in my face, ending with something nasty about my mother. His breath was as foul as his language, and his index finger flailed it front of my face.

"I had two men shot dead when they walked up on krauts they thought they killed. A soldier who knows he's about to die is gunna' fake it. Lie down and pretend he's dead. And when you let your guard down...Boom!" Boss shouted, clapping his calloused hands together. He laughed as I jumped back. "Don't ever give 'em a chance to go out a hero and take you along. You shoot a kraut once and put him down, then shoot him again two, maybe three times for good measure. Bullets is cheap. You understand, boy!"

"Yes, Sir," I shouted.

"Shit!" Boss yelled, swiveling his head around. Turning back in my direction, his nose inches from mine, his foul breath in my face again. "Don't ever say 'sir' in the field. There ain't nothin' more than a kraut wants is to take out an officer—even a lowly shit-for-brains sergeant like me."

"Yes..." I stammered, stifling the urge to add the respectful "sir" that had been hammered into my head as the appropriate response to a superior.

Again using his foot, Boss flopped the dead man onto his back. I peered down again into the lifeless eyes staring up at me.

"Smoke?" Boss asked, shaking a cigarette pack in my direction. "Take it," he said, acknowledging my hesitation. "It'll take the edge off." His Zippo flared in front of the cigarette I pulled from his pack and held with shaking fingers to my lips. I leaned into the flame and sucked in the numbing nicotine for the first time.

The camaraderie of enjoying cigarettes over dead bodies was repeated countless times as we fought our way through France and into the freezing forests of Bastogne. Long before V-E Day every man in the unit—me included—was hooked on cigarettes.

But that was years ago, back in the days when smoking was right up there with baseball as a national pastime. We smoked in movie theaters, between courses in restaurants, and lit up instinctively every time we touched a cup of coffee. Those days we smokers were in the company of heroes—Boss, Roosevelt, Babe Ruth, Cary Grant, Churchill. It wasn't anything like it is now when buying a pack of cigarettes at the corner store makes people look down their nose at you like you're some kind of perverted drug addict. To hell with them. They'll never know what I've been through and what got me started on the darned things in the first place.

I smoke outdoors on the high back porch—a ritual I acquired after I returned home and married Anna. She couldn't stand the smell of cigarettes and she pestered me to quit, which I wasn't about to do. So in the end we compromised. I would smoke outside, and she would stop nagging me about it. "It's your life," she'd say, mockingly.

Anna died suddenly and unexpectedly three years ago. Lung cancer. And she never touched a cigarette in her life. Now that she's gone I can smoke any time and any place I please—even in the living room if I want to—but I don't. I still do my smoking on the back porch, heavy into it at night when most civilized folks are in bed. And it was my late night smokes that had me out on the porch on May 14, 1965.

That's where this whole thing begins. This story isn't about me, in case you're wondering. This is Jack Dugan's story. My name's Tom Haggerty, and Jack's father was my best friend.

Looking back on it now and considering all the mischief kids get into these days with their drugs and guns and gangs, you might say that what Jack did that night was no big deal.

But seeing as how it involved Jimmy Creedon, that notched it up big time. Here's how it started.

Part I -- DEFIANCE

Chapter 1

I was into my second, maybe third smoke of the night when I heard the sirens. There were two of them. From the way the sound traveled I knew they were moving toward the same spot, coming at each other from opposite sides of town. The sirens died as the cars converged.

When I first heard them I listened for a bit, only to confirm that they weren't coming my way. But from the sound I knew they were headed somewhere uptown and were of no consequence to me.

It was Friday night, so police sirens were no big thing. Nothing to get excited about, unless you were the reason they were headed your way. Friday was payday, and that always seemed to bring out the worst in folks.

On any given Friday you could safely bet that some idiot would lose a week's worth of pay in a poker game or some back-alley craps shoot or that an imbecile would empty his wallet in a tavern buying rounds for the house. In either case they'd eventually end up home, penniless as the day they were born.

The wife would begin yelling that the grocer had cut off the credit or the rent was two months overdue. The manly response would be a drunkenly thrown punch, which would usually result in a busted door or a hole in the wall. A neighbor would call the cops and the sirens would wail. Not an unusual event. Not for a Friday night in Creedonton.

Standing with my left foot on the lower rung of the back porch railing, I sucked the last heady draw from the tiny butt pinched between my fingers. My lungs filled, I exhaled a plume of smoke into the cold night air. With a flick of my middle finger I shot the spent cigarette out into the darkness and watched the glowing arc the butt made as it headed toward the yard below.

That's when I saw him.

He was in the alley that ran behind my house, on the far side of the rusty wire fence that corralled my scrabbly patch of crabgrass and dandelions.

Bent over low to the ground, he slinked from one hiding spot to another, making moves that no one would see, or so he thought. From behind the fender of McFee's decrepit Ford he dashed out and circled to the far side of the gnarled oak at the edge of Sheehan's yard. His next move had him crouched down behind the burn barrel at the rear of Novack's place.

From the moment I spotted him I stood at the porch railing rigid as a statue, breathing though my nose so the vapor of my breath in the cool night air wouldn't give me away. Breathing through the nose was one of the things I remembered from my Army days playing a deadly game of hide-and-seek with the German infantry.

Who was he? And what was he up to?

Two more moves had him crouched at the fence at the end of the yard of the house next door. I stepped back into the shadows as he straddled the fence and dropped down, squatting on his haunches like a toad. Then he made a run that took him to the steps of the neighbor's porch.

He stopped at the foot of the stairs and I clenched my fists, ready to wallop the bastard.

He sucked down a deep breath then made his final move. He mounted the steps taking them two at a time. On the porch he cupped his hands to peer through the kitchen door of the duplex that adjoined mine, then dropped a hand to the doorknob.

I made my move quickly. Side-stepping over the railing I lunged at his back. Bringing my arms down around his midsection I pinned his arms at his sides. Lurching backward I kicked his feet out, and we fell together in a rolling heap on the floor.

"Who are you and what the hell are you up to?" I hissed in his ear as he clawed at my hands trying to break my grip. He was strong and squirmed furiously but was no match for me. "Keep it up and I'll break your ribs," I said, jerking my locked hands deep into his chest.

"My house," he gasped.

"Jack? Jack Dugan?"

"Yeah," he wheezed.

My memory of the kid next door was of a skinny little twerp chasing lightning bugs around the yard with a Mason jar tucked under his arm. Somehow the years had slipped by and I found myself wrestling on the porch with a gangling teenager.

I released my grip and lumbered to my knees as he rolled onto his back, sucking down air.

"You 'bout scared the crap outta' me, boy. What the hell's goin on?

"Nothin'," he said angrily between gulps.

"Nothin'?" I replied, rising to my feet.

Truth be told I was relieved knowing I was dealing with the boy next door and not some boozed up burglar—or worse.

"Whatta' you doin' out here this hour 'a the night?" I asked, nudging his side with my foot.

"What's it to you, Haggerty?" he replied, staring at me with a nasty squint.

His flippant reply hit a nerve. Bending down, I put a clenched fist in front of his face.

"I'll tell you what's it to me! You come slinkin' up the alley like the devil's on your tail. Try to sneak into your house like some friggin' burglar. Darn right I want to know why. What're ya' up to?"

"You seen me?" he asked, cocking his head defiantly.

I laughed.

"You're darn right I seen you, boy. You come movin' up the alley. Hidin' behind McFees old car and Sheehan's tree an' such. After workin' the mines for thirty years, I got eyes better'n a cat. Of course I seen you. So I'm gunna' ask you one more time: What're ya' up to?"

"Nothin!" the boy hissed back.

"Them sirens," I said, motioning into the air with my head. "You have anything to do with them? You in some kinda' trouble? Tell me boy," I said, "Tell me the truth."

Chapter 2

Harry heard the sirens just seconds before the phone on the nightstand began to ring. He snatched the handset and rolled to his side.

"The phone," his wife mumbled sleepily.

"I have it, honey."

"Who is it?"

"Never mind."

"Dewey?"

"Yes, it's Dewey," Harry replied, his hand over the mouthpiece.

"Damned Dewey," she said rolling to her side, punching her pillow.

Harry swung his legs off the bed and pressed the phone to his ear.

"Yeah, Dewey. Yeah, I can hear you. Slow down. Where? You're sure? Okay. Dewey...Dewey, calm down, damn it! Yes, I'll go. Yes, I'll go NOW!"

"Oh, for the love of God, hang up!" his wife hissed as she burrowed under the covers.

"It's all right, Dewey," Harry barked into the phone. "I know it's important. Yeah, you did the right thing. Thanks for calling. Yeah, it's okay. Good night. Dewey it's fine! Goodnight! GOODBYE!" Harry slammed the receiver down.

"Dewey alarm!" his wife squealed.

"What'd you say?"

"Dewey alarm. What is it? Cat stuck up a tree?" she laughed from her blankety cocoon.

"No. It's important," Harry said rising from the bed, stretching to relieve the sleep knots from his shoulders.

"Two cats stuck?" she replied, laughing.

If she was ever pressed to express her true feelings about Dewey—the old widowed officer who manned the night desk—Harry's wife would be in line at the Confessional immediately afterward for the language she'd use.

Dewey had interrupted their sleep, dinner, and special occasions more times than she wished to recall. To Dewey everything was a catastrophe. A fender bender, a peeping Tom, a kid who didn't make it home by curfew. For Dewey, every incident had to go to the Chief, and she hated him for it.

"So what is it?" she asked, throwing back the covers.

Harry was at the closet pulling slacks from a hanger. "Dewey said somebody attacked Creedon's place," Harry replied.

"Attacked him!" she said, suddenly interested.

"Dewey said it was a rock or somethin' hit the house."

"A rock or somethin'!" Mary exclaimed, punching a pillow up behind her. "Well holy hell, no wonder Dewey calls the police chief at midnight! A freekin rock! Goodness," she said with a giggle, "maybe we'd better call the governor!"

"Come on, Mary," Harry said sitting down on the bed. "Knock it off. You know Creedon has pull. He just says the word and I'd lose my job tomorrow. I have to go. You know that, right?"

Smacking her lightheartedly through the bedspread, Harry rose and grabbed a shirt from a hanger. He wrestled into it as he walked to the staircase. "I'll give you the details when I get home. Okay?"

"Don't wake me, Chief," she called back. "The horrible details 'bout a rock attack can wait till morning. Good night.

"Calling all cars, calling all cars!" Mary squealed as Harry tiptoed down the stairs. "Dewey alarm. Dewey alarm. Somebody lobbed a rock at Creedon's place! Call the chief!"

Harry shook his head and smiled.

"Dewey, Dewey, Dewey," he muttered to himself.

Chapter 3

"The truth!" Jack shouted, staring at me with narrowed eyes. "You want the truth, Haggery! The truth," he hissed. "How 'bout the truth 'bout how my dad died? How 'bout that? Is that what you wanna' hear?"

"Oh, God," I mumbled. There was a wrenching knot in my stomach as I dropped down to kneel at the boy's side.

"You wanna' hear it? You sure you want the truth?" Jack pressed.

"Go on," I said.

The boy scrambled backward, crab like, till his back was against the wall. Wrapping his arms tightly around his knees he stared at me.

"I was at Neely's."

"Go on," I said. I knew the place he was talking about. I spent a good bit of time there myself before I married Anna.

"Me an' Tommy Delaney an' some other guys was playin' pool. Then Steck showed up. He got his brother to sneak us some beers, so we went out in the back yard under the high porch."

"You were drinkin' beer?" I asked, somehow not letting go of my memory of him as a little kid with a jar of fireflies.

"Yeah," he said with a smirk, "Celebratin' my birthday, in fact. Tomorrow I'm eighteen. An' having a couple'a beers ain't no big deal anyway."

Eighteen? Damn, time sure flies.

"Go on," I said.

"We was just drinkin' the beers, mindin' our own business. Then Tony Levansky an' his pals came out on the porch up above."

Tony Levansky. I winced.

"Levansky an' his pals were drunk...an' mad, too, 'cause Neely tossed them outta' the poker game for sand baggin' their bets."

Tony Levansky drunk...and mad. This isn't going to be good.

Tony Levansky is about as worthless a human being as you'll ever find. Everyone in town knows his story. His father was a fast-talking salesman who blew into the next town over one day with a pocketful of money and one thing on his mind. In a little neighborhood tavern he found just what he was looking for.

Sarah Levansky and three girlfriends had been celebrating since noon. Sarah had just turned twenty-one and, more significant, she was leaving town in two days to start nursing school.

"I'm goin' a' nurschin' shoool," Sarah slurred, wrapping her arms around the salesman. "You wanna' join my goin' way parry?"

Indeed he did. With a wad of cash he kept it going long into the night. Just as he had planned, Sarah walked out of the place in the wee hours hanging onto his arm. It was a mistake she'd regret the rest of her life.

The salesman left town the next morning and never came back. Four months later Sarah quit nursing school and moved into a small apartment in our town. Tony Levansky came into the world five months afterward.

She was on her own to raise the boy, which wasn't easy for an unmarried woman in the coal region. Most folks didn't give her the time of day; treated her like she was a whore.

Sarah took a job in one of the sewing factories that opened up when the mines began shutting down. Sweatshops that paid a pittance is what they really were. She worked like a dog trying to make ends meet and had no choice but to leave young Tony pretty much on his own.

Now some will say there's no such thing as a bad boy, but I disagree. Tony Levansky was rotten to the core. You name it, that boy he did it. Only six and no bigger than a pipsqueak he shot cats and birds with a BB gun, smiling as he watched them die. He became a pretty good thief, stealing candy and bikes at first. Later he moved up to cars and whatever else took his fancy.

Tony became a big mean teenager with a tripwire temper. He picked fights for the joy of pounding smaller guys into the dirt, and he always won thanks to the dirty tricks he learned from the lowlifes he hung with. His favorite was to clutch a roll of nickels in his fist, making his hand hard and heavy as a hammer.

When he did show up at school—which was rare —he was nothing but trouble. In his senior year he was finally tossed out for good. A teacher had caught him carving his initials on a desk and confiscated his knife. Tony stormed out of the building and came back later with a baseball bat, demanding she give it back.

That was the final straw, and Tony was standing before old Judge Clacker for the umpteenth time.

"How old are you?" Clacker asked.

"Eighteen," Tony spat back defiantly.

"Eighteen, eh," the old judge said smiling, leaning back, steepling his fingers on his chest. "You're longer a minor, boy. And that means I don't gotta' coddle you no more. It's obvious your mama can't handle you, but I think I know who can. It's about time you got some real discipline. I'll give you one last chance to turn your life around. The decision's yours."

Clacker smiled at the thought that he might finally rid Creedonton of its worst nightmare. "You got a choice, son. Join the Army or go to jail for a good long time."

Tony took Clacker up on the offer. But less than a year later the Army gave him a dishonorable discharge for beating a prostitute almost to death. Unfortunately for us, Tony decided to come back home.

Now when Tony Levansky's not drunk and draped over a bar, you'll likely find him in jail. He's about the worst you can find in a man. And I should know; I had the unfortunate experience of working with him for a little while, and I use the word "working" loosely. That lazy slug would slink off any chance he got, and more than once we found him curled up, sleeping off a binge. Just shy of three months he was fired after a foreman caught him trying to make off with a crate of dynamite. God knows what he had in mind for that.

The boy's mention of Levansky's name made my skin crawl. "Go on, Jack," I said, girding myself for how Levansky fit into the picture.

"Levansky an' his pals had a bottle a' whiskey an' they were passin' it around, gettin' drunker'n all get out. They began tellin' stories about workin' the mines, trying to outdo each other. The others was tellin' about bein' freezin' cold an' wet an' dirty an' about seein' rats an' other nasty stuff. All the while Levansky was just leanin' against the banister lettin' 'em go on. Then outta' the blue he yelled, 'That's chicken shit! Ain't none a' you ever see a man die the way I did. The worst thing I ever saw was how Andy Dugan got killed.'"

"Oh, God," I mumbled.

"He went on sayin' how the roof fell on my dad. An' then he began laughin' when he told what happened next."

"What'd he say?"

"That dad was pinned under a rock. A rock big as a car was on him and he was stuck under it, lyin' in the mud. Just his head an' his arms an' legs were stickin' out. But he was still alive, 'squirmin' like a bug', Levansky said. Like a bug!" Jack cried. "And he said dad begged you to kill him to stop the pain."

"Jack," I whispered. It was all that would come out.

"Is what he said true? That he was crushed an' he didn't die quick the way you told us. An' he asked you to kill him 'cause he was hurt so bad?"

I still couldn't find the words.

"If what Levansky said is true, that makes you a damned liar," Jack shouted. "You were there. You saw it. Is what Levansky said true, Haggerty? Is it?" he sobbed, daring me to deny it.

"Jack," I said. I reached out to touch him, but he batted my hand away.

"Crushed like a bug!" Jack shouted. "An' you an' the others watched...just watched. Watched while he begged you ta' end it! That's the real truth, ain't it?"

I was shaking and I felt the tears running down my cheeks. I squeezed my eyes shut, trying to blot out the memory. But I'll never forget that day. Levansky hadn't left out a detail.

"Levansky wouldn't stop laughin' about it, so I whacked him," Jack said, bringing me back to reality.

"What?" I said, my mind wrestling with the boy's statement. "What'd you say?"

"I yelled up at him from the yard. I said, 'You're a liar, Levansky! That's my dad you're talkin' about! That ain't what happened! Just shut up, or I'll kill you, you stupid drunk.' But he just kept on laughin'. So I picked up a rock an' flung it at him. Caught him right in the forehead."

I couldn't believe it. "You hit him with a rock! What'd he do?" I exclaimed.

"He smashed the end off the whiskey bottle an' held the neck like a knife. He started for the stairs yellin' 'You bastard. I'll cut ya' ta' ribbons you stupid little shit! I'll get you, boy.'"

"And...And...," I blurted, urging him to continue.

"His buddies grabbed him an' kept him from comin' after me. He was yellin' 'I'll get you, you bastard! Your old man's life wasn't worth a shit. He died like a bug grubbin' two frickin' dollars worth a' coal outta' Creedon's mine. Just a stupid Irish bastard he was!'"

Jack pounded his fists on the floor and stared at me. "Is that the truth, Haggerty?" he demanded. "Tell me, Haggerty! Is that what really happened? Tell me!"

The truth.

Levansky hadn't left out a thing. Now it was my turn say something. Andrew Dugan was my best friend, and not a day goes by that something or other reminds me of him. Andrew and I grew up next door neighbors. As kids we spent every waking moment together playing ball, picking huckle-berries, swimming in the crick, hunting in the fall, building snow forts in the winter.

I remembered the time we found my old man's French postcards buried in a dresser drawer and were mesmerized as we discovered the opposite sex. I chuckled at the memory.

Our fathers were miners at Creedon Coal and our mothers were best friends. They'd gossip at the backyard fence and tell us to skedaddle so they could share giggly secrets over coffee at the kitchen table.

Andrew and I enlisted together right out of high school and went off to war. I went to Europe, Andrew to the Pacific, and for the first time we were worlds apart. Each of us had done our share of killing, and when we returned home we talked about it just once over beers at the VFW. That night we made a solemn pact never to talk about the war again.

We married our high school sweethearts, served as best man in each other's wedding and ended up living side-by-side in our old neighborhood.

Andrew and I worked the same shift our fathers had, and we got royally drunk celebrating on the night Jack was born. *Eighteen years ago, tonight.* I swallowed hard at the thought.

And, yes, I was there that day and watched helplessly as Andrew—my lifelong friend—died in that muddy mine shaft.

Just as Levansky had said, Andrew's death was slow, painful and agonizing.

Now it was my turn to speak and I weighed every word. "Your dad died in a roof fall," I said, "just as I told you and your mom on the day it happened. It was an accident," I added quickly. "Your dad was workin' alone, robbin' a pillar. You know what that means?"

Jack shook his head and I searched for the words to explain it.

"When you're drivin' a tunnel you hafta' support the roof. In small shafts we used timbers. But when the tunnel got wide—like in Creedon's mine—we sometimes built cribs. Wood boxes filled with rocks. And sometimes we'd drive smaller tunnels on both sides of the big shaft an' then bring em' together later on, leavin' a pillar to hold the roof. Seein' as how Creedon's Mammoth Vein was so big, we made a lotta' pillars.

"Then, when you finish diggin' the coal out in a section, they send the best men back to get whatever coal they can from the pillars. Robbin' the pillars it's called. It's dangerous as all get out, and you havta' know what you're doin'. That's why your dad was picked. He was the best, Jack. The very best. You need to know that."

Jack was staring at me, hanging on my every word.

"That day a terrible thing happened. The pillar your dad was workin' on wasn't as solid as he thought and it collapsed so fast he couldn't get outta' the way."

Although I wasn't there to see it, I have a pretty good idea of what probably happened.

That recollection is the reason I smoke out on the porch...by myself...late into the night. Staying up till near exhaustion, smoking till my throat is raw is how I put off sleep and the nightmares I have about that day.

The tunnel was low. Andrew was on his knees at the base of the pillar. He angled the beam of his cap light on it and ran his hand down the column searching for the right spot to attack it. The low roof prevented an overhead shot, so he had to come at it from the side, swinging his short-handled pick like a bat.

Andrew was a powerful man, and his pick went in deep. When he yanked it back, a huge chunk of the pillar came loose and Andrew lost his balance and landed flat on his back.

The pillar began to crumble and dirt and rock fell on his legs, pinning him to the floor. And when the pillar finally disintegrated, the roof began to give way. Flat on his back, Andrew stared up at a huge rock hovering above him.

The nightmare becomes vivid as my mind cobbles together the horrific scene. The roof is coming down, and all Andrew can do is watch it happen, unable to move as a massive slab comes crashing down on him.

We scrambled to his side, but we were helpless. The rock on top of him was enormous. All we could do was listen as Andrew did, in fact, plead for us to put an end to his agony. On my knees at his side I prayed that he would die quickly.

"Kill me. Kill me. For the love of God, Tom, kill me," he begged. "Kill me," he pleaded three more times until the crushing boulder snuffed out his life.

Kneeling around him in that godforsaken tunnel we made a pact not to tell anyone what happened. Andrew, we agreed to say, died in a rock fall. No one needed to know the details. No one would ever hear about his unbelievable suffering or his pleading to end it. We swore an oath never to tell. Anyone.

"It was an accident, Jack," I said. "A big rock came down on him while he was robbin' a pillar. A roof fall, Jack, just like I told you and your mom."

It was the simple—but incomplete—truth. Fighting back my tears, I hoped the boy would accept it.

"Did he suffer?" Jack asked. His stare demanded the truth.

"He died quick," I lied.

"Right away?"

"Very quickly," I said, lying again.

"Did he ask you to kill him?" Jack asked the question matter-of-factly, his eyes locked at mine.

Dear God in Heaven, give me an answer.

"He was hurt bad, and he knew he wasn't gunna' make it. In his pain he asked if we could put an end to it," I answered truthfully. "But he died before we could do anything."

Jack stared at me.

After what seemed like an eternity the boy spoke. "Tell me what robbin' pillars is about?"

I breathed in deeply. "What about it?"

"Levansky said dad died tryin' to scrounge out a couple 'a dollars worth 'a coal for Creedon. Is that what robbin' pillars is about? A couple bucks!"

Again I chose my words carefully.

"Coal minin' is what your dad an' me chose to do. No one forced us," I replied. "Robbin' pillars is part a' the job."

"No!" Jack shouted. "Sounds to me like it's about gettin' the last scrap of coal, even if a man's life is at stake!"

"Everything about minin's dangerous," I replied quickly. "Methane gas that explodes like hell fire. The Black Damp that creeps up an' suffocates you. You got roof falls, dynamite goin' off early. There's a hunnert ways ta' get killed. Robbin' pillars is just one of 'em."

"But sendin' a man in to dig a tad a'coal from a pillar, that seems *greedy* to me," Jack said, staring deep into my eyes.

Greed. I knew in my heart the boy was right. To the Creedons profit was everything, and it was their relentless pursuit of it that killed Andrew and countless others.

I mulled over that thought a good long while but didn't reply. I guess the boy knew that my silence meant that I agreed with him.

"Levansky was right," Jack said. "My dad died for almost nothin'."

How do you respond to that?

Jack and I stared at each other, both of us wrestling with the truth about how—and why—his father and my best friend had died.

"About them sirens," Jack said softly.

"What about 'em?" I asked.

Chapter 4

Harry rolled through empty intersections preoccupied with thoughts about Jimmy Creedon. His mindless drifting ended when he made the turn onto Maple Avenue.

As his headlights swept the corner he saw a throng of people in the street and hit the brakes. Given the time, he had expected a few curious onlookers. But it seemed like half the town jammed the sidewalks and spilled into the street. Some were in pajamas clutching blankets over their shoulders. Others had pulled on raincoats, topcoats, bathrobes —whatever was at hand. Harry laughed as he slowed the car to a crawl.

Crowds didn't faze him anymore. After nineteen years on the force he'd gotten used to them. At fires, gruesome auto accidents, domestic altercations. People relentless to get a peek at another man's adversity. "Amazing," Harry whispered to himself as he rolled slowly down the tree-lined street past the weirdly dressed mob.

Maple Avenue was aptly named. Eighty years earlier Charles Creedon had overseen the planting of silver maples along the curbs, marking the spot where each scrawny sapling went into the ground. The little twigs were giants now and their leaf-laden branches arched out over the street.

At high noon Maple Avenue was a shadowy tunnel. When the sun went down it became almost pitch dark. The street lamps along the curb were totally enveloped by the trees and the fixtures cast only little slivers of light through the branches.

There were no neon-lit taverns or corner groceries. Not in this section of town. And the folks who lived there were determined to keep it that way. A quiet, secluded enclave of Creedonton's elite.

Creedonton had only a handful of wealthy folks —a couple of doctors and lawyers, a half-dozen prosperous businessmen, and Jimmy Creedon, grandson of the town's namesake. All of them were clustered together on this small stretch of Maple Avenue.

Wrought iron fences encircled manicured lawns that fronted magnificent homes set back from the street. Expensive cars were parked out of sight in rear garages that in bygone days had been stables and carriage houses.

Even amongst the opulence the Creedon mansion stood out. The largest and finest home of all, it telegraphed the message that those who lived there were a cut above everyone else. Charles Creedon had seen to that. By dictating the size of neighboring lots and reviewing every building permit, Charles had ensured that no other home in Creedonton would ever be bigger or better than his.

The mansion was three stories high, built entirely of handcut limestone. Twenty Italian artisans had done the stonework. A dozen Amish craftsmen spent a year on the interior using the finest oak, cherry, and chestnut that money could buy. On the southeast corner a round turret rose a half story above the rest of the house.

Creedon's Castle, the locals called it. Home of the king of Creedonton.

Harry had never been inside the mansion, nor did he know anyone who had. His stomach churned at the thought that someone had the audacity to attack it.

Pulling to a stop in front of the grand home, Harry set the parking brake and leaned into the door. He managed to get his left foot out before a man appeared in the doorframe.

"Chief, what can you tell me?"

"Damn, Bobby," Harry said, recognizing the young reporter from *The Creedonton Call.* "You watched me just pull up."

"Can't you give me somethin'?" the reporter pressed.

"Bobby," Harry said impatiently, "if you don't let me otta' this car I'll never know what happened, an' neither will you. Now step back."

"Chief," the young man pleaded, "this is big news. I need somethin'. I gotta' file a story for tomorrow's paper."

"I can't say anything till I get inside," Harry said, putting his shoulder into the door.

"Any idea who you're lookin' for?" the reporter asked as he stepped back.

"Yeah," Harry said pulling his bulk from the car and jutting his chin in Bobby's direction.

"Who?"

"Some stupid ass," Harry laughed as he squared his shoulders and straightened his jacket.

"I can't print that!"

"You pushed me, Bobby!" Harry shouted, jabbing his finger in the young man's face. "Don't push me no more, you understand! And don't follow me," he added with a cold stare and another jab of his finger. "Take one step inside the fence and I'll throw you in jail for violatin' a crime scene."

Harry sidestepped the reporter and walked through the iron gate and up the walk to Creedon's porch. Punching the doorbell, Harry shifted nervously from foot to foot waiting for an answer.

A face peered from the curtained sidelight. Harry nodded and a deadbolt turned. The door opened just enough to let him slip inside.

The foyer was lit by a dim overhead fixture. Beyond it everything else was dark.

"Turn on some lights," Harry barked to the butler, who stood ramrod straight by his side.

"No, sir. Mr. Creedon's instruction," the butler replied curtly. "He wants the lights off until the...the situation...is under control."

The situation. Harry smirked and looked down his nose at the slight man.

"I'll call you when Mr. Creedon's ready to see you," the butler announced, diverting his eyes from

Harry's stare. The little man turned and walked quickly into the darkness.

Harry heard muffled pounding.

He glanced around but couldn't place where the sound was coming from. Moments later the noise stopped and there was a slight rap on the door behind him. Harry turned as the butler brushed by.

"Finished?" the butler asked, opening the door a crack. "Good, and goodbye," he said brusquely and closed the door.

"Chief Myers," he said, turning in Harry's direction, "this way." Harry glared at the little man and followed him.

The butler stopped at the end of a hallway and Harry heard the soft creak of rollers as pocket doors slid open. There was the click of a switch and brilliant light streamed through the doorway.

Harry stared over the butler's shoulder into the most massive and exquisite room he had ever seen. The butler turned. With his palm he made a sweeping gesture into the room. Harry didn't move. He just stared in awe at the opulence before him.

Later, when his wife asked him what it was like, Harry uttered one word: Phenomenal.

Oriental carpets with intricate parquet floors peeking out around the edges. A black lacquered grand piano in one corner, silk-covered chairs and sofas throughout the room, crystal chandeliers, and at every window heavy tapestries were pulled together shutting out the world. It was magnificent, like something from a magazine.

But there was something else. The room was glistening.

Harry walked to a marble-topped table and brushed his hand across the surface. He flinched at the pinpricks, and when he turned his palm to the light it sparkled.

Tiny pieces of glass. Little slivers that caught the light and diffused it like a thousand tiny prisms.

The shards were every color of the rainbow. Red, deep blue, turquoise, green, yellow.

Oh, my God!

Harry turned.

"*Oh, my God!*" he thought again as he eyed a gray canvas tarpaulin billowing into a round alcove off the main room.

The muffled pounding, Harry realized, had been workmen outside nailing up the canvas, covering up a gaping hole.

Harry's stomach went sour. "Oh, my God!" This time he said it aloud.

Forty years earlier Charles Creedon had commissioned the most renowned glass artisans he could find to create a window for the turret. A stained glass masterpiece that rivaled the finest window in any church, anywhere. Designed precisely to fit the curvature of the turret, it was a phenomenal work of art and craftsmanship.

Now, inside Creedon's magnificent home for the first time ever, Harry realized that the window had been the focal point of this extraordinary room.

Harry recalled the publicity the window had generated. Stories and photos in *The New York Times, The Baltimore Sun, The Philadelphia Inquirer, Life* and *Look* magazines. The window was that unique, that awesome.

The window told Charles Creedon's life story. One section, Harry remembered, pictured verdant fields and rolling mountains—Charles's birthplace in central Germany.

In the center of the window was a coat of arms: a shield bearing a lion's head crossed with golden swords. The Creedon family crest—or a regal symbol that Charles Creedon had conjured up.

The section beneath it depicted the coal industry that had literally taken Creedon from rags to riches. That scene pictured a muscled square-jawed miner with a pick over his shoulder, a mule at his side, a glistening mound of blue and black nuggets at his feet—representing a shimmering mound of anthracite coal.

Remnants of the stained glass masterpiece lay scattered throughout the room. In the curved—now splintered—window frame a mangled lattice of twisted lead hung down like arthritic fingers clutching onto little fragments of stained glass.

"Yo, Chief!"

Harry turned and saw two of his officers, Garver and Mains, standing against the far wall. Garver, the older of the two, jerked his head motioning for Harry to join them.

Harry took a step in their direction and stopped at the sound of crunching glass. He lifted his foot and held it aloft awkwardly.

"You can't help it, Chief," Garver yelled across the room. "There's glass everywhere. You can't take a step without bustin' it."

Harry tried to eye a clear path, but he realized there wasn't one. Gritting his teeth and grimacing with every step, he walked across the room grinding fragments of colored glass into the carpet.

"What the hell happened?" Harry asked.

"Me and Tom," Garver replied, nodding toward his partner, "was crusin' like we do Friday night. You know, jus' lookin' out for trouble."

Harry motioned with his hand to get on with it.

"Just before midnight Dewey radios us. 'Somebody attacked Creedon place' is all he says. So seein' as how it's Creedon's, I stepped on it. Me an' Tom got here a couple'a minutes later, then Cooper and Paulaski pulled up."

"Two cars?"

"You know Dewey," Garver replied, grinning. "He calls out the calvary."

"So where's Cooper an' Paulaski?"

"Well, seein' as how me an' Tom got here first, I figured we could handle it," Garver replied. "No use havin' the whole force caught up with this thing, so they went back on patrol. I called Dewey an' told him to give them anything else that came in."

"Good call," Harry said. Garver continued.

"Creedon was standin' on the porch yellin' 'bout how long it took us to get here. Then he told us the trouble was on the round part a' the house—tured or somethin' like that. Then he disappeared. After that, everything came from the butler.

"The street was empty when we first got here, just a couple'a folks starin' out their windows. But then people began showin' up in droves. I guess it was the sirens an' red lights, and probably people callin' their friends to come see, on accounta' it's Creedon's place.

"We went around 'an saw it was the fancy window that was busted. Then the butler came out and said some guys were comin' to cover up the hole. He said Creedon wanted us to tell the folks in the street to stay away, then he wanted us to wait in the kitchen."

"You find any evidence?" Harry asked.

"Like what!" Garver shot back.

"Hell, I don't know!" Harry barked. "Like whatever busted that frickin' window. A rock, brick, a damn bowlin' ball for all I know."

Garver and Mains couldn't help but laugh at the remark.

"No, Chief," Garver replied, still chuckling. "Like I said, we were told to wait in the kitchen. We weren't let back in here 'till just a minute ago. Then we saw you standin' over there gawkin' at the window...or what's left 'a it."

"Idiot sure picked one hell of 'a window to bust," Mains said.

Harry shook his head.

"There's not a lot you can do in here," Harry said. "Go on outside and talk to people; see if anyone heard or saw anything. I doubt you'll find much, but it's worth a try. After that, we need to get together to come up with a plan. I gotta' stay and talk to Creedon, but I wanna' catch up with you afterward. Meet me at Ann's in...say...half an hour. But wait for me if I'm late," he added quickly. "You okay with that?"

"What the hell," Garver replied scrunching his shoulders. "We'll see ya' at Ann's."

Harry watched the two officers tiptoe across the room trying to avoid the litter of glass. He wished he could go, too, and avoid the inevitable encounter with Jimmy Creedon.

The officers' crunching footsteps brought the butler to the door and he ushered them out. Turning the lock, he walked to the threshold of the opulent room and announced curtly in Harry's direction: "Mr. Creedon's on the phone. You need to wait."

Harry shot the little man a dirty look.

"When Mr. Creedon's finished I'll tell him you're here." Message delivered, the butler disappeared.

Harry glanced at his watch. *On the phone at twelve-thirty in the morning?*

As he waited for his meeting with Jimmy Creedon, one thought rolled through Harry's head: *What am I gunna' say?*

Scanning the room trying to get his mind off the question, his eye settled on a portrait of Charles Creedon hanging in a gilded frame above a huge intricately-carved marble-framed fireplace.

Apple don't fall far from the tree, Harry chuckled to himself, recalling Jimmy's likeness to the hardened old man in the painting: Charles Creedon, the King of Creedonton.

His lightning-fast rise to wealth and power was legendary, and like everyone in town Harry knew the story.

Charles was born in Germany, the second son. As second-born, he would inherit nothing; everything would pass on to his older brother. So at nineteen Charles headed to America. All he had to his name were four gold coins, his father's pocket watch, and his seventeen-year-old pregnant wife at his side.

Minutes after walking onto the docks in Baltimore, Charles was approached by a fast-talking con man who preyed on immigrants. The shrewd hustler used pictures to show them his wares. His eyes wide as saucers after seeing the photos, Charles gave the man his four gold coins for a deed to twenty acres of Pennsylvania land.

The deed, Charles discovered three days later, was for a worthless parcel of Pennsylvania hillside. Clear-cut of all its timber, it was a barren wasteland —a dismal plot of rocks and tree stumps.

Charles and his young wife barely survived the first year on their land. They lived on potatoes, turnips and an occasional snared rabbit or groundhog. Home was a tar paper shack that Charles built himself.

Stubborn as an ass and twice as strong, Charles began clearing the land. He traded the heirloom watch for a tired old mule and spent months wrenching out stumps and rocks, working tirelessly to gain a leg up on his dream of creating a farmstead from the wasteland. All he wanted was a simple place for himself, his wife, and their newborn son, Joseph.

One stump—the remnant of a huge oak—stood mid-field. Its roots spread out like a gnarled hand laying claim to a good portion of the land around it. Two weeks of digging, tugging, and prying at the oak's roots almost killed both Charles and the mule.

In a final act of desperation, vowing not to be outdone by a tree stump, Charles bartered the near-dead mule for a half case of dynamite. As the sun broke the horizon on July 14, 1861, Charles packed the base of the stump with dynamite. Face down on the ground, he touched a match to the fuse then covered his ears. The explosion was deafening, followed by a rain of rock, dirt, and shattered roots.

After the smoke and dust cleared, Charles slowly crept forward. On his knees, looking down at the spot where the oak stump had laid, he saw bowl-shaped crater that glistened in the sunlight.

Charles was staring at the uppermost tip of the largest cache of anthracite coal ever discovered in Pennsylvania. But at the time, he had no clue what it was.

Germany was rich in coal; *die kohle*. Brown coal, lignite. Dull, dark brown and crumbly, it looked nothing like Anthracite. Black as pitch, shiny as a mirror and hard as a rock, Anthracite was often referred to as "black diamonds." Charles had never seen anything like it before.

Taking a piece of it to the man who had traded him the dynamite for his mule, Charles asked, "Vos is dis?"

"Coal," the man laughed.

"*Kohle?*" Creedon replied, questioningly. "*Es it goot kohle?*"

"*Ya, iss goot,*" the man mimicked in reply. Grabbing the immigrant's arm, the man pulled Charles toward a cold pot-bellied stove in the corner. He unlatched the door and shoveled his cupped hands toward the opening.

"Coal in," he said. Then he held his hands up, as if warming them by the stove. "*Aaah, goot,*" he said, rubbing his hands together. "*Coal goot,*" he said. "*Ya?*"

"*Ya,*" Charles replied, nodding. "*Iss goot.*"

"Where'd you get it?" the man asked.

Charles just stared back, then turned and walked away.

Out of sight of the man, Charles ran home.

Charles began digging into the crater and was constantly amazed. The deeper he dug, the wider the coal vein got.

He worked the mine alone for a year. At night he'd cart the coal out and sell small wagon loads of it in towns miles away where no one knew him.

Then, in cash-only deals, he bought up land that adjoined his.

As the transactions were made he would stare blankly and feign ignorance. When asked why he wanted their hardscrabble fields, he would shrug and reply, "I donnoe." His neighbors were overjoyed at their good fortune in selling him whatever land he wanted, and Charles heard them laughing as he walked away. He would just smile, knowing that someday he would have the last laugh.

After he had bought almost every farm around his, Charles announced his find. The coal vein under his land was phenomenal, and in time it came to be called The Mammoth Vein. Eight foot high in places and twenty yards wide, it extended more than a mile underground. Eventually Creedon's mine would produce more Anthracite coal in a month than other mines did in a year.

The town of Creedonton grew quickly as men and machines were brought in to work his growing empire. Shrewd and calculating, Charles reigned over it all. He was the major shareholder in the bank. He owned the company store, every downtown property and most of the houses. And he literally controlled the lives of more than four hundred Irish, Italian, Lithuanian, and Polish immigrants who came to work for him.

A year later both his wife and their unborn second child died at the hands of an Irish midwife. The event left Charles with an unquenchable hatred of both God and the Irish.

To him the immigrant miners—especially the Irish—were despicable and dispensable, yet necessary. He charged them outlandish rent for ill-kept houses that were slightly better than shacks. His paymaster withheld wages from them for overpriced goods from the company store and for any broken tools. Any remaining wages were paid in company script worth fifty-cents on the dollar at anywhere other than Creedon's store.

Bad as it was above ground, below it was a thousand times worse. There was only one tunnel. One way in, one way out. No way to escape if something went wrong. And the list of things that could go wrong was a long one. Roof falls, flooding, poor or no ventilation, open flames lanterns that touched off the explosive methane gas, clouds of thick dust that settled deep in their lungs for years, and the Black Damp. The only good thing about the Black Damp was that it knocked you out first; then it killed you.

In the mid eighteen-sixties a group of Irish miners rebelled. Their intent was to hobble Creedon's operation and force him to better their conditions, above and below ground.

The press dubbed them The Molly Maguires. It was a name British landlords in Ireland had given to a band of men who disguised themselves as women when they harassed—and often times killed —the landlords' agents. To the coal barons, the Mollies in Pennsylvania were just a bunch of thugs.

Creedon formed a private police force to put down the insurrection, but the effort only strengthened the Mollies' resolve and they struck back harder. The beating of a miner by Creedon's men would be revenged by the derailment of a coal train. An unjustified firing would result in the dynamiting of a company outbuilding. The violence escalated on both sides and culminated in an all-out riot in which two of Creedon's men were killed. By whom, no one would say. Snitches, everyone knew, were knee-capped—a crippling fate worse than death.

Never one to yield—not to an oak stump or to what he publicly denounced as a band of hooligans and killers—Charles enlisted a Philadelphia detective agency to infiltrate the Mollies. An Irish agent was assigned the case.

Working as a miner side-by-side with his countrymen, the beguiling agent eventually won the

Mollies' friendship. Welcomed like a brother, he attended their secret meetings and gathered damning evidence against them. With the agent's testimony, six Mollies were found guilty of the murder of Creedon's henchmen and were sentenced to hang.

Charles, with his son Joseph at his side, stood in the prison courtyard in Pottsville and watched the Mollies go to the gallows.

Charles died two years later from a brain aneurism, and Joseph inherited everything. Twenty years later Joseph and his wife died in the flu pandemic of 1918. Their only son, Jimmy, became the sole heir to the Creedon empire at the age of twenty.

The company expanded beyond Creedonton as Jimmy used the volume of Creedon Coal to manipulate pricing, forcing several small mine owners to sell out to him. It was either that, or go bankrupt.

Harry also recalled a story alleging Jimmy's involvement in union busting.

Six years earlier at Creedon's Gilberton mine a foreman was found shot to death. An out-of-town policeman passing through testified to having seen a volatile argument between the foreman and another man in an alleyway. As it turned out, the 'other man' was an Irish miner who allegedly had ties to the union.

It was a golden opportunity for Creedon to drive a wooden stake into the heart of the union. With Creedon's power and push and the policeman's testimony, the hapless miner was hastily tried and sentenced to life for murder. There was no more union talk in Gilberton after that.

The old man put down the Molly Maguires, and Jimmy successfully fought off the union. Now I'm going to confront him about the destruction of his grandfather's beloved stained glass window. What am I going to say?

The thought was overwhelming, and Harry's stomach churned.

"Mr. Creedon will see you now." The butler's voice came from the shadows of the hallway.

Harry turned and saw the butler smirking, his palm pointing the way to a paneled door. As Harry started toward the door it was no longer the shattering of glass underfoot that caused him concern. Every step took him closer to his face-to-face meeting with Jimmy Creedon. *What will I say?*

Harry had no answer to that question as he slowly turned the knob.

Chapter 5

"What about the sirens?" I asked. "Was it the cops comin' on account 'a your mix-up with Levanskly?"

Jack didn't answer immediately. He stared down then spoke.

"It wasn't that."

"Then what?"

"What Levansky said about my dad...'bout him robbin' the pillar to get a couple buck's worth a' coal for Creedon. He died robbin' that damned pillar!"

"We talked that out, Jack," I replied. "Your dad's death was an acci...:"

"Jimmy Creedon killed my dad!" Jack shouted, cutting me off.

"It was an accident, a bad accident," I shot back.

"No, it wasn't!" Jack shouted. "Riskin' my dad's life for a tad a' coal wasn't no accident! It was greed. Greed, pure and simple!"

"OK!" I shouted in frustration. "Maybe it was Creedon's greed that got your dad killed."

"Good," Jack replied.

"Whatta' you mean, 'good'?"

"'Cause tonight I made Creedon pay. I made him pay for what he did."

"Whatta' you mean you made Creedon pay? What're you sayin'?"

"I wanted to make Creedon pay for killin' my dad," Jack replied, looking into my eyes.

"You lost me boy."

"I busted a window at his house," Jack said, watching me carefully for my reaction. "That's what the sirens were about."

"You busted a window?"

"I snuck down Creedon's street hidin' behind the big trees. An' when I was in front of his place I yelled, 'Creedon, you bastard!' Then I hurled a rock through his window."

"Did anybody see you?"

"I don't think so. I ran an' was a coupla' blocks away when I heard the cop cars headed toward Creedon's. So I just kept on runnin'."

"Well it ain't like you killed someone," I laughed.

"But I busted his special window," Jack said, smiling.

"Whatta' you mean?" I asked. But no sooner were the words out of my mouth, it dawned on me what he meant. "Oh, my God, no! Tell me you don't mean the stained glass one."

Jack didn't say anything, but I could see the answer in his eyes.

"Good Lord! You're sure?"

"Yeah, I'm sure," he said, smiling impishly.

"You have no idea what you done, boy," I said shaking my head. "That window's like a'...a'...a' damned treasure to Creedon. He'll skin you alive if he finds out you're the one that broke it. You an' your mom'll be on the street with nothin' to your name!"

"I didn't think...." Jack began.

"You're darn right," I interrupted him. "You didn't think at all."

"You ain't gunna' tell, are you?" Jack asked.

"Hell no," I replied. "And you'll never breathe a word about it either."

Both of us fell silent. There was nothing more to say. Jack just sat staring at me.

As I recall I smoked another cigarette, maybe two as I paced the porch, my mind going a mile a minute. *You have no idea what you done, boy.*

"You go to bed now," I finally said.

As Jack clambered to his feet, I reminded him yet again, shaking my finger in his face. "Don't you ever tell anyone what you did tonight. You hear me, boy? There'll be hell to pay. Believe me."

I watched as Jack slipped into his house.

I lit another cigarette and stood alone on the porch. My mouth on fire, my lungs raw, I wrestled with a new thought that was plaguing me. *Tony Levansky.*

Levansky broke our oath and told the boy the truth about his father's death. It was Levansky who caused Jack to strike out at the most powerful man alive.

And you threatened the boy, too, I thought.

There wasn't anything I could do about Creedon, but I could take care of Tony Levansky. Flicking my cigarette off the porch, I crept down the stairs and made my way into the alley.

Chapter 6

Harry stood outside the paneled door of Creedon's study, took a deep breath and with a sweaty palm turned the brass knob. The room was illuminated by a banker's lamp with a green shade angled downward.

"Come in," a voice inside the room directed, "and close the door."

Harry pulled the door shut and walked slowly into the room feeling thick soft carpeting underfoot. As his eyes adjusted to the darkness he saw a figure —Jimmy Creedon, he guessed—slip into a chair on the far side of the desk. Light reflecting off the desk illuminated just the bottom half of the man's face. It reminded Harry of a kid holding a flashlight under his chin at Halloween. The light created dark circles around the man's eyes and made his cheek bones stick out ghoulishly. His demon-like look didn't help Harry's acid stomach.

"Mr. Creedon?" Harry asked softly

"Chief Myers," Creedon offered back softly as his answer, "take a seat."

Harry edged sideways in front of the desk till his knees bumped into a wooden chair. Dipping into it he found himself sitting low, forced to gaze up at Creedon. Harry knew the subtleties of interrogation, and he knew that the low-slung chair put him in a subordinate position. For the first time in his life Harry was on the wrong side of the desk, and he peered up like a whipped puppy.

"So..." Creedon said slowly, letting the word languish. "You've seen the damage?"

"It's a real shame," Harry replied softly.

"A shame?" Then louder, "A shame!" Creedon shouted. "Some lowlife bastard sneaks up to my home in the middle of the night and attacks me and you call it a 'shame'! It's an outrage is what is! A damned outrage!"

Harry had expected a reaction, but Creedon's outburst had him pressed back against the unyielding spines of the hard wooden chair.

"Thank goodness no one was hurt," Harry offered quickly.

"Yes, Chief Myers," Creedon replied in a patronizing tone, "No one was hurt. And as you say, thank goodness for that. Had anyone been hurt," he shouted, "I would be insane!"

As if you're not, Harry thought to himself, awed by Creedon's wild mood swings and changing voice inflections.

"So, Chief Myers," Creedon continued, lowering his voice to the point that Harry found himself leaning in toward the desk to hear, "what I want from you and your police force...what I want...," his voice rising rapidly in octaves, "NO...what I demand," he shouted, "is the son of a bitch who attacked my home with THIS!"

As the words left his mouth Creedon brought his hand from under the desk and slammed a rock down.

Harry ducked as the rock gouged the desk in front of him then clattered off into the darkness.

Harry righted himself in the chair and looked up to find Creedon standing, leaning across the desk, glaring at him.

"Do you understand what happened here?" Creedon thundered.

"I think..." Harry stammered.

"Quiet!" Creedon shouted. "Do you really understand what happened? We're NOT talking about some petty act of vandalism. No, Myers. Not in the least." Then lowering his voice to a whisper, "We're talking about the destruction of an irreplaceable, priceless work of art. My link to my grandfather...my heritage. Do you understand that?" he thundered.

Creedon cocked his head waiting for Harry to reply. But Harry didn't take the bait.

Extending his index finger to within inches of Harry's face, Creedon continued. "We're talking about a violent attack against me," he said, his voice rising again. "That's what we're talking about!" he shouted. "Now, I ask you again! Do you understand?"

"Absolutely, sir," Harry replied, feeling a cold rivulet of sweat run down his spine.

"Good," Creedon replied softly. "Now we know what we're talking about."

Plopping into his seat he swiveled around, leaving Harry staring at the shiny leather back of his chair.

"Not vandalism," Creedon whispered toward the ceiling. "Not misdirected anger," he added softly. "No, Chief Myers," he said, spinning in the chair then leaning across the desk, "we're talking about an attack with a deadly weapon...right? And that would make it....attempted murder."

Attempted murder? What in the world are you saying? Surely you must be kidding.

As that thought flashed through his head, Harry squirmed in his seat, searching for a response.

"Mr. Creedon, with all due respect," Harry began, then suddenly wished he hadn't. But he was beyond the point of stopping. Creedon was waiting for his response, hanging onto his every word. "Attempted murder is....harsh," Harry offered.

Harsh. Where the hell did that come from? Harry thought as he reflected on his choice of words. But it was better than what he really wanted to say, which was *ridiculous.*

"Harsh? Harsh, you say?" Creedon replied, laughing. "Well then, I disagree with you."

The next exchange came softly as Creedon spun in his chair, again putting his back to Harry.

He's truly insane, Harry thought.

"You know the power and influence I wield in this town, don't you, Myers? So if I say it's attempted murder with a deadly weapon, then we'll agree to call it that, won't we?" Creedon whispered up at the ceiling.

"Yes sir," Harry replied in defeat.

"I want every man you have working on this. Leave no *stone* unturned, as they say," Creedon added, chuckling at his inference to the rock.

"Every man on the force will be on it."

Creedon swiveled in his chair. "But not that idiot you have answering the phone. What's his name, anyway?"

"Dewey."

"Dewey? You might as well call him 'Sleepy'. It took five rings before he answered the phone," Creedon replied. "But that's your business. As for now, go, get out. Get to work," he said as he reached across the desk and pulled the chain on the banker's light, plunging the room into darkness. Creedon's chair creaked as he rolled it back from the desk. Soft padded footsteps followed.

"Good night, Mr. Creedon," Harry whispered into the darkness. No sooner had the words left his lips he regretted having uttered them.

"NO!" Creedon's voice boomed from the darkness. "It is certainly NOT a good night!"

A door slammed on the opposite side of the room. Harry waited a minute then rose from his chair and moved slowly, his back against the wall, feeling for the doorknob in the pitch black room. Finding it, he turned the knob and backed into the hallway.

"I'll show you out." The butler's grating voice, coming from the far end of the hall.

"No need," Harry said as he moved quickly toward the door. "I know the way."

Harry drove faster than he should have down Maple and his tires squealed as he made a sudden right onto a cross street. He made a slightly slower left a block later and was on Oak. Normal breathing and a regular heartbeat had returned by the time he pulled into a slot next to the squad car parked in front of Ann's all-night diner. He ran his hand slowly down the side of the black and white as he walked by it, thankful that Garver and Mains had waited for him.

Chapter 7

I had resolved that Tony Levansky would pay for what he had done. Exactly what that meant I didn't know for sure as I made my way through the yard and ran down the alley.

Where would Levansky be? Neely's? No, not after the fight. Neely would have told Levansky and his drunken pals to scram.

Winded, I stopped and checked my watch under a streetlamp. One fifteen. The bars and social clubs would be closed. Even joints like Neely's didn't stay open past one.

Where would Levansky go? He's drunk, smacked with a rock, and he's mad. Even his low-life friends would want to be rid of him before he did something else stupid and brought the police down on them, too.

I don't remember how I arrived at the answer. I don't recall thinking it through, but somehow it dawned on me. I began running again.

Back in the mid 50's the abandoned mine tunnels under the west end of town began to collapse as their timber supports finally rotted away. Knowing that the tunnels would eventually cave in completely, Jimmy Creedon quickly sold off his company houses directly over them. With bad luck—the only type of luck she ever had—Sarah Levansky bought one.

As Creedon predicted, the tunnels did collapse several months later and the homes above them began to disintegrate. As the land over the tunnels subsided, basement walls failed, windows shattered, door frames buckled, walls bowed, floors heaved, and in a matter of weeks two blocks of homes on Quince Street had to be abandoned. Sarah Levansky's was one of them.

No one in his right mind would venture into those places now. One wrong step could have you plummeting through rotting floorboards into a mine shaft so deep you'd never be found. But Tony Levansky was never in his right mind, and if my hunch was right, his mother's abandoned house might be where I'd find him.

As I approached the lopsided wreck of a house I checked behind me frequently, peering into the darkness. *Eyes like a cat.* I smiled, remembering the expression I uttered to Jack earlier. No one saw me, I was sure of that.

A sagging set of wooden stairs led to a tilting front porch with half of its railing missing. Overgrown shrubbery and high grass surrounded the place like a jungle.

Mounting the rotting stairs carefully, I slipped into the shadows on the porch. *Come on, Tony. Come on.*

I crouched in the darkness, hoping he'd eventually show.

Maybe he's already inside.

That thought crossed my mind and I debated whether I would dare venture inside to look for him, alone, and in the dark no less. *Give it a minute,* my rational side argued.

That gamble paid off, and I smiled when I saw him coming. He was walking awkwardly through the deep grass, approaching the house in a whiskey-induced stumble—one step forward, a half step back—his arms waiving at his sides. "Sheeit," he called out laughing, flapping his arms like a bird to keep his balance. Finally he grabbed the weathered newel post at the foot of the stairs.

Come on Tony. Come on.

Levansky stumbled up the stairs sloppily, hand over hand on the railing as he made his way to the porch. At the top of the stairs he turned, burped loudly, smiled, and stood with his hands on his hips celebrating his assent like a climber having made it to the top of Everest.

Springing from the darkness, I threw my right arm around his neck and jammed my left knee into his spine bending him backward.

"Whaa!" Levansky squealed, clawing at my arm with his hands.

I pulled tighter, choking off his words.

"You son of a bitch," I hissed into his ear.

"Whaa," he managed. I tightened my forearm across his windpipe.

"You broke the oath about Andy Dugan," I whispered. "We promised not to tell. But you did, you bastard! And I hear you threatened his boy, too." I relaxed my hold so he wouldn't pass out.

"What the hell!" he shouted.

"Shut up and listen to me, Levansky, and listen good," I said, cinching my arm again. "You so much as look sideways at Andy's boy and I'll hunt you down like a dog. And you won't be the first man I killed. You hear me! And if you think I'm kiddin', here's somethin' to help you remember, you bastard."

I released my grip and plunged my knee into his backside. Levansky went careening off the porch.

He flapped at the air wildly with his arms as if he might fly and seemed to flounder in mid-air before landing in a heap on the crumbling sidewalk below. I grimaced at the sound of bone hitting concrete and heard him moan. I knew he was hurt bad, but I didn't care. I vaulted the railing and ran into the darkness.

It was around two when I finally made it home, slinking down the alleyway behind my house, darting back and forth from the same hiding spots Jack had used.

On my back porch I fished my last cigarette from the sweat-damp pack in my pocket and lit it with shaking fingers. Blowing jets of smoke into the air, I finished the cigarette in record time. I flicked the dying butt off the porch and watched the sparks as it headed into the yard below. "That," I announced to the darkness, "was for you, Andrew, and for you, too, Jack. Oaths ain't made to be broken. Ever."

Chapter 8

Harry walked into Ann's and squinted as his eyes adjusted to the brightness of the fluorescent-lit restaurant.

"Your boys are in the back, Chief," a waitress announced from behind the worn Formica counter. She angled her head toward the back room, pointing the way with a pile of puffed up bleached blond hair. "Coffee?" she asked as Harry walked past her.

"Black," Harry called over his shoulder as he moved toward the booth where Garver and Mains were seated, hunched over coffee mugs. Harry pulled a chair to the end of the booth and waited while the waitress set a mug on the table and filled it. "Thanks," Harry mumbled as the woman shuffled back toward the front counter.

"Thanks for waitin' for me," Harry said, nudging his chair close to the table.

"No big thing," Garver replied. "So, how'd it go with Creedon?"

"Bad," Harry said, cradling his mug.

"Real bad?"

"Real bad. Creedon's a nut case."

"I could'a told you that. Saved ya' the trouble a' talkin' with him," Mains replied with a smirk.

"It ain't funny, Tom," Harry said shooting the young officer a hard glance. "He wants this to go down as attempted murder, assault with a deadly weapon."

"What?" Garver replied incredulously.

"You heard me. Creedon says whoever did this was out to kill him. He wants the bird put away for a good long time."

"Good Lord," Garver gasped.

"Just tellin' you what's on the man's alleged mind," Harry said, staring at the two officers. "You find out anything? Got any ideas who would'a done it? You guys got any clues?"

"We didn't learn nothin' from the folks in the street!" Garver shouted, throwing his hand up to stop the barrage of questions. "They was just there to see what happened. The one who did it could'a been standin' right there with 'em."

"Sorry," Harry said shaking his head. "I didn't mean to come on so hard. Creedon just got me riled up is all."

"I think we gotta' figure out who might have a gripe with Creedon." Mains offered.

"Could use the phone book," Garver replied with a laugh. "Everyone in town hates that S.O.B. It'd be a lot easier makin' a list a' people that like him...it would be a heck of a lot shorter."

"This still ain't no laughin' matter," Harry said.

"Sorry," Garver replied quickly. "But it's the truth. There ain't a lot of people who like Jimmy Creedon. But it takes a lot a' gumption to do what this guy did," he added.

"So where does that take us?" Harry asked in frustration. "Someone with a lotta' gumption an' a lotta' attitude. You got any idea who that might be?"

"The way I see it," Garver replied, "whoever did it was pretty riled...and pretty strong. It takes a good arm to heave somethin' that would do that much damage. Did you find out what it was? A brick, a rock...a bowlin' ball maybe?" and he chuckled.

This time even Harry managed a slight laugh.

"It was a rock, a damn big one," Harry replied. "Creedon 'bout crowned me with it. The moron slammed it down on his desk a couple a' inches in front a' me. So we're lookin' for someone who had a thing for Creedon... and someone with a powerful arm. Problem is, this town's full 'a old miners who hate Creedon and got powerful arms," Harry mused. "I think Mains is right. We start lookin' for someone who has a gripe with Creedon and put the powerful arm angle on the back burner. Could be the guy got someone else to lob the rock. We go for motive first, and maybe 'means' will follow. So the question is: Who has it in for Creedon?"

"I'll get the phone book," Mains said, feigning a rise from his seat.

"Knock it off, Tom," Harry replied, laughing a bit again.

"Truth is," the young officer offered as he slumped back in his seat, "there's about a hunnert people I know like'd to lob a gooney at Creedon given half a chance."

"But how many of 'em got the guts to do it?" Harry shot back.

"Let's try this," Garver offered. "My niece does some part-time bookwork for Creedon. Me and Tom'll try to catch her in the mornin' and see if she knows a' anybody who has a bone to pick with Creedon. Might give us some names to go on."

"Good idea," Harry said.

"And I think we should check out the bars," Mains said. "It is...or was...Friday night. Payday. A lotta' liquid courage flowin'. Maybe we can find out if someone was juiced up, spoutin' off about Creedon."

"Now you're talkin' like a cop," Harry said, nodding at the young officer.

"So we'll check with my niece in the mornin' and see if we come up with some names, and then me an' Tom'll start checkin' out the bars," Garver said.

"Sounds 'bout as good as anything right now," Harry said, downing the remains of his coffee. "The bars are closed now...or should be," he said, checking his watch. "Cooper and Paulaski'll cover the rest of the night, so you guys go home. I'll call Dewey and tell him to sign you off. Get some sleep and we'll start out fresh in the morning. Agreed?"

"Sounds like a plan to me," Mains replied.

"Start at the bars closest to Creedon's place and work your way out," Harry said. "I'm thinkin' this was a spur-of-the moment thing. Impulsive. I'll make a list a' bars in the morning."

"Works for me," Garver said, draining his cup.

"Me, too," Mains replied, relieved at the idea of calling it a night.

"Thanks for bein' here for me," Harry said as he scooted his chair back to let the men out of the booth. "I'll get the bill."

Garver stopped in the aisle and turned to Harry. "If I knew you was buyin', I would'a had me a cheeseburger an' some fries."

"Last thing you need is a greasy cheeseburger," Harry said, shooting a glance at the paunch that hung over Garver's belt.

"Thanks, Chief," Garver laughed over his shoulder as he pushed through the screen door with Mains following.

Harry waived off the waitress when she started toward him with her carafe'. As he moved toward the door, Harry laid two dollars on the counter. "Keep the change," he said to the waitress, who smiled as she stuffed the bills into her apron.

At the door he met a big man in the threshold. The man held the door open and stepped back to let Harry pass.

Harry walked to his car, turned the ignition and drove toward home. On the way he radioed the station. When Dewey finally answered, Harry told him that Garver and Mains were done for the night. All calls were to go to Paulaski and Cooper. As he clicked off the radio, Harry smiled. He had finally turned the tables...and interrupted Dewey's sleep.

Chapter 9

Bo cradled a paper sack in the crook of his arm and pulled the heavy glass door open. Stopping the door with his foot, he slipped inside, careful not to jostle the bag.

The place was lit by the greenish glow of fluorescent tubes. "Hello" Bo called, standing before the unmanned counter. No one answered.

He walked around the counter and made his way slowly down the tiled hall passing a nest of cluttered gray steel desks separated by half-high walls. "Hello," he called again.

At the end of the cubicles he turned and saw the old man, feet crossed, propped on an open desk drawer. The man was in uniform more or less. Grease stains spotted the front of his dingy white shirt. A black clip-on tie had slipped from its moorings at his neck and hung down on his round belly, anchored in place by a tie clip. His hands were entwined atop the twisted tie and he was snoring loudly.

Bo smiled as he backhanded his ring against the cubicle's metal frame. "Hey there."

The old man blinked awake and struggled to disengage his feet from the drawer. His back-tilted chair finally banged forward as his feet came free. "Don't get many visitors this time a' night," the old man stammered, rubbing his eyes.

"Hey, brother," Bo said, smiling. "Don't think nothin' of it. I did my share of catching Z's when I pulled the night-owl shift."

"Brother?" Dewey replied, squinting.

"Brothers of the badge!" Bo said as he set the sack on the desk. He reached into his breast pocket and pulled out a black leather wallet. He flipped it open just long enough to let the old man catch a glimpse of the gold shield inside before snapping it shut.

"You're a cop!" Dewey exclaimed.

"Darn straight, and proud to be one. You and me, both officers of the law...brothers," Bo replied, playing up to the old man.

"Well I'll be," Dewey said, staring back wide-eyed. "Take a seat...brother," nodding to a chair opposite his desk.

"Thanks, officer," Bo replied, placing emphasis on the title. Bo settled back in the chair. "And you are?"

"Dewey," the old man replied, thrusting his hand across the desk.

"Officer Dewey, I'm Bo," as he shook the old man's hand.

"Bo?"

"Bo's the name, gettin' bad guy's the game." He watched the old man's eyes sparkle at the rhyme.

"Hey!" Bo shouted, releasing the handshake and slapping a meaty palm on the desk. "I got us some good old Joe that's goin' cold," pointing to the sack on the desk.

"Coffee?"

"Yes sir. Coffee it is, Officer Dewey. Black and strong," Bo said as he ripped the bag open. "Good old Joe keeps cops on their toes," he replied, laughing as he slid a cup in front of the old man.

"For me?"

"You bet'cha, partner. Hope you like it black. That's the way the guys in my precinct take it. Hope it's okay."

"Black's fine," Dewey said smiling, prying the lid off his cup. "You're really a cop?" he asked, peering over the edge of the steaming cup as he took a sip.

"Yes sir. From Philadelphia."

"Philly?"

"Yes sir, Officer Dewey."

"So what brings you here?"

"Vacation," Bo replied, carefully watching the old man's reaction.

" Here?"

"No. Not here. Just passin' through. Takin' a little time off. I just finished up a case down in Harrisburg."

"Harrisburg?" Dewey said, cocking his head. "What's a Philly cop doin' on a case in Harrisburg?"

"You're quick on the draw there, Officer," Bo said, winking at the old man. "Here's the deal. Two days ago we heard that a Philly cop killer was hidin' out in Harrisburg. Since I know what the guy looks like, they teamed me up with a detective there. After about six hours of beatin' the bushes—and one of his dirtbag pals—we tracked him down to some two-bit flea-bag apartment. We had the bozo surrounded, but the jerk just wouldn't give it up. He started firin' at us out the window. Four rounds hit the car we were crouched behind, so I had to do it."

"You shot him!"

"Had to. The man's a cop killer and he was aimin' to get me, too. It was either him or me."

The old man's jaw dropped.

"Ever shoot a man, Officer Dewey?"

"No, can't say that I have."

"It ain't pretty. Not something you forget," Bo said, casting his eyes down. "So after the paperwork went through and I was cleared for takin' the shot, my Captain told me to take a few days off. Get it off my mind. So that's why I'm here. I'm goin' fishin' up state. Tioga County. Ever been there?"

"Can't say that I have."

"North of Williamsport. There's trout water there like you only dream about," Bo offered, smiling. "Slate Run. Brookie stream; runs into Pine Crick. Nestled between the mountains, they call it the Grand Canyon of Pennsylvania. Hemlocks all around. I swear, it's the place for a man to lose himself for a while. No better place to be than Slate Run with a fly rod in your hand. That's where I'm headed."

"So how's come you're here?"

"Got about two more hours to go I figure, but I'm beat," Bo answered. "Gotta' pack it in for the night. Don't wanna' fall asleep behind the wheel and find myself in some ditch. Wouldn't look good for a cop to be rollin' off the road."

"No sir," Dewey replied, wiping a dribble of coffee from his chin with his sleeve.

"So I thought I'd stop a while and look for a nice clean, quiet place ta' bunk down. Don't want no rif-raf next door partyin' it up, keepin' me awake all hours a' the night."

Dewey nodded.

"So I'm thinkin', who's better to ask about a decent place than a fellow officer of the law. I figured I'd find the local stationhouse somewhere along the main drag. And here you are, just as I suspected. So seein' as how it's the middle a' the night and I'm comin' in here askin' for advice, I thought I oughta' bring you somethin' for your trouble. I got the coffee at an all-night place down the street."

"Real thoughtful a' you," Dewey said, nursing his cup.

"Ain't nothin'," Bo said with a flip of his hand. "Now, about that place to stay?"

"If I was you, I'd see if they got any rooms at The Pines. It's 'bout a mile outside 'a town headin' west on the main road. Real clean place, no rif-raf, as you say."

"Pines. I'll remember that, friend."

Bo leaned back in his chair and sipped his coffee.

"Now you know my story," Bo said, setting his cup on the desk. "So what about you, Officer Dewey? Anything goin' on tonight? You know, crime-wise?"

Bo smiled as the old man warmed to his *spiel*.

"Matter of fact we did have a busy night," Dewey said, puffing up in his seat.

"Really?"

"Started out like a regular old Friday. First thing we got was a report 'a some nonsense at Neely's."

"What's Neely's?"

"Neighborhood tavern. Joe O'Neil's place. He sells beer under the counter an' usually got a nine-ball game for money goin' an' a nickel/dime poker game in the back room. It's illegal as all get out, but we turn a blind eye to it. As long as the neighbors don't complain, we let it go."

"What happened?"

"Some woman, a neighbor I guess—wouldn't give her name—called in an' said she heard glass breakin' and shoutin' goin' on. Maybe a fight. So I rolled a car over. Told 'em no siren, no lights. Didn't wanna' scare 'em off."

"Good move. What'd your boys find?"

"Nothin'. If there was a fight, it was over when they got there and nobody could remember nothin' about it."

"It's the same way in the city," Bo laughed. "No one wants to get involved, but in the next breath they're complainin' that the police can't stop crime. Hell's bells, we aren't magicians or mind readers!"

"You got that right," Dewey chuckled.

"So what else happened? You said you had a busy night. Somethin' more'n this non-existent fight."

"Yes sir. Now we come to the good part," Dewey replied, smiling. "This was big. I even called out the Chief."

"Really? What happened?"

"Round 'bout midnight some fool attacked the richest guy in town."

"Attacked him? You're kiddin' me! What'd they do?"

"Donnoe for sure," Dewey replied.

"But somebody definitely attacked the guy?"

"Yes sir. Jimmy Creedon."

"Creeton?" Bo replied.

"Cree-don," Dewey said. "Jimmy Creedon. Richest guy in the whole damn town. In fact, his granddaddy built this place. At's why it's called Creedonton. He owned most a' it all by hisself. Jimmy's his grandson. He's the last a' the line, an' he inherited everything. Yes sir, he's the richest man around."

Leaning over the desk, Bo whispered. "I know this is police business, so if you can't give me the details I'll understand. But just out of curiosity..." Bo let the sentence dangle, like bait.

"Heck, Bo," Dewey replied, smiling. "Like you said, you and me's on the same side. Brothers of the badge, right?"

"So....?"

"I don't know a whole bunch more," the old man replied. "'Bout midnight the call came in. It was Jimmy hisself. He's all excited, and he says somebody attacked his house."

"Was he hurt?"

"He didn't say. He was just yellin' at me, demandin' the police come immediately. So I sent em'. Two cars."

"Two?"

"Two cars, and I called the Chief, too."

"And the Chief?"

"We're talking about Creedon here," Dewey said.

"Oh, I see what you mean. Account a' he's the rich guy."

"You got it," Dewey nodded.

"You get any follow-up from the Chief about what happened?" Bo asked.

"Naw," Dewey replied shaking his head. "I suspect he was too busy. Jimmy Creedon's not one to mess with. I wouldn't wanna' be in the Chief's shoes, that's for sure. The Chief called in a bit ago and pulled the two guys who was with him off duty. Said they'd be workin' with him on the Creedon thing in the mornin'. He didn't give me no details.

Left me with only one squad car till mornin', but I'll make it work."

"I'm sure you can handle it, officer," Bo said. "That's quite a night you had there."

"Ain't done yet!" Dewey replied.

"No!"

"Yes sir, there's more," Dewey said leaning back in his chair, reveling in the admiration his new friend was shuffling his way.

"Around one-thirty another a call comes in."

"Another!"

"Yes sir. Some guy was out chasin' his dog that ran off. Imagine that, chasin' a stupid dog at that hour. Anyways, he heard this moanin' and found a guy lyin' on the ground busted up pretty bad. So I dispatched the boys over to see what it was all about. Again, no sirens I told 'em. This time on account 'a it was so late."

"Boy, for a small town you officers sure see a lotta' action. More than I see on a night tour in Philly."

"You're kiddin' me?" Dewey replied.

"Heck, no," Bo said smiling. "You boys are really earnin' your keep. Tell me more!"

"Well, turns out it was just a regular drunk... Tony Levansky."

"Lesansky," Bo laughed, "that's a mouthful."

"Le-van-sky," Dewey replied. "Anyway, my guys found him lyin' on the sidewalk. Had himself a bellyfull 'a booze. Poor bastard broke his arm real bad. Paulaski—one a' my guys—even said he thought he saw bone stickin' out.

"But Levansky told my boys he just tripped and didn't want no police involved. Then he shut up tighter 'n a clam. Refused treatment and said he'd fix his arm hisself. Yeah," Dewey laughed, "he'll fix it all right...him an' Jim Beam."

"I hope your boys filed a report," Bo said. "That's the kinda' thing'll come back and bite you in the butt. Especially if his arm was bad as your guy said. You know... this Leksanky gets himself a slick lawyer and tries to make the police look bad for not taking him to a doctor."

"The man's name's Le-van-sky," Dewey said, smiling. "An' Tony Levansky don't want nothin' to do with the law. He's got a record a mile long goin' back to when he he was a pup. He even got hisself tossed outta' the Army. Imagine that. You gotta' be pretty damn bad for them not to want ya'. With his record, Tony ain't gunna' say nothin' that might tie him back to some other shenanigans. Not Tony. He may be a good-for-nothin' drunk, but he ain't stupid neither."

"So let me get this straight. You got this fight... whatever...at that Neely's place, then the thing at the rich guy's place, and then you got a drunk all busted up. In one night!"

"Yes sir," Dewey replied. "One hell of 'a night."

"You got solid write-ups on all of 'em?"

"In the basket there," Dewey said, nodding toward a wire tray on the corner of the desk. "Not much to report on the thing at Neely's. Just that we rolled a car on account 'a that lady callin' in. Then I wrote down pretty much word-for-word what Creedon said when he called. And after that, Paulaski radioed in the details about the Levansky thing. I just wrote down what he said—'specially the part about Levansky refusin' treatment. The boys'll check out the reports and make sure they're okay before they sign 'em. Saves them havin' to do a bunch a' paperwork 'emselves. We do it all the time," he said with a wink.

"Did you get a chance to tell the Chief about the thing at Neely's or about that Leska...Lesvan... whatever...the drunk guy?" Bo asked, laughing.

"No, I didn't," Dewey replied. "The thing at Neely's wasn't nothin', and findin' Tony Levansky drunk ain't news either. I figure the Chief got his plate full with the Creedon thing. He can read the reports in the mornin'."

"You're one heck of a cop," Bo said, standing. He extended his hand toward Dewey and knocked over his half-empty cup, sending lukewarm coffee across the desk toward the old man.

"Oh, shit!" Bo shouted. "You got some towels or somethin'!"

Dewey skidded his chair back as the coffee began dripping over the edge of the desk.

"Got paper towels in the men's room!" Dewey shouted, jumping from his chair and moving quickly toward the rear of the station.

Bo watched the old man scamper down the hall. When Dewey turned the corner, Bo dug into the wire basket. He plopped onto the edge of his seat as Dewey returned with a wad of paper towels.

"Sorry about that," Bo said as Dewey swabbed up the coffee.

"Don't think nothin' about it," Dewey replied as he guided the wet mess into a wastebasket. "No harm done."

"Well, I better be goin' now. I did enough damage here for one night. Sorry," Bo said. "The Pines. That's where you said I should stay, right. That's the place?"

"Yeah, The Pines. Nice clean place...no rif-raf," Dewey replied smiling, leaning back in his chair.

"Thanks," Bo said as he rose and started down the aisle. "You're a good cop, Officer Dewey," he said over his shoulder as he pushed through the glass door. *Thanks a bunch you old fool.*

In his car Bo scribbled two names on a pad. *Neely's* and *Levansky.*

Two blocks later Bo turned into the empty parking lot of the Acme grocery store. Dousing the lights he drove slowly around the store and coasted to a stop at the loading dock. He walked back to the phone booth at the entrance and flipped through the pages of a dog-eared phone book hanging inside. *Neely's.* Nothing in the yellow pages. He checked the whites. O'Neil, Joseph. Bo jotted down the address. 502 North Vine. There was no listing for Levansky.

Bo walked back to his car and set the alarm on a wind-up Big Ben for five-forty-five. Pulling a blanket from the back seat, he curled up and went to sleep.

*****

Harry tiptoed into his living room, tossed the throw pillows off the couch and covered himself as best he could with his uniform jacket. The last thing he wanted to do was wake his wife and have to recount his meeting with Jimmy Creedon.

Sleep came hard as his mind returned to Creedon's ridiculous demand. *Attempted murder, assault with a deadly weapon.*

Around three a.m. exhaustion overtook him and he dozed off. His body clock had him wide awake staring at the ceiling three hours later. He didn't bother to change, just finger-combed his hair in front of the mirror in the foyer, pulled on his jacket and left. In the car he jotted *9 a.m. - Mary* on a dashboard pad, a note to himself to call his wife later in the morning and promise to see her at home for lunch.

Chapter 10

Bo stood on Creedon's porch before the sun came up and punched the doorbell three times. As he waited for an answer he turned to scan the neighborhood. *Hurry the hell up.*

Curtains at the door sidelight parted slightly and Bo caught the movement. Pressing his face close to the glass he mouthed "Bo Lufkin" to the face peering out at him through the narrow window. The curtains fell back and he heard the lock turn. The door opened a crack.

"Mr. Lufkin, I presume?"

"Yeah, you presume right," Bo whispered through the opening. "Come on, hurry up."

The butler opened the door allowing Bo to step inside then closed it quickly and turned the bolt.

"I'll tell Mr. Creedon you're here. Please wait in his study," the butler said motioning to the paneled door to his left.

Bo pushed the door open and squinted into the low-lit room. There was a single light on, a green-shaded banker's lamp on a desk. Stepping inside, Bo scanned the dark room as best he could then took a seat on the Windsor chair that faced the huge wooden desk. Bo noted a deep fresh gouge in the surface. Arms folded across his chest, he sat back in the low seat and waited.

This was a power play, Bo knew, smirking. Creedon would make him wait, signaling who was in charge. But for the money he would make he would wait all day playing Creedon's game, and he chuckled at the thought.

A short time later a door opened on the far side of the room. Footsteps followed and Bo watched as Jimmy Creedon, he assumed, walked toward him then stopped and rested his hands on the top of a large leather desk chair.

In the meager light reflecting off the desk Bo eyed him up. It was Jimmy Creedon all right. Aged some from the last time he had seen him; his hair was grayer, his belly a bit bigger. He was dressed to the nines. Suit, crisp white shirt, silk tie, and a sparkle reflected off a huge diamond tie pin he wore for show.

"You make a grand entrance," Bo remarked.

Creedon held his spot behind the leather chair. "It rattles some people."

"Some people," Bo replied, smiling.

Creedon swiveled the desk chair, plopped down, and spun around.

"I'm glad you came quickly."

"Money has a way of motivating me," Bo laughed.

"Had a pleasant drive up from the city?"

"Not much traffic in the wee hours. But we're not here to talk about my late night foray into the hinterlands are we?"

"You never were one for small talk," Creedon replied with a tone of indignation.

"When the meter's running, I really don't care. It's your money, Mr. Creedon, so if you want, we can talk about the drive, what I ate on the way, where I stopped to take a leak ...anything you want."

"So down to business," Creedon said, miffed at Bo's reply. "You know why I called you?"

"'Cause I'm the best money can buy."

"Modesty—and small talk—not your strong suits."

"Not by a long shot."

"I called you," Creedon said curtly, "because you're probably the best for what I have in mind. And you've proved yourself capable of, shall we say, 'completing the job'."

"Just like before, I'll do what needs to be done, for the right price," Bo replied, smiling. "On the phone you just said somebody attacked you, but you didn't want to elaborate. You look pretty unscathed to me."

"No one was physically hurt."

"So what exactly was this 'attack'?"

"Have you seen the turret?"

"Turd?" Bo laughed.

"Turr-et. The round tower on the corner of the house."

"No," Bo replied, still chuckling. "I haven't seen it. In fact, I was never in your house before. Last time we met in your downtown office, remember?"

"Follow me," Creedon said.

Creedon led them down the dark hallway then stopped suddenly, forcing Bo to check his step to avoid bumping into him. Bo heard the click of a switch, and a room to his left burst into light. Bo turned toward it quickly.

Responding just as Harry did earlier, Bo was awestruck by the opulence.

Creedon gave him a moment to ogle the splendor then motioned with his head toward the south side of the room. A gray tarp billowed through a shattered window frame and into the room, like a Santa Claus belly.

"There," Creedon said nodding. "What do you see?"

"Canvas over a busted window."

"Yes!" Creedon replied angrily. "Dirty canvas covering a hole...a hole that until last night held a masterpiece!"

"Masterpiece?"

"A stained glass window was in that...that...hole! A phenomenal work of art!" Creedon bellowed.

"From the looks of the rest of this room, I'm guessing it was expensive," Bo replied.

"It was priceless!" Creedon shouted. "A one-of-a-kind stained glass window! Commissioned by my grandfather as a tribute to his extraordinary success! An irreplaceable masterpiece! And now it's destroyed! Do you understand what this means?"

"What happened to it?" Bo asked, walking closer to the window and glancing down as his feet crushed glass into the carpet.

"Someone attacked my home and destroyed it!" Creedon shouted. "That's why you're here. I want you to find out who did it and why. And I want you to find out before the police do!"

"You called the cops?" Bo asked softly as he stared at the canvas-covered hole.

"When I heard a crash, I called the police from upstairs. But I had no idea it was this," Creedon said, walking to Bo's side, his hands outstretched toward the shattered frame. "Had I know it was this…"

"You did the right thing," Bo said, still staring at the wrecked window frame.

"Why do you say that?" Creedon asked.

"You can't pretend it didn't happen. I'd bet a hundred people know by now."

"Way more than that," Creedon replied. "The crowd in the street last night was huge."

"Tell me about the police," Bo asked, aimlessly reaching out to twist a piece of lead wire from the frame.

"Two officers came first, and later the Chief of Police."

Bo turned and stared at Creedon. "So why don't you let the local cops handle it? Two cops plus their Chief show up. I'd say they're taking this seriously."

Creedon laughed.

"The truth is, Mr. Lufkin, I don't want the local cops to find the guy who did this; I want you to find him."

"Why? If the cops find him or I do, either way you get the guy," Bo said.

"But if the cops find him, I won't get justice," Creedon replied.

"Justice?"

"Let's assume the local yokels bumble onto the guy," Creedon said. "We'll have some hoodlum

---

64

facing a misdemeanor. He'll say he was drunk or pissed off at me for some reason. He'll get a slap on the wrist, maybe start to pay a pittance in restitution before he disappears. But as sure as hell that won't be enough. I won't see him just walk away. Not after doing this," Creedon said, pausing. "That's why I told the police chief I expect the charge to be attempted murder, assault with a deadly weapon."

"For a busted window?" Bo said, incredulously.

"A destroyed masterpiece!" Creedon shouted.

"To you, maybe. But at the end of the day, it's just a window, and breaking a window ain't attempted murder any way you cut it," Bo pressed.

"Just hear me out," Creedon shot back. "I only said it to slow them down. Make them think, then double-think every step they take. I want them figuring they have to be one-hundred percent sure they have the right guy, thinking that I'll be pushing for serious charges.

"You see," Creedon continued, chuckling, "when I told the police chief I wanted the charge to be attempted murder and assault, I could tell he thought I was crazy. But I guarantee you he's <u>not</u> sure I won't pull out all the stops and try to make the charge stick. So the cops will be very, very cautious, and that'll slow them down, giving us time to find out who did it. Then we—you and I together —will ensure that real justice is done."

"So what you're saying is that if we find the guy, you could fix it to come out any way you want to. A broken window somehow becomes something a hell of a lot bigger."

"What I'm saying," Creedon shouted, "is that I own this town! If I say pigs can fly, I can get ten people to swear that they saw them do it. You catch my drift?"

"Sounds like you're the master of your own destiny."

"Like I said, I own this town and I control almost everyone in it. You have any idea what it's like to be that much in charge?"

"Probably a heady thing," Bo laughed.

There was a pregnant pause. Bo studied Creedon. The smirk, the glint in his eye. Creedon was basking about the extent of his power.

Bo broke the silence.

"Actually, the local police don't have much information about this," Bo said softly, waiting to see if his comment would get Creedon's attention. It did.

"How do you know that? And since you do, I take it you already knew I called the police. So... earlier...why'd you ask me if I did?"

"I asked if you called them to see if you were on the up-and-up with me. If you said you didn't, I would have walked out the door. No one's going to pit me against the local cops without my knowing it.

"As to your question: 'How do I know about how their investigation's going?' I paid a visit to the police station before I came here. I always wanna' know what I'm up against. And I can tell you this: The cops'll be starting from square one with nothing, and they won't be able to get any leads from other events that happened last night. Things that just might be tied in to what happened here."

"I don't understand." Creedon said.

"An old cop at the police station told me about some other events that happened before and after your incident here. Maybe, just maybe," Bo cautioned, "they could have something to do with you and your precious window. You know, one thing leads to another. I'll check them out, and if there's a common thread, we'll be miles ahead of the police in finding your man."

"What 'events'"? Creedon demanded.

"There was some ruckus earlier tonight at a neighborhood bar called Neely's. You know it?"

"Yeah, I know it. It's a hole-in-the-wall poolroom on Vine Street."

Bo nodded. "That's it. Anyway, someone— probably a neighbor—called the cops about a fight at the place. But when the cops showed up, everyone suddenly got amnesia. They didn't give the cops anything to go on. But from my experience, little fights can lead to bigger things."

"I still don't get the connection," Creedon said.

"Think about it this way," Bo replied. "Maybe the fight at this Neely's place involved someone you had dealings with, and tonight the guy was humiliated in front of his drinkin' buddies. He gets thinking about how someone else kicked the pins out from under him. Maybe yesterday, maybe years ago, who knows. So he decides to strike out —salve his shattered ego. And maybe that someone he goes after is you. I'm sure you alienated a few folks over the years."

"I deal with business people!" Creedon shouted. "Not low-life scum that sneak around in the dark hurling rocks!"

"You're telling me you never canned a miner or closed down a shopkeeper for not paying the rent?" Bo asked, staring at Creedon.

"I hear your logic," Creedon replied, nodding. "But you said 'events'. More than one. What else happened?"

"Some local rummy got busted up pretty bad. The cops showed up and he told them he tripped and fell down."

"What in the world would that have to do with me?" Creedon shouted.

"I seen a lot of drunks in my day, and most of them bounce," Bo replied, laughing.

"What the hell does that mean?" Creedon shouted.

"Drunks fall down all the time, but they don't get hurt bad. Like I said, most of them just bounce. I saw one fall out a two-story window and land in some bushes. He got up, pulled a pint from his pocket, took a hit, and walked away like he stepped off a curb," Bo replied, laughing at the memory.

"The guy last night told the cops he tripped. But he was hurt pretty bad. Worse than taking a little juiced-up spill. So my guess is someone else might have been involved in his little 'accident'. Maybe trying to shut him up about something he saw...or did.

"Maybe the guy who was out to get you talked the drunk into tossing the rock and now he wants him out of the picture...for good. Hey," Bo added, "it might be nothing, but then again, it might be related to what happened here. But knowing about the fracas at the bar and the drunk getting busted up later, that gives me two things to start checking out. And the police don't know anything about them."

"How do you know but the police don't?" Creedon asked, his eyes locked on Bo.

"Like I said, the old cop at the station told me what happened. The cops that were called out to investigate radioed their reports to him. But the Chief and the two officers trying to find your guy don't know anything about them. The old cop at the night desk wrote up the reports, but the Chief hasn't read them. And he won't be seeing them any time soon."

"How do you know that?"

Bo smiled. "Because before I left the station, I made sure the reports were...let's say...not readily available."

"You did that?"

"Did what?" Bo replied, with a wink.

"You are good."

"And expensive," Bo added.

"What do we do now?" Creedon asked.

"We?" Bo replied smirking. "For now, let's leave it to *me*, not *we*. You stay out of it. I'll keep you updated, and when it comes time for a tough decision to be made it'll definitely be your call. Now if you'll excuse me I've got work to do. And I don't like using the front door. I take it there's a rear entrance to this wonderful house of yours?"

"Through the kitchen. The door leads to the garage and the alley behind the house."

Bo followed Creedon into the kitchen. At the door Creedon stopped and turned. "About your fee?"

"Let's work on a sliding scale, depending on what I find...and what needs to be done about it. We can talk about it later. I'm sure we'll come to an agreement."

Bo walked through the kitchen door leaving Jimmy Creedon in the threshold.

Chapter 11

Harry stopped for a coffee to go at Ann's and pushed through the glass door of the station house at six forty-five. "Yo, Dewey!"

"Hey," Dewey replied, turning in the hallway as Harry walked toward him. "Hang on a minute Chief, I gotta' get rid of some coffee. Now!"

Harry laughed as Dewey squirmed in the hallway wide-eyed and crossed-legged.

"Anything up?" he called as Dewey headed toward the men's room.

"Everything's in the basket," Dewey yelled over his shoulder.

Harry picked up a half-dozen sheets from the top of the wire tray on the corner of Dewey's desk and thumbed through them quickly. Dropping them back in the basket, he walked to his office and plopped down at his desk.

Dewey stopped outside Harry's door. "You seen the reports?"

"Yeah," Harry mumbled.

"Okay," Dewey shrugged. "See you tonight."

"Yeah, I'll catch you later Dewey. Sleep tight."

As he waited for Garver and Mains, Harry used the phone book to make a list of stops then numbered them according to their proximity to Creedon's. Fifteen minutes later Garver and Mains reported in.

"First, talk to Garver's niece. After that, hit the bars. Here's a list to start with," Harry said.

"This is only bars," Garver said, scanning the sheet. "You didn't write down the Moose or the Elks or the VFW. You even left off the hosies. How's come? All of them serve booze."

"I know," Harry replied, sighing. "We got a shitload 'a bars but we don't have the manpower to hit 'em all. Remember, Paulaski's best man in his brother's wedding today and Cooper finished off the night shift. Man's gotta' get some rest. That leaves just you two for now. So I'm figurin' we focus on the little places. The clubs keep a pretty close eye on their customers...try not to let them get too outta' hand. The neighborhood bars are in it for the money. They're less apt to kick a guy out who's emptyin' his pockets. I may be wrong, but I think for now we gotta' focus on them. Check out as many as you can, then let's meet up here at eleven for a status check, okay?"

"Hey, at least it's a plan," Garver said, stuffing the list into his pocket. "Come on, Tom."

"Good luck!" Harry said as they moved toward the door.

"Luck. That's what we're gunna' need," Garver replied, laughing.

Chapter 12

Bo got breakfast in the restaurant next to The Pines Motel then checked into a room. Showered, shaved, dressed in a fresh white shirt, suit and tie, he drove off at nine.

In town—and frustrated—he pulled to the curb and rolled down his window, watching in the mirror as a boy on a bike came his way. "Hey," he shouted as the kid rolled by. Skidding to a stop, the kid walked his bike back to Bo's window.

"Whatch'a want mister?"

"I'm lookin' for a place called Neely's. Five hundred and two North Vine."

"Right there," the boy said, motioning with his head. "Catty-corner."

Bo looked where they boy was pointing and saw a house, the first in the block of shoulder-to-shoulder row homes that lined the street.

"I'm not lookin' for a house. I'm lookin' for a place called Neely's. It's a bar...poolroom."

"That's it," the boy insisted, gesturing again to the house on the corner. By his insolent tone the kid could have added *idiot* to his reply. Cranking hard on the pedals, the kid took off down the street.

Bo drifted his car to a spot around the corner. Mounting the porch he asked "Neely's?" through the wood-framed screen door. He was certain the kid was mistaken.

"Door's open," came from inside.

Bo pulled the door handle and stepped through the threshold, squinting into the darkness. "Is this Neely's?"

"Is the Pope Catholic?'

"You open for business?" Bo asked.

"Door was unlocked wasn't it? I'd say that means I'm open."

The musty smell of stale beer and old smoke permeated the place. In the dim light Bo saw a bar running the length of the far wall in what had once been a living room. Behind the bar was a big man, palms down on the counter.

Bo walked in slowly and slid onto a backless chrome stool.

"Can a man buy a beer?"

"Is the Pope Catholic?" the big man replied, laughing as he plugged a well-chewed cigar into the corner his mouth.

"I suspect he is," Bo said, shifting his weight on the stool to extract a money clip from his pocket. He peeled off a twenty and laid it on the bar. "So, seein as how the Pope *is* Catholic and you *are* open, I'll have a beer."

"What's your pleasure?"

"Whatta' ya' have?"

"You got two choices. The beer's Yuengling, and your choices are warm or cold.

"Cold," Bo said, laughing. "And a glass."

"A glass?"

"And a glass," Bo replied. "Are you Neely?"

"That's what they call me," the bartender replied.

"Mornin' mister."

The voice startled him and Bo swiveled on his stool. In the darkness at the far end of the bar a wild-haired rumpled old man smiled at him with a happy half-drunk grin.

"Don't mind Stubby," Neely said waving his hand in the old guy's direction. "He jus' 'bout lives here."

"Stubby?" Bo asked as the old man quickly slid down four stools and settled in at his side.

"Jus' Stubby."

"Get my friend a beer," Bo said. "On me."

"Cold one, no glass," Stubby said quickly.

"You don't need to buy him no beer," Neely said.

"Don't need to, but I want to," Bo replied.

"Suit yourself."

Sliding the top of a red Coke cooler aside, Neely reached in and brought up two dripping bottles . He wrenched the caps off and set them down. "Two cold Yings." Turning, he pulled a scarred tumbler from the shelf behind him and smacked it on the bar. "An' a glass."

He scooped up Bo's twenty and punched the keys on a brass cash register on the far wall. After setting Bo's change on the bar, he retreated to a low stool.

"Thanks mister," Stubby said, upending his bottle and sucking down half its contents in a gulp.

"Call me Bo."

Stubby set his bottle down and extended his hand. He made a snorting laugh as Bo offered his hand, then slowly drew it back. His right and the old man's left didn't line up.

Stubby snorted again as he raised his right arm from his lap. At the end of his wrist was a mangled protrusion of what had once been a hand. Just a gnarled piece of thumb and four short nubs.

"It's why they call me Stubby."

"I see," Bo said, eyeing the deformity.

"Lost it when I was twelve. In the breaker."

"The breaker?"

"Coal breaker," Stubby replied as he finished off his beer.

"Another?" Bo asked.

"Sure!"

"You don't need to be buyin' him more. He'll gladly tell you his life story for free," Neely said as Bo nodded toward Stubby's empty bottle.

"I don't need to, but I want to," Bo replied, dismissing the bartender's remark.

"You ain't from 'round here, are you?" Stubby asked, reaching quickly for his fresh beer.

"What makes you think that?"

"'Cause you ain't never heard of a coal breaker, right?"

"You're in for an earfull, stranger," Neely said as he took the money for Stubby's drink from Bo's pile of change.

"Breaker boys," Stubby said after slugging from his bottle. "We was eight, ten, maybe twelve years old. Too young to be miners, so we worked the breaker. At's where they crush the coal and sort it out. They got names for the different sizes... buckwheat, rice, pea.

"Our job was to pick out rocks, slate, wood 'an other junk from the coal. We was sittin' on wood slats over the chutes and reached down to pluck out the crap. Ten hour shift, two bucks," he added.

"So I'm reaching down one day an' the coal's comin' down the chute like a black river. Afore I know it my hand gets stuck. Then zip," he said, snapping the fingers on his good hand. "A piece 'a slate comes whizzin' by and off goes my fingers. Cut 'em off better'n a knife."

"Good God!" Bo said, choking on a sip of beer.

Stubby laughed at Bo's reaction.

"Now blood...it's squirtin' out like water from a spigot. The boss man comes over an' wraps a dirty rag around what's left 'a my hand, then he says, 'Go on, git. You're fired.'"

"No!"

"Yes sir. As fast as that coal comes down the chute you coulda' had three hands and barely keep up. But now I got jus' one. Ain't no way I coulda' done that job no more. So I got me no right hand, no job, no nothin'."

"You sue them?" Bo asked.

Stubby laughed out loud.

"You sure as hell ain't from 'round here! Sue Jimmy Creedon?" Stubby bellowed. "Hell, Bo, Jimmy Creedon is the law. Anyone stupid enough to try an' sue him is dumber'n a rock!"

"I can't believe it. You just let it go!"

"Wasn't nothin' I could do. It's the cards I got dealt."

"You believe that?"

"Believe it or not, it's the truth. Nobody forced me work the breaker," Stubby replied.

"But you were only a kid! You lost your hand for God's sake."

"Mister," Stubby said solemnly, "I wanted that job...begged for it in fact. There was eight kids in my family and I was the oldest. I had ta' work. Had ta' do my part. T'was an accident is all. Wasn't nobody's fault but my own."

Bo stared at the old man.

Stubby stared back then spoke. "A couple'a years later I moved out. Didn't wanna' drag down the family no more. One less mouth ta' feed."

"So whatta' you do? How do you get by?" Bo asked.

"The regular thing I do is sweep up at the Wilson shirt factory. Five till midnight durin' the week, Saturdays eleven-thirty ta' five. Other than that I pick up soda bottles for the deposit. Sometimes I go to the slag heaps an' bag up any coal I can find. I get good money for that.

"So how's about you?" Stubby asked, finishing off his beer and wiping his mouth with his sleeve. "You got a pocketful a' money, and we already 'stablished you ain't from 'round here. What brings you to these parts?"

"Give him another," Bo said to the barkeep as he framed up how he would answer.

"You sure?"

"Is the Pope Catholic?" Bo replied. Both he and Stubby laughed at Bo's one-upping Neely at his own game.

Neely reluctantly shoved another beer in front of Stubby then retreated to his stool. Bo watched as he opened a newspaper and pretended to read. *He's a lousy pretender,* Bo thought.

"Me," Bo said, watching as Neely cocked his ear to hear. "I'm from Philly. Was just driving up this way on business, headin' to Shamokin. I was never up here before, and I came down the road and saw the sign saying 'Welcome to Creedonton'. And whatta' you know, I met a guy in the Army who came from here. I haven't seen him in years, so I thought I might stop by and try to look him up. I remembered him talking about a place called Neely's, so I asked a guy at the gas station a couple of blocks over and he gave me the address. So here I am."

"What's your Army buddy's name?" Stubby asked.

"Tony," Bo said, tilting his head back as if searching his memory for the rest of the name. "La...La-nan..."

"Levansky, Tony Levansky?" Stubby asked, excitedly.

"Yeah! That's it! Tony Levansky," Bo said. "You know him?"

"Hell, yeah!" Stubby said, slapping his good hand on the bar. "I know Tony. Knowed him all my life."

"You're kiddin' me!"

"Heck, no. Me an' Tony's like that," Stubby said, holding up the intertwined index and middle finger of his good hand.

"You're puttin' me on!" Bo said.

"No sir."

Bo stared at the old man, thinking about how he'd capitalize on the goldmine of information sitting next to him.

"Well then set me straight," Bo finally said. "I wanna' see if ole' Tony was bullshittin' us with his stories. All the time he was braggin' about how good an athlete he was in high school."

"Athlete!" Stubby laughed. "Tony Levansky ain't no athlete, less you count liftin' a bottle to be a sport."

"No!" Bo replied. "Tony told us all the time how good a ball player he was. Said in his day he could throw a baseball a hundred yards."

It was Bo's second cast at fishing for information that might tie Levansky to Creedon. Stubby's next remark derailed the connection.

"'Bout the only balls Levansky plays with is the ones on a pool table, and only if he's playin' some sucker for money."

"You're tellin' me his baseball story was bull?"

"Tony couldn't throw a ball ten feet. Like I said, the only exercise he does is this," Stubby said, pumping his beer bottle overhead like a dumbbell. "Fact is, drinkin's about the only thing Tony does good. That and get in trouble. Got hisself in a mix-up last night right here, out back."

"Really?" Bo asked, trying hard to keep his enthusiasm in check.

Bo knew he was onto something as he caught Neely looking over the top of his newspaper as Stubby continued.

"Didn't see it myself, but what I heard is Tony was tellin' 'bout seein' Andy Dugan get killed in the mines robbin' the pillars. Trouble was, Andy's kid was out back unner' the porch with some a' his pals. The kid heard Tony, and he went off on him."

"That thing the kid's dad was doing...robbin' pillars. What's that mean?" Bo asked.

"It's when you go inta' a worked out mine and dig out the coal from the pillars holdin' up the roof. You go in hopin' to grub out some coal an' skedaddle 'afore the roof caves in."

"Shit! That sounds dangerous," Bo said.

"'Bout the most dangerous job there is."

"So why'd they do it?"

"For the coal," Stubby laughed. "At's the name a' the game. Get as much coal as you can."

"It sounds stupid!"

"Like tellin' a kid to stick his hand inta' a' roarin' coal chute," Stubby replied, raising his gnarled hand.

"Anyways," Stubby continued, "from what I hear, the kid and Levansky was yellin' at each other. Then the kid picked up a gooney and beaned Tony with it. Caught him right in the forehead," Stubby laughed. "Tony's buddies held him back from goin' after the kid with a busted bottle."

"That kid must'a been scared to death. The Tony I remember was a tough egg. The kid must'a been pretty big...or pretty stupid," Bo said.

"The Dugan boy's pretty big, ain't he, Neely?" Stubby blurted out.

Neely threw the newspaper down and glared at the old man.

"Dugan kid's pretty big, right, Neely?" Stubby repeated.

Neely ignored the question and moved to the edge of the bar, staring hard-eyed at Stubby, shaking his finger in his face. "You said enough Stubby. Just shut up."

"Just tellin' the man what happened las' night is all," the old man replied.

"You said enough," Neely barked again, and he turned to Bo. "Listen mister, you're askin' a lotta' questions for a stranger. I don't know what you're after, but I don't want no trouble here. Stubby's had enough to drink. He's cut off, and you are, too. So take your money and go."

"I didn't mean any harm," Bo replied, returning the bartender's icy stare. "I'm just interested in tryin' to find my old pal Levansky."

"Well he ain't here now, and there's nothin' more to tell you," Neely shot back.

"Thanks for your hospitality," Bo said sarcastically, sliding off his stool.

"You forgot your change," Neely called as Bo walked away.

"Give it to Stubby," Bo said.

Stubby waived his mangled right hand as Bo stepped off the porch.

Chapter 13

"We caught up with my niece," Garver reported when he, Mains and Harry met at the station at eleven o'clock.

"Anything?" Harry asked.

"Zilch. Accordin' to her, Creedon didn't fire anyone in months. Coal ain't worth squat any more, an' the mines are down to skeleton crews. Anyone that got a job is glad to have it 'an they ain't gunna' do nothin' ta' rock the boat."

"Learn anything at the bars?"

"Nothin'," Garver replied glumly. "We hit about a dozen places and talked to the bartenders and some guys gettin' an eye-opener. Nobody we talked to said anything outta' the ordinary happened."

"We heard about a couple'a guys pissed off about their bad luck. You know, losin' at poker, craps, nine-ball, the usual stuff," Mains added. "But nobody said anything about anyone bad mouthin' Creedon."

"So we got nothin'," Harry replied dejectedly, massaging his forehead.

"There's some places on the list we haven't hit yet," Garver offered. "I say we keep checkin' the bars. I still think it's our best bet."

"I sure wish we had somethin' more to go on," Mains added.

"Wishin'," Harry said, shaking his head and laughing softly. "My grandpa used to say people in Hell wished they had ice water. That's about all wishin' is worth. Since we don't have anything yet, I agree with Garver; keep knockin' out the list. I'm going home for lunch in a little bit. Call me if you find anything. Anything at all."

Chapter 14

Bo checked right and left as he slowly rolled through the intersections. At Third and Chestnut he spotted what he was searching for. Next to a three-story red brick school kids were playing softball in the schoolyard.

He parked on the far side of the street and walked toward them, pulling two dollars from his fold.

"Hey kid," he shouted to a boy who was swinging a bat at the air getting ready for his turn at the plate. "Come here a minute. Gotta' ask you a question."

"I'm up next."

"I got two dollars that says it can wait," Bo said, holding the bills up.

The boy dropped the bat and jogged toward him, ignoring the angry shouts of the other players.

"Whatta' ya' want mister?"

"You know a kid named Dugan?"

"Who wants to know?"

"Me and two George Washingtons," Bo said, sliding the bills together between his upraised fingers.

"I know Jack Dugan," the boy replied, moving for the money.

Bo lifted the bills out of the boy's reach. "Is he in the game there?"

"Jack Dugan don't play with us. He's too big. And too good. He was varsity and he'd burn that ball in 'afore you even seen it leave his hand. College scouts was even watchin' him," the boy added, eying the bills.

"One more question and the money's yours. Who does Jack hang around with?"

"Tommy Delaney, George Stoke an' some other big kids."

"You know where I might find them?"

"No fair!" the boy protested. "That's another question!"

"Worth another three bucks?" Bo asked, reaching into his pocket and peeling three more bills from his clip.

The boy's eyes lit up. "For sure?"

"For sure."

"Tommy Delaney works in his pop's hardware store on Saturday."

"And another five bucks will get me the name of the store?"

"Delaney's!" the boy squealed.

"Thanks," Bo said, pocketing the singles and pulling out a ten. "Here you go, pal."

Bo watched the boy scamper back to the school yard, waving his fortune over his head.

Delaney's, Tommy Delaney, George Stoke, college scouts. Bo scribbled the notes on his pad. Before he drove off he added another line: *Jack Dugan—hot arm.*

Bo rolled down the main street checking the signs. He spotted Delaney's Hardware and drove past it and pulled into a parking spot a block away. Meandering down the sidewalk, he paused at several stores. Feigning interest in the displays, he eyed the reflection in the windows to see if anyone was watching him. Two more stops and he was satisfied that no one was paying him any attention.

In front of Delaney's Bo paused briefly to study the store hours posted on the door. The storefront held a display of handyman stuff. A pyramid of boxes of grass seed, a garden sprayer, shovels, dirt claws—things Bo didn't own nor ever cared to.

Pulling the door open, he was accosted by a stew of odors. The smell of linseed oil, musty burlap, and the sweet tang of pesticides assaulted his nose.

The place was a throwback in time. White milk glass globes hung from a pressed tin ceiling. The side wall was filled with small drawers with hardware items stapled to them. An old man in a denim apron was perched on a stool behind the counter.

"Something I can help you with?"

Bo squinted at the old man then did a quick check of the nearby shelves. "Paint?" he asked.

"In the back room," the old man replied, pointing with his head. "My grandson's back there. He can help you."

Bo's gamble at seeing neither paint nor a boy in the front of the store paid off. He smiled as he walked slowly in the direction the old man had gestured.

"Hello," Bo called out as he entered a small alcove crowded with cans. A young boy peered from around a shelf.

"Lookin' for paint?"

"Matter of fact, I am," Bo said, picking a can off the shelf and pretending to read the label. "Wall paint. Is this right?"

"No," the boy laughed, reaching for the can. "That's enamel. You use it on floors or to keep metal from rustin'. For walls you want latex. Over here."

"You're a smart young man," Bo said.

"There ain't a whole lot to know about paint. Not if you work here," the boy added quickly, realizing his remark might be taken as an insult.

"Well, you saved me from buying the wrong stuff. Thanks there...," Bo paused, hoping the boy would offer up his name. The kid missed the cue. "What's your name, son?" Bo asked.

"Tommy. Tommy Delaney".

"Pleased to meet you, Tommy."

Bo waited until the boy put the can in a shaker and hit the switch, knowing that the racket of the vibrating machine would cover their conversation. Walking to the boy's side, Bo whispered in his ear.

"I heard you were with Jack Dugan last night."

The boy jumped back and stared at Bo with deer-in-the-headlight eyes.

Bo reached into his breast pocket for his wallet and flipped it open. The boy gasped when he saw the gold badge.

"I didn't do nothin'!"

"I didn't say you did, Tommy," Bo said, turning his head, making sure no one could see them. "But I heard you were at Neely's with Jack Dugan last night. And you saw what happened between him and Tony Levansky."

The boy inhaled, and Bo smiled.

"You aren't in trouble, Tommy," Bo said, and the boy exhaled. "But I want you to tell me what happened. The truth."

The boy shuffled his feet and stared at the floor.

"The truth, Tommy!" Bo hissed. "Now!"

"Jack got riled when he heard Levansky talkin' 'bout how his dad was killed," the boy replied softly.

"What'd Jack do?"

"He yelled at Levansky. Told him to shut up."

"That's all? Jack just yelled at him?" Bo pressed. The boy wouldn't look at him.

"What else!" Bo hissed. "The truth, Tommy!"

"Levansky wouldn't shut up, an' he was laughin', too, so Jack flung a rock at him. Hit him square in the head."

"You're sure?"

"Yeah. I seen it."

"What happened after that?"

"Levansky went nuts. He smashed the end off a bottle an' was yellin' at Jack, sayin' he'd cut him to ribbons. He was wavin' the bottle like a knife." The boy gestured the movement with his hand. "But Levansky's pals grabbed him an' held him back."

"Did Jack say anything else?"

The boy paused.

"What! What did he say!"

"He told Levansky to shut up or he'd kill him. Then he took off."

The kid was shaking, breathing hard.

"It's okay, Tommy," Bo said reassuringly. He put his hands on the boy's shoulders and stared into his eyes. "I have one more question: Do you know where Jack went?"

"No, no I don't. All I know is he ran off."

"Did you see which way he went?"

"No."

"Honest?" Bo pressed.

The boy stared away.

Bo reached around and cranked the timer on the paint shaker to keep the machine rattling, then he patted the breast pocket where he had put the badge.

"I'll ask you one more time...here and now. But if you don't tell the truth, Tommy, the next stop will be the police station. So, one more time: Did you see which way Jack went?"

The boy blinked back tears. "He ran down Fourth Street. I tried to follow him, but he's a lot faster than me."

"He was running toward his house?"

"At first, but then he turned the corner."

"Corner of Fourth and...?"

"Chestnut," the boy replied.

"He turned down Chestnut?"

"Yeah. I guess he wasn't goin' home."

"Did you see where he went after that?"

"I saw him in the streetlight go left at Third."

"Going further away from his house?"

"Yeah," the boy mumbled.

"Turning onto Third had him headed downtown. He would cross...." Bo paused, letting the boy fill in the blanks.

"Cherry, then Beech, Oak, Hickory," the boy rattled off the cross streets.

"And after that is?"

The boy paused before answering. "I think Maple's next, if he ran that far. But like I said, he was ahead a' me and I don't know which street he mighta' turned on."

"You're sure?"

Bo watched the boy's eyes, listened to his breathing.

The timer on the paint shaker ran its course and the machine wobbled to a stop.

Bo knew the boy was holding back, but he wasn't going to press his luck. The last thing Bo wanted was to have the kid start wailing and have the old man up front call the cops.

"The paint's done," Bo said, nodding to the shaker. "But listen up, Tommy," he whispered as the boy nervously turned the crank to release the can. "This is serious business." He patted his breast pocket again. "You don't tell anyone about our conversation. Not your grandpa out front, not Jack Dugan, no one. Understand?"

"Yes sir," the boy replied, searching Bo's eyes. "I ain't in trouble am I, mister?"

"Not if you keep this to yourself."

Bo took the paint can and walked down the aisle. He knew Tommy was staring at him, scared to death.

At the counter the old man in the denim apron rang up the sale.

"That's a real smart grandson you have there," Bo said, handing the man a twenty.

"He helped you find what you wanted?"

"Yes sir, he did," Bo replied. "Absolutely. And give that to the boy," he added, pointing to the change in the old man's hand. "Real nice store you have here. Been here long?"

"Thirty some years. First my pop, now me and my son. Maybe some day the boy back there'll take 'er over," the old man replied.

"Must be nice owning a place like this... something to pass on," Bo said.

"We don't own the store," the old man chuckled. "Just rent it from Jimmy Creedon. As long as we pay him the rent on time, we're fine. Just pay the rent when it's due, that's the deal."

"Still, I bet it's nice having the family involved. And, by the way," Bo added, "in case I need something else small...like a paint brush or somethin'...does the boy ever make deliveries? Could I call in and have him bring it?"

"Absolutely. He does it all the time," the old man said.

"He knows his way around town?"

"Oh, yeah," the old man replied.

"That's good to know," Bo said, smiling. "Very good to know."

"Hope to see you again," the old man said as Bo moved toward the door.

Chapter 15

Bo was looking for somewhere to grab an early lunch when he spotted a police car in front of a place with a swinging tin sign. Alma's. Neon beer signs hung in the front window.

Bo pulled into a parking spot and unfolded a road map. Glancing over the top of it, he watched until two cops walked out of the place and drove off. Bo waited until the black and white turned the corner.

"Mornin'," Bo said as he entered the place. He slipped onto a swivel seat and quickly scanned the room. He was the only patron.

"Good mornin' to you, too," the lone barkeep said, rising from a stool.

"Heck!" Bo said, laughing. "In a place called Alma's, I was expectin' a cute little gal, not some ugly mug like you." Bo knew it was a lame line, but he gambled that it might break the ice with the guy.

The barkeeper did one of those 'ha, ha, haven't heard that one before' laughs.

"I really need a drink. A real drink," Bo said. "Jim Beam, double, on the rocks."

"Bad day?" the bartender said as he set a glass with ice on the bar and poured generously.

"That's a double?" Bo remarked, eying the brimming drink.

"Sounds like you could use a heavy pour."

"You got that right. Thanks," Bo said, toasting the bartender with his glass before taking a swallow. "The company sent me up here from Harrisburg to close a sale. 'In and out' they said. 'Slam dunk," Bo said, rolling his eyes.

"Didn't quite go that way?" the bartender laughed.

"Not by a long shot," Bo said, slapping his glass down. "The guy negotiating the deal tried to beat me down with everything but a stick."

"Folks around here are real careful with their money."

"Careful my foot. That guy has his pants pockets sewed shut," Bo said, taking another hit on his drink as the bartender laughed at his remark.

"Welcome to the coal region," the bartender chuckled.

"So," Bo said, "I saw two cops coming out a couple'a minutes ago. Something wrong?"

"No," the bartender replied, swabbing a towel across the bar. "They were just lookin' for information. Last night somebody busted some expensive window at Jimmy Creedon's house. He's a high falutin' rich guy," the bartender added, remembering Bo wasn't a local. "The cops asked if I heard anyone bad mouthin' him. You know, spoutin' off 'I'll get that SOB'."

"Seein' if somebody found a little bravery in a bottle?" Bo asked.

"Yeah, somethin' like that," the barkeep laughed. "A buddy a' mine at a place a couple'a blocks away called me 'bout a half hour ago. He said the cops were at his place askin' the same question."

"Checkin' out bars sounds like a decent plan," Bo replied, voicing the uneasy thought what was going through his mind. "You have anybody here match up?"

"No, just the usual Friday night crowd. Neighborhood guys celebratin' payday. Pretty quiet group...for a bunch a' guys suckin' down beers," the bartender added, laughing. "Another?" motioning toward Bo's drink.

"No more," Bo said after draining the dregs from his glass. "You got a menu?"

"No, sorry. We don't get enough lunchtime traffic to make it worthwhile. Try Ann's downtown, the food there's pretty good."

"Thanks for the advice," Bo said, rising from his stool. "How much do I owe you?"

"Buck fifty."

Bo set a five on the bar. "Keep the change."

"Thanks," the bartender beamed.

"You're welcome. Nice talking with you," Bo said. At the door he stopped and turned back. "You got a phone book I could use?"

"Sure, pal." The bartender reached under the counter and flopped a well-thumbed book on the bar.

Bo pulled out his pad as he flipped through the pages. He jotted down an address. "Thanks," he said, sliding the book across the bar.

"Good luck with your sale."

"Oh, yeah, luck. I'm gunna' need it," Bo said as he pushed through the door.

Bo sat in his car drumming his fingers on the steering wheel.

The cops are checking out bars looking for someone mouthing off about Creedon. Pretty good plan. Something I'd probably do if I was in their shoes with nothing else to go on. Try to find someone mad at Creedon and with enough juice in him to take a shot. Maybe Jimmy Creedon had underestimated the local police.

He also recalled what Stubby and Tommy Delaney said: *Levansky's pals held him back.*

Levansky's pals. If the cops latched onto one them in the bars they were canvassing, they might learn about the fight at Neeley's. Guys like them were always ready to trade information for a 'get out of jail card' they could redeem down the road. Then the cops would be onto the Dugan kid, and I lose my lead. I'm not going to let that happen. No way.

Bo cranked the ignition and drove back downtown to a liquor store he had seen earlier. A typical state-run store, the bottles on the shelves were only for show. A clerk went to get what Bo ordered from a stockroom in the back and returned with two fifths of Jim Beam. As the clerk bagged the bottles, Bo asked for directions to the Wilson factory, nonchalantly mentioning that he was making a round of stops trying to drum up business.

"A little gift for the purchasing agents," Bo said, nodding at the bags. "Sometimes it helps make the sale.

"Packing boxes," Bo replied when the clerk asked what he was selling.

Five minutes later Bo parked at the loading dock.

"Yo, Stubby!" he called when he saw the one-handed man walking across the lot. "You got a minute?"

Stubby squinted then smiled and walked to Bo's car. "Hey, Bo, how ya' doin'," the old man said, extending his good hand through the window. Bo grabbed Stubby's left hand in an awkward shake. "Got a couple of questions for you, pal."

"I only got a minute. Gotta' get in before they lock er' up. Eleven-thirty sharp."

"When we were talking about Tony, I didn't get a chance to ask where he lives, and he's not in the phone book. Can you help me out?" Bo asked.

Stubby chuckled. "Tony don't got no real place, Bo, so he ain't got no phone number. Most times he mooches a bed from one a' his drinkin' buddies or shacks up with some whore. He did get his mom's place when she passed, and I know he stays there sometimes. He spends a bunch a' time locked up, too," he added with a laugh.

"You know where his mom's place is?"

"Quince Street," Stubby replied. "It ain't much of house, though. In fact, it's condemned. All the places there'r fallin' down."

"You know the house number?"

"Sorry, Bo, I don't," Stubby said, shaking his head. "I could take you there in a heartbeat. Walk you right up to it. We can do that later if you want, after work. You wanna' wait for me?"

I don't have the time, Stubby. I gotta' get back on the road; I got a real job, you know. But you're sure Lavansky's mom's place is on Quince."

"For sure."

"How about where Tony works? Could I find him there?"

"Tony don't have no real job," Stubby replied. "He worked a couple months for Creedon years ago, but they let him go. Caught him stealin' stuff. Nowadays he just picks up odd jobs."

Damn. Bo cursed his luck.

"You're one heck of a friend, Stubby. Here's a little something for your trouble," Bo said, handing the old man a brown paper bag.

Stubby peered into the sack. "Thanks Bo!" he exclaimed, tucking the bottle of bourbon into his jacket.

Bo reached out and caught Stubby's arm as he turned. "I wanna' keep this conversation between just you and me, okay?" Bo said. "Anyone else comes around asking questions about Levansky, you just play dumb. Agreed?"

"Say what?" Stubby replied.

"Just play dumb, like you don't know anything!"

"Say what?" Stubby said again with a wink.

"You got it, friend," Bo replied, smiling. "And don't be late!" he shouted as Stubby turned and ran toward the dress factory door.

Bo found a phone booth and checked a listing in the blue pages. Five minutes later he was standing in front of the lobby desk at City Hall. "Property records?" he asked the matronly woman seated behind it.

"Second door on your right," she replied, peering up at him over half glasses perched on her nose. "But you have to hurry, we close promptly at noon. You only have fifteen minutes."

Bo opened the frosted-glass door and confronted another woman who looked like the spinster twin of the lady at the front desk.

"I know I don't have much time before you close, but I'm hoping you can help me," Bo said with as much charm as he could muster.

"Perhaps."

"I'm trying to find the address of a family that lived on Quince Street."

"Those properties are condemned. Nobody lives there anymore."

"I know. I heard what happened. What a shame," Bo said, shaking his head. "You see, I'm doing some genealogic research, tracing my mother's...."

"Geneology?" the woman interrupted. Bo's ruse hit home with the old lady.

"Yes. I'm tracing our roots for my children, and I learned that relatives might have lived on Quince Street years ago. I just want to confirm if it's true."

"How nice," the woman gushed. "What can I help you with?"

"The name's Levansky."

"Quince Street, Levansky," the woman said to herself as she walked to a shelf of ledgers. "Yes," she said, pulling down a leather-bound book. "This shouldn't take long at all." She thumbed through the pages. "Here," she said, turning the book so Bo could read it, her finger pointing to a line.

Bo saw the handwritten entry which was partially obscured by CONDEMNED stamped over it in red ink. Sarah Levansky. 213 S. Quince Street.

Bo pulled his notepad out and scribbled the address.

"You have a lot of names there," the woman said, eying the pad.

In his haste, Bo hadn't thought about her seeing the list, but another lie came easily. "Lots of marriages, lots of names," he said smiling as he quickly pocketed the pad.

"My children are going to be very happy." He extended his hand across the counter. "Thank you."

In the doorway Bo paused and turned. "Just one more thing. Quince Street is which way from here?"

"Those properties are condemned," the old woman scolded with a shaking finger.

"I just want to take a picture of the place."

"West. Go West, young man," the old lady giggled. "Good luck with your search."

Bo swallowed hard to keep from laughing until he made it to the sidewalk.

Chapter 16

Bo mounted the rotting steps carefully. On the porch, he cupped his hands and yelled through the broken glass pane on the front door. "Levansky! Tony Levansky! You in there?"

"Whatever you're sellin', I don't need it!"

Bingo, Bo said to himself, smiling.

"I'm not selling anything," Bo said as he cautiously stepped into the room.

Levansky was sprawled on a filthy couch, an empty whiskey bottle nestled in the crook of his arm, a crumpled cigarette pack and a half-empty matchbook lying on his chest.

"You a preacher?" Levansky asked, eyeing Bo's dark suit.

Bo laughed. "I might be dressed like one, but I'm not."

"Wha'cha doin' here?" Levansky said, lumbering painfully to sit up, his right arm bent at a wicked angle, wrapped in dirty towel. A nasty gash had congealed on his forehead.

"Just want to talk with you for a minute."

"'Bout what!" Levansky yelled.

"Your head, your arm," Bo replied. "That's your good arm," he added, nodding to the wrapped one.

"Not now it ain't," Levansky laughed. "How'd you know that anyway?"

"Matches torn off the right side tells me you're right-handed," Bo replied, nodding at the match pack that had fallen to the floor.

Levansky stared back.

"What'cha want? I told you I don't need nothin'."

"Not even this?" Bo asked, pulling a bottle of bourbon from under his coat.

"Who are you?" Levansky asked, reaching for the bottle.

Bo pulled the bottle out of his reach. "We need to talk."

"'Bout what?"

"How you got hurt."

"You a cop?"

"Not a cop, not a preacher."

"I sure could use a drink," Levansky said, nodding toward the bottle.

"And you'll get one," Bo replied. "If, in fact, you play your cards right, you'll get the whole bottle. But we have to talk first."

"You give me that bottle an' I'll talk till your ears hurt."

Bo laughed as he twisted the cap and handed him the bourbon. Levansky took a gulp and Bo wrenched the bottle away.

"What happened to you? How'd you bust your arm and get that gash on your head?"

"I fell," Levansky answered, nodding toward the bottle.

"You fell?" Bo held the whiskey just out of Levansky's reach.

"Yeah, I fell."

Bo handed over the bottle and Levansky took a hefty hit, wiping what escaped his mouth on his sleeve.

"That isn't what I heard," Bo said. "I heard some kid nailed you in the head with a rock at Neely's."

"Little son of a bitch," Levansky hissed, then took another drink.

"About your arm?" Bo asked.

"What about it? I told ya' I fell."

"Did the kid help you take a tumble, too?"

"No !" Levansky shouted, taking another slug. "It wasn't 'at lil' shit," he said, starting to slur his words. "The guy who grabbed me was big...strong. Somnabitch 'bout choked me ta' death."

Bo pulled the bottle away.

"I heard the kid threatened to kill you for somethin' you said about his old man. You sure it wasn't the kid?"

"That lil' shit said some'n like 'at. But it waschnt him. Guy 'at pushed me offa' porch was a big somnabitch."

"Somebody pushed you off the porch?"

"Gimme' 'at bottle!" Levansky bellowed.

Bo let him take another hit.

"Who pushed you?" Bo asked, pulling the bottle away. "Who?"

"Hell if I know, but I g'arntee it washn't that redhead kid! Was shomebody a hell'a lot bigger. A big somnabitch. At's for damn sure," Levansky said, dropping back on the couch.

"How much would it take for you to say it was the kid that pushed you? Say the cops show up asking. A hundred, maybe two hundred bucks?"

"You shittin' me? Two hunnert buschks! I'd schwear it was who'er you wan'!" Levansky yelled.

"I'll keep that in mind. Here," Bo said, handing Levansky the near-empty bottle. Bo moved toward the door.

"Wha' 'boutta' money!" Levansky shouted. "Two hunnert buschks!"

"Sleep tight," Bo replied.

Chapter 17

Kate backed through the kitchen door and dropped a basket of wet laundry onto the porch. She caught the smell of smoke in the air and turned in my direction.

"You still smokin' them things?" she asked, staring at me.

"Since I was nineteen," I replied, smiling back at her from my bench, blowing a jet of smoke into the air.

"They'll kill you, Tom."

"So'll lightnin', but you won't find me hunkerin' down the cellar every time a thundercloud comes by. I'll take my chances."

"You're a fool, Tom," Kate laughed.

"Old fool. How's that boy of yours doin'?" I asked, changing the subject.

"Okay, I guess. Typical teenager."

"What's that mean?"

"Means he don't say much. I ask him how's school and he says 'fine.' I ask him if he has plans and he says 'I'll let you know when I do.' Ask where he's goin' and he says 'out.' Any damned fool knows if he's headed out the door he ain't goin' in," she laughed.

"Boy givin' you trouble, Kate?"

"No. Not at all. He's a good kid. Just feelin' his oats is all."

"Is he around now?" I asked.

"No. He left this morning, just said he was goin' 'out'. Wherever that means. But he'll be back in time for dinner. Like I said, he's a good kid."

Kate began hanging laundry on the pulley line, slowly wheeling a kite of garments out over the yard.

"Say, Kate," I asked sheepishly. "You have plans for dinner tonight?"

She lowered a wet shirt she was holding up in front of her. She had two clothespins stuck in her mouth like walrus tusks.

I burst out laughing, and she pulled the pins out and laughed along.

Then somehow the words just babbled out, and I was surprised they did.

"West End hosey's putting on a feed tonight tryin' to raise money for a new truck. Gunna' have some good eats. Pierogies, bleenies, kielbasi. Starts around six. If you wanna' go along, it'll be my treat."

I was breathing hard, nervously waiting for her reply.

Kate smiled back real pretty. "Oh, Tom, that's very kind of you."

"So?" I asked.

"I'm sorry," she said, shaking her head as she pinned up the shirt. "I got called in to cover for a gal who went home sick. In fact, I have to go in a couple a' minutes. I won't finish up till eleven tonight."

"You'll be missin' out on some mighty good grub," I told her.

"I'm really sorry," she said.

I believe she was sincere.

"I'll take a rain check," she added.

"Sure, some other time," I replied as she picked up her basket and fumbled with the door.

Chapter 18

Jimmy Creedon sat in his high leather chair, hands entwined behind his head, staring at the ceiling.

Always wants to be in charge, Bo thought as he stared across the desk at the back of Creedon's chair.

"Here's what I know," Bo said. "There was a fight...more of a shouting match...last night at Neely's. I went there and got the lowdown on what happened from an old drunk."

"Go on," Creedon said coolly, still staring at the ceiling.

"It was between one of your former miners and a kid. Seventeen...maybe eighteen."

"You have names?" Creedon asked, swiveling around.

"The kid's name is Jack Dugan."

"I know the name. High school baseball player. Pretty good, too, according to the paper."

"His dad, Andy Dugan, died in your mine."

"I don't recall that," Creedon replied nonchalant. "And the miner?"

"Levansky. Tony Levansky."

Creedon laughed. "Everyone in town knows Tony Levansky. Half the time he's drunk and the other half he's in the hoosegow for what he did when he was drunk."

"Hoosegow?" Bo asked.

"Jail," Creedon laughed.

"Levansky was drunk last night at Neely's and he was telling stories about working for you," Bo said.

"So we got a drunk miner telling tales," Creedon said dryly. "I expect this is eventually going somewhere?"

"Levansky took some kind of perverted pleasure telling about how the Dugan kid's dad was killed robbing the pillars. He was crushed to death, and Levansky was laughing about it."

"Robbing the pillars?" Creedon raised an eyebrow. "You're up on the jargon of the coal region."

"I learned what it means, and it sounds barbaric."

"It is what it is. Part of the process!" Creedon shouted.

"No kid needs to hear his dad got crushed to death as 'part of the process'. And certainly not from the town drunk," Bo replied.

"Levansky laughing about it made the kid go nuts. The kid called him a liar and flung a rock at him; got him good...right in the forehead. The kid threatened to kill the bastard if he kept making fun of the way his old man died."

"Good for the kid!" Creedon replied. "But how's any of this important to me?"

"The kid heard that his dad's life wasn't worth a shit to you!" Bo shouted.

"Miners are miners!" Creedon roared back, slapping the desk. "They do the work they're hired to do! Some die in the process! It's not my fault!"

"Tell that to the dead man's kid!" Bo shot back. "That's what we're talking about! The Dugan kid learns his dad was crushed to death so you can make a few more bucks! He certainly might have it in for you!"

"So you're telling me it was this Dugan kid who attacked my home?" Creedon asked softly, as if the shouting match seconds earlier had never occurred.

Bo didn't reply immediately. He just sat back gathering his thoughts.

The clock was ticking. The local cops were working a good plan and they might get lucky. Latch onto one of Levansky's pals and learn about Levansky's fight with the Dugan kid and what set it off. Thanks to Levansky, the kid certainly had a motive to strike out at Creedon. If Dugan was the one and if he admitted it, the ballgame would be over. No jury would convict the boy of anything more than a misdemeanor. End of story. End of job.

"I'm not a hundred percent positive," Bo said slowly. "But the Dugan kid's a very likely suspect. He's got a hot arm...star pitcher on the baseball team. It wouldn't take much for him to bust your beloved window. And thanks to Levansky, he knows his dad died died robbing a pillar trying to make you a little bit richer. Yeah, I think the Dugan kid might be the one."

"Thinking he might be isn't good enough. We need proof."

"Agreed," Bo said. "But for the moment, let's assume I get proof Dugan's the one. Let's talk about what happens next."

"We'd need to tie him into something bigger," Creedon said. "Something that would get him serious time. Remember, I don't want whoever did this walking away easy."

Creedon paused, but Bo could almost hear the wheels turning in his head.

"Didn't you say the Dugan kid threaten to kill Levansky?" Creedon asked.

Bo stared at him. *You son of a bitch. You would actually consider having Levansky killed, and then frame the boy for it because of a broken window.*

"Your silence is intriguing, Mr. Lufkin," Creedon said. "You didn't have any reservations about taking care of those two guys in Gilberton a few years ago. Are you going soft?"

"That was different," Bo shot back. "You steered me toward the foreman. You suspected something was up...that the guy was living a good bit above his means."

Creedon stared back, arms crossed, saying nothing. Bo continued.

"I found out the guy was robbing you blind, overloading trucks after they went over your scales. He was pocketing the difference between what was owed you for the weigh-out and what he got for the overload. And when I confronted him about it, he pulled a gun on me. A very stupid move."

"But you had no trouble pinning his death on the miner," Creedon smiled.

"Yeah, the miner," Bo smirked. "The one trying to bring in the union. We needed a scapegoat, and you fingered the miner. You got rid of two problems at the same time. But you know," Bo said, "more than once I wondered if that was your plan all along."

"Levansky's scum," Creedon replied, ignoring Bo's comment. "Nobody would lose any sleep if anything happened to him. How much will it cost me?"

"Five grand."

"That's more than double what you charged for the Gilberton thing!" Creedon bellowed.

"I was new to the game then, and you got a real bargain. Five's the going rate now. And I have an expensive hobby to maintain," Bo replied.

"Is your new bimbo worth it?" Creedon laughed.

"Every penny of it," Bo replied. "Give me half now, and I'll trust you for the balance."

Creedon opened a desk drawer and pulled out a thick envelope.

Bo fanned the bills Creedon shoved across the desk before stuffing the money into his pocket. "Done," he said, extending his hand toward Creedon.

"Seems like I'm making a deal with the devil," Creedon said, reaching across the desk.

"That's exactly the way I see it, too," Bo said as he turned and walked toward the kitchen door.

"Remember, we need confirmation! You make sure Dugan's the one who destroyed my grand-father's window!" Creedon shouted.

"Understood," Bo replied from the doorway.

*****

Bo was parked in front of the hardware store. Tommy waited until his grandfather locked the door then walked with him to his car. "See you Monday," Tommy yelled as the old man backed out. The boy waved then went into the alleyway and walked his bike toward the street.

Bo cranked down his window and yelled.

Tommy stared as Bo flung the car door open and stepped out.

"Hi, Tommy, remember me?" Bo asked.

The boy nodded.

"I gotta' tell you something, Tommy," Bo began. "You're not a very good liar, boy. When you were telling me about following Jack last night after his fight at Neely's, pretending you didn't know what street came after Hickory was a dead give-away... especially for a kid who makes deliveries all over town."

Bo laughed as the boy's jaw dropped.

"You followed Jack and you saw him cross Cherry, Beech, Oak, and Hickory...and finally turn onto Maple. You followed him, and you saw him smash Creedon's window last night, right? You followed him and you saw him do it! Right?"

The boy glanced at his feet.

"I know he's your pal and you want to protect him, but think about this, Tommy. Jimmy Creedon owns this store. If he finds out you knew what Jack did and didn't tell, your family will be finished. He'll shut this place down in a minute. Throw you out. Your father, your grandfather. Thirty years down the toilet. Finished! You understand!

"You followed Jack last night, and you saw him break Creedon's window! You saw him!"

"Yes," the boy sobbed. "I saw him do it!"

Chapter 19

I was on the back porch on the bench, leaning against the wall enjoying a smoke when I heard the Dugan's doorbell ring, and ring, and ring.

Persistent SOB, I thought to myself as I made my way to the front door.

"Is this the Dugans' house?" a man asked, stepping back from their door.

I sized him up. *Dressed nice. Briefcase. For sure he's sellin' somethin'.*

"I'm here to see Jack Dugan," he added.

"Jack?" I said, not expecting that. "What for?"

"That's personal."

"Have a nice day," I replied, turning toward my door.

"Hold on a minute," he shouted. "I'm sorry. Look, I didn't mean to be rude. I just wanna' keep my business with the boy quiet, don't want to get a lot of folks yappin' about it. My name's Rick Johnson. I'm from Slayton College.

"College? You a scout?"

"Yes, sir, I am. I tried to call earlier but nobody answered. Since I was in the area, I took a chance I might find him home. Looks like I struck out...if this is his house. "

"It is, but he ain't home and his mom's at work. She won't be back till late tonight, and the boy probably won't come home till he's hungry," I replied.

"What about his dad?"

"His dad's dead."

"Sorry to hear that. Friend of yours?"

"Best friend."

"I'm truly sorry," he said, shaking his head. "You know, this could be Jack's big ticket. A college scholarship maybe. Just by chance, you know someplace I might catch up with him and talk a bit. Ball field, maybe?"

"He ain't playin' ball now," I replied.

The man looked at me, puzzled.

"The boy's cap and glove are there." I nodded at the glider on the Dugans' porch.

The man walked over and saw Jack's glove and cap nestled in the corner of the metal seat.

"Son of a gun," he laughed. "Guess it's pretty obvious he isn't playin' ball. You think they'd mind if I waited a while, try to catch up with him when he comes home? I don't relish the thought of driving back home without talking to him. I have some time before I have to hit the road."

"You wanna' wait, it won't bother me none. I got the newspaper if you want somethin' to help pass the time," I offered.

"No, thanks. I'll just sit here and relax a bit," he said, taking a seat on the glider

"Suit yourself."

He was rocking back and forth on the glider twirling Jack's cap around on his finger. I went out back for another smoke.

When I left for the hosey shindig at around five-thirty, the man wasn't on the porch. The lights were on in the Dugans' place, and I thought about knocking on the door to see if Jack met up with the guy. But on second thought, that was Jack's business, not mine. And anyway, there were mighty good eats waiting at the fire house.

Chapter 20

Bo punched a pocketful of coins into the payphone outside The Pines.

"Say exactly what I told you, then call me back. You got this number, right? You call me back one way or another. Just let me know how you make out."

Bo leaned against the phone booth. Five minutes later he caught the phone on the second ring.

"Perfect," he said. "Now I need you to make one more call exactly one half hour from now unless I call and tell you otherwise. If you don't hear from me, you make the call. Got it? Okay. Listen up. I'm going to tell you exactly what to say. Here goes."

Bo meticulously wiped down everything he had touched in his room then checked out, paying the bill with Creedon's cash.

Chapter 21

Harry, Garver and Mains were in Harry's office around the conference table. "So we got nothin'," Harry said as the officers recalled their day. "Whatta' you think we do next?"

"We been checkin' bars all day and we come up empty," Garver replied. "I say we switch gears an' do somethin' different tomorrow."

"The bars aren't open on Sunday, but the Vets' an' the Eagles' an' the other clubs are, and we ain't been to any of them yet. How 'bout we try them?" Mains offered.

"Better'n nothin'," Harry said. "Garver, whatta' you..."

The ringing phone on his desk stopped Harry in mid-sentence. Dewey picked up the call in his cubicle.

"Dewey, what is it?" Harry yelled from his office.

Moments later Dewey was in the doorway. "Hospital switchboard. A lady called in for an ambulance. It's on its way."

"Why? Where?" Harry barked.

"The lady that called the hospital said her kid took a shortcut home and went by them condemned places on the west end. She said her kid heard someone moanin' inside one of 'em. Said it sounded like they was hurt real bad. The hospital sent an ambulance then called here."

"Where?" Harry demanded.

"They didn't get an address before the lady hung up. She told 'em it was on Quince somewhere 'round Second. I guess the ambulance guys'r gunna' hafta' try 'an find the place an'... Shit!" Dewey yelled, smacking his forehead with his palm.

"What? Whatta' you mean 'shit'!" Harry said.

"It just dawned on me. The two hundred block 'a Quince Street...it might be Levansky...about his arm."

"What're ya' talkin' about?"

"The report last night, about Tony Levansky bustin' his arm," Dewey replied. "The write-up was in the basket on my desk. You said you looked at the reports this mornin'."

"What friggin' reports!" Harry shouted.

"In the basket!"

"The only new thing on top was about Creedon's call. The next couple of reports underneath were at least two days old! So what're ya' talkin' about?"

"Levansky. He hurt hisself last night at his old lady's place. Cooper an' Paulasky checked it out an' called it in. Levansky told 'em ta' leave him the hell alone. I wrote it down an' put it in the basket with the write-up about the thing at Neely's."

"What thing at Neely's?" Harry yelled.

"It was in the basket!"

"What's Levansky's address?" Harry barked.

"Quince Street. Two-thirteen South."

"Go. Check it out!" Harry shouted at Garver and Mains. "Dewey, call the hospital and give the dispatcher Levansky's address. Then get me the report basket. Now!"

Dewey handed Harry the wire tray and retreated to his back-room desk. Harry rifled through the basket and was swearing a blue streak when he found the buried reports.

"Dewey," Harry bellowed, "get Cooper and Paulaski in here. Now!"

"Paulaski's off...brother's wedding...remember," Dewey yelled back.

"Then just get Cooper!"

Ten minutes later Cooper barely made it through the door before Harry was in his face.

"Get your ass back to Neely's and don't leave without the truth. You hear me! I wanna' know what the hell happened there last night!"

Chapter 22

Bo was on his stomach in the high grass just beyond the sweep of the ambulance lights. The crew had gone into the house earlier then came out for a stretcher. There was another screaming siren coming his way, and Bo inched deeper into the cover. A police car screeched to the side of the ambulance, throwing more pulsing red light onto the scene.

Two cops scrambled from the car but quickly checked their pace when they hit the rotting stairs. When Bo saw the sweep of their flashlights inside the house, he moved quickly and got as close as he could to the squad car, still hidden by the weeds.

Minutes later the ambulance crew came out with the stretcher, the two cops trailing behind them. While his young partner helped the medics hoist the gurney into the ambulance, the older cop walked to the black and white and tossed something into the back. Climbing into the driver's seat, he put his hands together at twelve o'clock on the steering wheel and rested his forehead on them.

The ambulance doors slammed shut and the squeal of tires was followed by the wail of the siren as it pulled away.

"Can you believe this, Tom?" Bo heard the old cop ask, looking up when his partner opened the passenger's door.

"Frickin' unbelievable," the young cop replied as he got in and shut the door.

Bo watched the old cop bend down, reaching for the mic on the two-way.

"Dewey!" Harry shouted down the hallway after getting Garver's report. "I'm goin' to meet Garver and Mains at the hospital. Patch any calls for me over there!"

"What's goin' on?" Dewey shouted back. He got no answer. Harry was already out the door.

Chapter 23

Neely stiffened behind the bar and the place fell silent when Cooper walked through the door. Cooper smiled as the word "cop" began to fly around in whispers.

Poker players in the back room reached across the table to scrape back their share of the pot while folks at the bar stuck beer bottles between their legs in a feeble attempt to hide them. The nine-ball players swept their bets off the side rails.

Cooper laughed, staring at Neely. "Got you dead to rights, Neely. Poker game, sellin' beer without a license, bets on the pool table."

Neely hunched his shoulders and grinned.

"Over here, we need to talk," Cooper said, nodding his head to a corner of the room.

Everyone watched as Cooper backed Neely into the corner. "Stay put," Cooper barked as several patrons began moving toward the door. "Everyone stays."

Cooper pointed his finger in Neely's face.

"No bullshit like you gave us last night when you went stupid and couldn't remember nothin'. The call we got last night was about a bunch of yellin', like a fight. Who was in it and what was it about?"

Neely stared at his feet.

"Have it your way, but the Chief said he'll shut this place down in a heartbeat if you don't spill."

"Whatta' you wanna' know?" Neely replied.

"Tell me what happened and who was involved, simple as that."

"Hell, it wasn't even a real fight," Neely whispered. "A mouth battle. Two guys yellin' at each other. One smashed a bottle. At's all it was."

"Listen, Neely. I don't care if it was two kids squabblin' over a cupcake. The Chief wants details an' names."

"I don't recall..." Neely began.

"Well, you better recall if you wanna' stay in business," Cooper hissed. "Come on, Neely. All we're talkin' about is a fight, not a murder. Who was it?"

"Levansky. The freekin' drunk," Neely replied.

"And?"

"Some kid."

"Kid's got a name?" Cooper asked.

Neely stared back at the floor.

"Everyone against the wall," Cooper shouted over his shoulder. "I'm callin' in help and you're all goin' uptown. We'll sort it out there."

"Wait!" Neely said through clinched teeth.

"You got ten seconds to give me a name," Cooper replied. "Ten, nine, eight…"

"Dugan, Jack Dugan. Andy's kid."

"The baseball player?"

"Yeah."

"What happened?"

"I didn't see it myself, happened out back," Neely replied.

"But I bet the fine clientele you got in here had a lot to say about it afterward. I'm sure you heard the details."

"So if I tell you want I heard, it's business as usual? You don't shut me down. Jus' leave me alone?"

"The Chief said he wants information. You give it, he'll probably be appreciative. But if I come back with nothin'…" Cooper twirled his index finger like a revolving cop car light.

"Here's what I heard," Neely began.

"So the Dugan kid bonked Levansky with a rock for mouthin' off about his dad?" Cooper asked when Neely finished.

"That's what they say. The kid whacked him good. Right on the noggin'. The kid's got one hell of an arm," Neely laughed.

"And they say the boy threatened to kill Levansky if he didn't shut up?"

"Yeah, that's what they say. But, hell, that was just talk."

"Who heard him say it?"

"Levansky's pals, I guess."

"Worthless bunch a' liars. How 'bout Dugan's pals? Who was with him?"

"The Delaney kid. Steck's little brother. I don't know the rest."

"You done good, Neely. I'll be sure to tell the Chief," Cooper said as he started toward the door. "Enjoy your evening," he said to the crowd.

Back in his car Cooper radioed the station for Harry.

"Chief's at the hospital," Dewey responded.

"How's come? Cooper asked.

"Hell if I know. You gotta' ask him yourself. Channel fourteen'll get you hospital dispatch. Ask 'em to get the Chief on."

It took a few minutes, and Cooper could hear the echo of the hospital's PA system paging Harry.

When Harry finally picked up, Cooper gave him a quick rundown then asked, "What's goin' on at the hospital?"

"I'll tell you later," Harry replied tersely.

From his tone, Cooper knew to let it go.

"Here's what I want you to do," Harry continued. "Go to the Dugan kid's house. Ask kinda' friendly-like where he was tonight. Get him talkin' before he gets scared and starts makin' up lies. Then bring him to the station. Radio Dewey if you need the boy's address," Harry added.

Cooper heard a click and the radio went silent.

Chapter 24

Jack jumped when the doorbell rang.

"Jack Dugan?" Cooper asked when Jack came to the door.

Jack stared at the cop through the screen.

"Jack Dugan?" Cooper repeated. The question was protocol to get the boy to identify himself for the record. Cooper—and everyone else who followed high school baseball—knew Jack.

"What's wrong?" Jack stammered.

"Nothin's wrong, son."

"Is it my mom? Somethin' happen to her?"

"No. There ain't nothin' wrong. Just want to ask you a few questions is all."

"'Bout what?"

"Jack, you mind if we take this inside?"

Jack fumbled with the screendoor hook.

"Is your mom home?" Cooper asked, looking around as he stepped into the living room.

"She's at work at the hospital. Is she all right? What's wrong?"

"Your mother's fine, believe me. Are you here alone?"

"Yeah," Jack replied. "I got home a little before five-thirty. My mom left a note; she was called in to work 'cause some other lady got sick. A little bit later, a lady called askin' me to stay here an' wait for Mr. Johnson. In fact, I thought you was him when the doorbell rang."

"Wait a minute. Slow down," Cooper said. "You gotta' go over that whole thing again. First off, who were you waitin' for?"

"Mr. Johnson," Jack replied.

"Who's Mr. Johnson?"

"A baseball scout from Slayton College. A lady from his office called just after I got home, and she said he wanted to stop by later tonight and talk to me, maybe 'bout a scholarship," Jack added, smiling. "She said he was gunna' come around seven."

"So you were here from just before five-thirty till now, by yourself, waitin' for this Mr. Johnson to show up?"

"That's right. Why? What's wrong?"

"Anyone else see you? Anyone stop by?" Cooper asked.

"No. Remember, my mom was called in to work before I got home. Then I got the call from the lady, ate some dinner, and I been waitin' here by myself ever since."

"So between five-thirty and now, no one saw you?"

"That's right. I was here alone," Jack repeated. "What's this about, anyway?"

"I ain't sayin' anything more, Jack," Cooper replied. "All I know is I got orders to take you to the station. We'll talk more there."

"The police station!" Jack shouted.

"That's right," Cooper replied. "I got orders to take you to the station."

"I'm in a mess a' trouble, ain't I. You found out, right?" Jack stammered.

"I can't say no more," Cooper said. "Just come along."

"What about my mom? I don't want her comin' home and not findin' me here. It'll scare her to death," Jack protested.

"Chief Myers is at the hospital. I'll radio him when we get in the car and I'll have him bring her along," Cooper replied.

"How's come the cops are at the hospital?" Jack asked.

"Hell if I know," Cooper replied, shrugging his shoulders. "Just come on, son."

Cooper closed squad car window that separated the front seat from the back. When he turned to latch it, his heart sunk. Jack, sitting alone in the back seat, looked scared to death.

Just what the hell is goin' on? The thought frustrated Cooper, as he reached down for the radio mic.

"You're sure about his mom?" Harry asked when Cooper finished telling him what Jack had said.

"Yeah. He said she's workin' at the hospital. He also said he thinks he's in a mess a' trouble and that we somehow found out what happened. What's he talkin' about? What's goin' on?" Cooper asked.

"We'll talk about it at the station," Harry replied.

Cooper heard a click, and the radio went silent again.

Damn! Cooper muttered to himself as he threw down the radio mic and jammed the car into gear.

****

Bo pulled from a shaded spot up the street after Cooper's black and white squealed away. On the outskirts of town, Bo stopped at a pay phone.

"Call the police station in about an hour. Say you're just checking in to see how the investigation's going. I think you'll be pleased with what they say. And about the money; send cash. Good night, Mr. Creedon."

Chapter 25

Cooper put Jack in the conference room and then questioned Dewey. "What the hell's goin' on?"

"Darned if I know," Dewey replied.

Steaming mad, Cooper was leaning against the counter nursing a coffee when Garver and Mains came through the door.

"Will somebody tell me what the hell's goin' on?" Cooper barked.

Garver shook his head and silently mouthed 'not now' as he gestured with his head toward the front door. Harry walked in seconds later holding Kate's elbow. He ushered her into his office and closed the door.

"Cooper," Harry said, nodding toward the cubicles in the back room. Cooper followed him. Given the Chief's posture and tone, Cooper didn't push his luck and ask anything.

"That's exactly what he said," Cooper replied to Harry's question after he finished retelling his conversation with Jack. Harry jotted something on a pad and tore the sheet off.

"I need you to check somethin' at the library. Come on," Harry said as he walked toward the front of the station.

"The library's closed," Cooper called after him.

"Won't be for long," Harry replied as he stepped behind the counter and made a call.

"Margaret'll come over and open up," he said, hanging up the phone. "She should be there in about ten minutes. Here's what I want you to check out," handing Cooper the slip of paper. "Margaret can help you find what you're lookin' for. Don't dawdle."

After Cooper left, Harry called Garver and Mains aside. The two officers nodded as Harry gave them instructions. After Harry walked away, they leaned against the counter.

"This is feekin' unbelievable," Garver whispered. Mains said nothing, he just shook his head in agreement.

Cooper came back twenty minutes later and huddled with Harry off to the side.

"You're certain?" Harry asked, and Cooper nodded. "Ok, come with me."

Stopping in the hallway outside his office, Harry turned to Garver. "Bring the boy in, then wait till I call for you, just like we planned."

Cooper followed Harry inside. A minute later Garver brought Jack to the office and closed the door.

"Jack!" Kate shouted as her son entered the room. "What's this all about?"

"Oh God, Mom, I'm sorry," Jack cried.

"Sorry about what? What'd you do?"

"I busted Creedon's window. I'm really sorry, Mom, honest."

"Say what?" Harry shouted, stunned.

"Creedon's window. I broke it. That's what this is about, isn't it," Jack stammered. "You found out, right?"

Jack glanced at the cops, trying to get acknowledgment from Harry or Cooper.

"You? You're the one that busted Creedon's window?" Harry finally said.

"That's why I'm here, isn't it. You found out, right?"

"No, Jack! That's not why you're here and you know it!" Harry shouted.

"Know what?" Jack shot back.

"Quit the nonsense, Jack!" Harry barked.

"What nonsense? What're you talkin' 'bout?"

"We're talkin' about tonight, Jack. Not about Creedon's window."

"What about tonight?" Jack shouted.

"Cut the crap, Jack! You told Officer Cooper you were at home tonight, alone. Is that your story?"

"Yeah! I was waitin' for Mr. Johnson to come'n talk to me."

"Who's Mr. Johnson?" Kate asked, staring at Jack.

"He's a college scout, Mom, from Slayton College. A lady from his office called and said he wanted to talk to me. I was waitin' for him to show up when the cop came."

"Mrs. Dugan," Harry said softly, "your son is lying."

"Lying about what?" Kate pleaded.

"Yeah, what?" Jack said.

Harry walked over and opened the door. "Garver, Mains!"

Garver walked into the room; Mains waited in the doorway. Neither said a word.

Harry nodded and Mains stepped back into the hallway. When he returned, he had a baseball cap in one hand and a banister railing in the other. Harry motioned toward the table, and Mains set them down.

"We found these at Tony Levansky's house tonight, Jack. The cap's yours," Garver said. "Your name's on the headband."

Jack just stared.

"Your name, right there," Harry said, pointing to a scribble on the headband. "And there," nodding to the railing, "that's blood on the end. Tony Levansky was bashed with it a little bit ago... like someone up an' whacked him in the head with a baseball bat."

"I...I don't know..." Jack stammered.

"Your cap puts you at the scene, boy!" Harry shouted, slamming his fist on the table.

"What are you saying?" Kate cried.

Harry stared at Jack shaking his head, then he spoke.

"We heard you threatened Levansky last night at Neely' for what he said about your dad. Do you deny it?"

"I was pissed off at him!" Jack shouted.

"So you admit you threatened him."

"He was sayin' shit about my dad!" Jack yelled.

"And you said you'd kill him if he didn't shut up!" Harry yelled back.

"That was just talk!"

"For the love of God, will you please tell me what this is about!" Kate sobbed.

Harry turned to her and sighed. "I'm sorry Mrs. Dugan." He went on, softly.

"A man named Tony Levansky was attacked tonight with that banister there," nodding toward the bloody railing. "And last night your son threatened to kill him for saying...crap...about your late husband.

"We found Jack's cap in Levansky's house, and the attack happened around the time your son says he was home alone with no one to vouch for him."

"I was waitin' for Mr. Johnson to show up. I swear!" Jack yelled.

"Officer Cooper," Harry said.

"We had the library open up," Cooper said. "There's a book that lists all the colleges in the country. I checked it myself a little bit ago. There is no Slayton College."

"But I swear a lady called me!" Jack shouted. "Askin' me to wait for Mr. Johnson. He was supposed to come around seven."

"There is no Slayton College! No Mr. Johnson!" Harry replied sternly, glaring at Jack. "But there is your threat, and now Tony Levansky's got his head bashed in. Your cap was at the scene. The evidence speaks for itself."

"I didn't do it! I didn't!" Jack yelled, taking a step toward Harry.

Cooper moved quickly and pinned Jack's elbows behind him.

Kate doubled over, sobbing.

"I'm sorry, Mrs. Dugan," Harry said as Cooper led Jack from the room.

Garver and Mains drove Kate home and walked her to the door. "Can we call a neighbor, get someone to come over and be with you?" Garver asked.

Kate glanced at my place. The lights were off. The hosey shindig was still goin' strong.

"No," Kate said as she closed the door.

*****

Harry was in his office when the phone rang. Dewey answered it at his desk and buzzed the Chief. Harry picked up the handset.

"Mr. Creedon. Yes, we do have news," Harry said. "We found the person who attacked your home. No, sir," Harry said, finding the nerve to cut Creedon off in mid sentence. "It's not good news. He admitted breaking your window, but that's minor now. We believe that he attacked a man this evening. No, no, sir, he didn't kill him, just hurt him bad, but it'll certainly override the window incident."

His name? Harry paused at Creedon's inquiry. *It's public record and will be headlines tomorrow.*

"Dugan. Jack Dugan," Harry replied. "Yes, the baseball player.

The charge? Harry contemplated Creedon's question, then answered. "The charge most likely will be attempted murder, assault with a deadly weapon. Yes, sir. Good night to you, too."

Chapter 26

I went to Jack's trial for Kate's sake. We sat beside each other the whole time, but she barely said a word. I know she was heartbroken and just couldn't believe what was happening to her son.

They got right down to it. They put Jack on the stand and asked him to account for his whereabouts the night Levansky was attacked. Jack told about the call he got from the lady asking him to stay home that night and wait for a college scout to come by.

"And this scout's name was?" the prosecutor asked.

"Mr. Johnson," Jack replied.

"And he was allegedly from?"

"Slayton College."

I was on the edge of my seat.

"That's your story?" the lawyer asked. Jack swore it was and he was dismissed.

The cop, Cooper, was next and he confirmed Jack's story. Then he told how he checked the library and couldn't find any Slayton College.

"So there is no Slayton College, no Mr. Johnson," the attorney concluded. "It appears that Mr. Dugan has concocted an alibi."

I raised my hand like a third-grader asking to go to the lavatory. Nobody noticed, so I stood up. That got everyone's attention and the judge nodded at me.

"I got somethin' to say."

"For the prosecution or the defense?" the judge asked.

"For the boy," I said. The judge nodded at Jack's attorney.

"I don't know what this is about, Your Honor," Jack's lawyer said, staring at me. Then he asked for a recess. *Recess*, I thought, laughing to myself. *Just like third grade.*

Jack's attorney took me aside and I told him about the man I saw on Jack's porch. Next thing I know I was in a conference room with Jack's lawyer and the other one.

"Mr. Haggerty, this is Michael Vernon," Jack's lawyer said, introducing the other man. "He's the prosecuting attorney, and you have to tell him exactly what you just told me. It the law; it's called 'discovery'."

"What Jack said about a college scout wantin' to meet up with him?" I asked.

"Yes, tell me about it," Vernon replied.

I told them both about how I talked with the man.

"And he said his name was?" Vernon asked.

"Johnson, just like Jack said. He said he was a college scout and he said he was gunna' wait a while till Jack came home so he could talk to him, maybe 'bout a scholarship. Last time I saw him he was sittin' on Jack's glider."

"Did anyone else see this Mr. Johnson?" Vernon asked.

"Not that I know of."

"And what's your relationship to Jack Dugan?"

"We ain't blood relatives, but I was best friends with his dad. I'm a good friend of the family," I replied.

Vernon stared at me over his half glasses. He said nothing, but I knew what he was thinking.

"You think I'm lyin'," I said.

"No sir, Mr. Haggerty," Vernon replied. "I'm not the one to pass judgment on what you say. But if I put you on the stand, here's what it sounds like to the jury: The Dugan boy said he was waiting at his house...alone...for this Mr. Johnson to show up. That's his alibi for the time-frame when Mr. Levansky was attacked.

"And you say you saw Mr. Johnson earlier that day at the boy's house, but you were the only one.

"The police, however, learn there is no Slayton College, so there couldn't have been a college scout.

"Next question: Your relation to the boy. You answer: Not blood, but you were his father's best friend.

"No, I'm not calling you a liar, Mr. Haggerty. I'm just pointing out the logical conclusion the jury might come to: That you might be trying to cover up for the boy. For your best friend's son."

I glared at the man. He wasn't calling me a liar outright, but from the way he put it, it sure seemed like he was.

"Let's talk about this," Jack's lawyer said, and the two attorneys backed into the corner whispering. A couple a' minutes later Jack's attorney walked over to me.

"He's right," Jack's lawyer said. "Having you testify won't do Jack any good, and it might do him more harm, in fact. Sorry," he said, shaking his head.

Back in the courtroom it all came out. Jack's fight with Levansky, his threat, his cap in Levansky's place, the bloody banister railin'.

That Vernon fellow put together a real strong case against Jack.

Attempted murder, assault with a deadly weapon. The jury was unanimous: guilty.

Part II-- RETRIBUTION

Chapter 1

Jack looked out the window as the bus slowed almost to a stop, and his stomach churned when he saw the sign painted in the Commonwealth's trademark blue and yellow: Rockville State Prison.

The bus turned and lurched forward. A half mile down a rutted asphalt road, it ground to a halt in front of a foreboding gray limestone fortress that looked like something from a medieval fairy tale. Armed guards in high towers on both sides of a wire-topped gate signaled, and the gate slid open. The bus moved through and Jack heard the metallic clang as the gate closed behind it. Two hundred yards ahead, the bus stopped for the final time and the driver got out. "They're all yours," he said to a guard waiting by the door.

The burly guard mounted the bus and stood cross-armed in the aisle, smiling as he glanced around at the occupants. "Tony, Hank, Bobby," he said, nodding at men who glared back at him. "Welcome home. Looks like you won the prize there, Hank," he said, setting his stare on a man seated in the fourth row. "What's it been, a month?"

"Three weeks 'n four days," Hank replied, rising from his seat and taking a small bow, acknowledging the clapping and catcalls from some of the men on the bus.

"Three weeks 'n four days since you were let out and now you're back," the guard laughed. "What'd you do this time, steal another car?"

"Got two," Hank replied.

"You're gettin' better," the guard laughed. "But you got some work to do on the stayin' un-caught part. Well, Hank, we missed ya' for almost four whole weeks."

"I missed *you,*" Hank said, blowing a kiss across his open palm.

After letting the laughter go for a minute, the guard brought it to an abrupt stop by slamming his baton sharply on the driver's seat.

"Shut up and listen. Here's the drill, girls," he shouted, hitting the seat again for effect. "You come off the bus single file. No pushin', no talkin'. Line up outside and take one step forward when your name is called. Once every one a' you losers is accounted for, you walk single file into the buildin' yonder," pointing his baton at a steel door in the grey limestone fortress across the yard.

"For those a' you ain't been here before, listen up. This ain't no ho-tel. Every guard has a club an' a gun, and they ain't afraid to use em'," he said, tapping his free hand against the holstered pistol on his hip. "Make a wrong move and you'll get whacked," raising his baton. "Make a fast move and you'll probably get shot," tapping his holster again. "You got it?"

"Yes sir!" half the men on the bus shouted.

"Let's try that again. Got it!"

"Yes sir!" This time every one of the prisoners, including Jack, replied back.

"That's better. Now let's move."

As Jack stepped off the bus he felt as if a thousand men were staring at him. Shielding his eyes from the bright sun with a cupped hand, he watched the inmates gather in groups, keeping measured space between them.

"Hank! Hank's back!" someone shouted as Hank stepped off the bus waiving his hand like a home-coming queen. "Yo, Hank, what's it been?"

"Twenty-five!" Hank yelled to the crowd.

Jack watched as the groups broke rank and converged around an inmate with thick glasses. Holding a dog-eared notebook, the man flipped through the pages as the crowd gathered.

"What's goin' on?" Jack whispered to the man next to him.

The man slowly checked right and left to see if the guards were watching. Cocking his head he whispered. "They laid bets on which one would come back first. You hear them callin' Hank's name. He's the one. Now they're checkin' with old four-eyes there to see who came closest to pickin' the number."

"What number?"

"How long till Hank came back. They're seein' who came closest to how long he was outside. What'd Hank say...twenty-five...so that's the winnin' number. If one of em' bet it'd be Hank comin' back in twenty-five days, he could win a whole lot of somethin'."

"Win what?"

"Could be smokes...could be dope...could be lovin'...whatever he bet. But it looks like nobody won," he added.

Jack watched as the bettors drifted back and reassembled with their groups, again keeping their distance from each other.

"What's that about?" Jack whispered.

"Cell blocks," the man whispered, motioning with his head. "Far left," and Jack glanced in that direction. "That's C block. The guy with the wicked grin in the middle is Duffy. Head gorilla in C. If you like boys bettern' women, C block's your choice.

"Over there, in the middle," and Jack turned his head slightly. "That's B. The big man in front, that's Malloy. He's a straight shooter, an' Duffy hates his guts. Guys in B won't have nothin' to do with C's."

On the right, that's A. E's in back. But all you gotta' know is to stay clear a' C an' Duffy. That's one bad bunch."

The last man stepped off the bus, a heavy fellow with thick glasses. Stumbling as he hit the yard, he shuffled slowly toward the far end of the line.

"That one don't stand a chance," the man whispered as they watched the fat man amble by. "Look at Duffy, but don't stare."

Jack glanced and saw Duffy smile as he watched the fat man with the awkward gait.

"Duffy's got his eye on him. He wants him. Duffy wants the fat man."

"Whatta' ya' mean?" Jack whispered. There was no reply.

Snapping his shoulders back, arms against his side, eyes forward, the man next to him had jerked to attention. Jack glanced and caught sight of a guard looking their way.

Jack straightened likewise and stared ahead as the guard began reading off names from a clipboard. When his name was called, Jack stepped forward. When everyone from the bus had done the same, the guard barked. "Turn left and move to the door. No talkin'. No pushin'. Just move. MOVE!"

Jack again felt that every man on the yard was watching him. *Duffy wants the fat man.* The words rolled through his head, and he couldn't help but wonder if Duffy was watching him, too.

They walked single-file across the yard and through the metal door. Inside they queued up behind a scarred metal desk and gave their names— last name first—to a guard with thick glasses. The guard checked the names on his clipboard and read off cell assignment.

"Dugan, Jack," Jack said when it was his turn in front of the desk.

"B, 128," the guard mumbled, nodding his head toward the hallway to his left. Jack joined a group of men assembled against the wall. Finally the fat man staggered to the desk.

"Name?"

"Larry," the fat man mumbled.

"Last name!" the guard barked.

"Ta-ta-toomy," the fat man stuttered, bringing laughs from everyone in the room.

"Ta-ta-toomy" the guard laughed, mimicking the fat man's reply.

"Too-my," the fat man replied slowly, straining not to stutter, staring down at his feet.

"Looks like you're in…"

"C," came a quick reply from the back of the room.

Jack turned toward the voice and saw Duffy standing cross-armed in the doorway.

"La-la-larry's goin' to C, right?" Duffy said, smiling at the guard.

"Yeah, that's right," the guard said, casting a quick glance at Duffy. Turning his pencil upside down he erased something on his sheet and scribbled "C" next to the fat man's name.

"Toomy," the guard said, not looking up, "C Block. Over there," motioning with his head.

Jack stole another glance and saw that Duffy was no longer in the doorway. He watched the fat man shuffle away to join the others assigned to C.

They moved slowly in a line, like cattle to slaughter. Ordered to strip, then into a shower. Disinfected with a foul-smelling spray. Next stop their hair was indelicately shorn to the scalp. From a window in a wire cage they were issued soap, a razor—no blade—underwear, socks, jeans, a denim shirt with a number stenciled over the pocket and shoes with the flexibility of cardboard. Under the watchful gaze of guards they dressed then marched single file into the tiers. A thousand eyes stared at them through the bars. Jack was placed in a cell by himself at the far end of B block.

A static-filled voice from crackling speakers directed their every move. It woke them up and told them when it was time for work. When the voice said it was time to eat, Jack silently followed the line of men walking before him. He went through the chow line and took his tray to a table in a far corner of the dining room. With his back toward the wall, he poked at the horrible food on his tray and ate little.

In a couple of days Jack felt his clothes bagging around him. At night, alone in his cell, he forced himself to exercise. He did push-ups, sit-ups, and chin-ups on the iron bars of his cell door. No one, he vowed, would touch him. He ate alone at the table in the corner and kept to himself in the exercise yard.

Chapter 2

"You gunna' join us?"

Jack looked up from his breakfast tray and saw the one they called Malloy standing opposite him. "Join the rest a' us in B," Malloy said. "You won't make it here on your own."

"Says who?" Jack replied, his eyes focused back on his tray as he shuffled the slop with a fork.

"You got no protection," Malloy said.

"Protection from what?"

"From Duffy an' his bunch in C. They prey on weak ones...and loners...like you."

"I can take care a' myself."

"Not in here you can't," Malloy shot back. "Duffy has connections and he gets what he wants doin' favors for some a' the guards," Malloy said, carefully picking his words.

"Favors?"

"I'll put it this way," Malloy said. "You got men in here for years. Locked away. Haven't been with a woman for God knows how long. You get my drift?"

Jack stared at Malloy.

"You saw how Duffy can get weak ones assigned his way," Malloy whispered.

"The fat man?" Jack replied.

"Yeah, the fat man. Duffy and his crew will have their way with him, then barter him to guards who like that sort a' thing."

"That's sick!" Jack shouted.

"It's the truth!" Malloy hissed. "Like it or not, it's the way it is. That's why everyone in B gotta' stick together. Join up!"

"No one ain't gunna' touch me," Jack shot back, pushing his tray to the center of the table.

"In time Duffy will tire of the fat man," Malloy replied. "Then he'll be on the prowl for someone to take his place. He'll look for someone with no one watchin' his back. A loner...like you."

Jack crossed his arms and stared at the table.

"Have it your way," Malloy whispered. "But watch the fat man," he said as he walked off to join the rest of B at their table. "Watch the fat man," he repeated over his shoulder.

****

Jack watched the fat man. He watched him shuffle into the dining hall, watched him in the exercise yard, and he watched the bruises comes and go.

"You're Larry?" Jack asked one morning, walking to the fat man's side in the chow line.

""Don...don't talk to me. The...The...They're wa...wa...watching."

"What happened to you, Larry?" Jack asked, reaching out for man's arm.

"I fe-fe-fell," the man replied, jerking away from Jack's touch, his eyes cast down at his feet.

"Hey, Dugan!"

Jack turned and saw Duffy moving in his direction.

"Whatta' doin', Dugan?"

"Just talkin' to Larry here," Jack said, staring into Duffy's eyes.

"He's a C man'," Duffy said, staring back. "And C's don't talk with B's in case you ain't heard."

"I talk to whoever I want to," Jack replied. "What happened to him?" pointing to the purple bruises on the fat man's face.

"What happened to you, fat man?" Duffy yelled.

"I fe-fe-fell."

"See, the man says he fell," Duffy hissed.

"And I say you're full'a shit!" Jack yelled.

"You watch yourself, boy," Duffy replied angrily. Turning, he nodded toward the table where the rest of C was seated. The one they called Rabbit rose quickly and moved to Duffy's side.

"I don't want no trouble," Jack said as Rabbit brought his clenched fists up and threw a series of lightning-fast jabs out into the air in front of him.

"Then you best go back to your seat in the corner and shuffle your food like good boy," Duffy said, smiling. "Me and my friend La-La-Larry here are goin' to our table now. Right, Larry?"

Duffy draped his arm around the fat man's shoulders. The man was quaking.

Jack heard footsteps on the tile floor behind him and turned. A guard was walking toward them slapping a baton against his leg.

"What's goin' on?" the guard asked.

"Mr. Dugan was just askin' 'bout our clumsy friend here," Duffy replied.

"Looks like you took a bad fall there, fat man," the guard said, laughing.

"He took a terrible fall," Duffy chuckled.

"Fat people can be kinda' awkward," the guard replied, poking the fat man with his baton. "Right?"

"Ya-ya-yes sir," the fat man stuttered, his eyes riveted to the floor.

"You get back to your place now," the guard said to Jack, pointing his baton toward the corner table.

Jack backed off slowly as everyone watched. Back to his table in the far corner of the room.

*****

Jack continued to watch the fat man. Watched him show up in the dining room with purple bruises that faded to green, only to be replaced with fresh ones. Watched as the fat man shed the weight that had earned him his nickname, his clothes hanging loosely around him. Watched his gait become a slow shuffle, his eyes constantly cast down at his feet. Watched as a group from C block always surrounded him and directed his every move.

Chapter 3

Jack was in his corner, back against the wall, toying with the miserable stuff they called 'food'. Malloy slipped into the seat opposite to him.

"The fat man's not comin'. He's gone," Malloy said.

"Whatta' you mean he's gone," Jack said standing, scanning the room.

Malloy stood up and whispered. "The fat man killed hisself last night. Used a pencil to open up a vein in his wrist. Bled to death on his bunk. He couldn't take it no more. Just the thought a' how he done it gives me the willies...diggin' inta' his wrist with a dirty pencil."

"Stop it!" Jack shouted, bringing the attention of the entire dining room.

"You know why the fat man was here?" Malloy whispered. "For cheatin' on taxes...that's all. He screwed the state outta' 'a couple'a bucks, and now he's dead. No one deserves a death sentence for that."

"He didn't get no death sentence!" Jack shouted.

"He sure as hell did," Malloy hissed back. "The minute Duffy got him into C, he was doomed. And now he's dead because a' Duffy. So, Dugan, you wanna' go down like the fat man, or are you ready to join us?"

"His name wasn't Fat Man!" Jack shouted. "His name was Larry. Larry Toomy!"

Duffy and his crew stood up at Jack's outburst. Malloy stared at them then turned to Jack.

"You're right, it *was* his name." Malloy said. "Now, my question to you is this, Dugan: Are you ready to join up with B? Duffy's gunna' be on the prowl for a replacement. Remember, he has connections. He'll be lookin' for a loner, for someone with no one watchin' his back. You want to end up like the fat man? This is the last time I'll ask you.

You ready to join us...or you want me to get ya' a pencil so you'll be ready if you don't."

Jack turned and stared at Duffy and the crew of deviants standing around him, smiling. "Count me in," he said, turning to Malloy.

Guards with their batons out were moving toward them. Malloy raised his hands in 'surrender' then slowly reached down for Jack's tray.

"No trouble here. Everything's calm. Man's just movin' over to join us," Malloy said as he started toward the B table with Jack following. Duffy and his crew just glared.

"This here's Jack Dugan," Malloy said as he set Jack's tray down. "Jack, meet your new best friends."

Jack edged into an open seat and cautiously eyed the men who stared back at him.

"I know you seen most 'a these guys before," Malloy said, sliding onto a chair. "But I suspect you don't know much about 'em."

Jack nodded and Malloy went around the table giving the names and brief descriptions of their crimes.

"And if you can ever get those two straight," Malloy said, coming to two men seated across from him, "you're a better man than me. That's Joe," Malloy said, nodding toward one.

"No, I'm Jim," the man replied, laughing.

"Okay, so that's Jim," Malloy laughed, shaking his head. "And next to him's his twin brother Joe. Those two had a real good smash an' grab thing goin' till they got caught."

"Smash an' grab?" Jack asked.

"Damn, Dugan, you're one young pup," Malloy said. "It's what jewelry thieves do. Smash the case an' grab up the goods. But these two added a new twist. Here's how they done it: One of 'em'd saunter inta' a' jewelry store an' at the same time the other one'd walk into the police station and begin spinnin' a yarn with the cops, reportin' somethin' stupid, like maybe he lost his wallet. Next thing you know, the one in the store does the smash an' grab. The alarm goes off and he skedaddles. A couple a' minutes later, the other one comes runnin' down the street with the cops, like he just wants ta' see what's goin' on. Now comes the good part," Malloy said.

"The store owner sees the one with the cops and says, 'That's him! Good job! You got him!'"

"What?" the cops say, "This guy was with us when it happened.'"

"Damn, I'd swear it was him!" the jeweler says."

Everyone at the table was roaring as Malloy continued the story.

"So the cops are just lookin' at each other, dumb like. And you got the jeweler starin' back all confused, wondrin' if he's goin' crazy. In the end the cops come up with nothin'. The twin just drifts off and joins up with his brother down the road.

"They pulled that trick off a couple dozen times in three states. Got pretty lucky, and pretty rich. Then they got either cocky or clumsy an' decided to try it close to home. That's when they got caught."

"So how did you get caught?" Jack asked, staring at the twins.

"School teacher," Joe replied.

"School teacher?"

"Yeah. Our third-grade teacher. We hit a place where she was workin' durin' the summer. She was in the back room and saw everything. After I made the grab, Jim shows up with the cops. The jeweler and the cops are standin' there scratchin' their heads like always. Then she comes outta' the back and says to the cops, 'I believe the thief was his twin brother'."

"You were done in by your third-grade teacher!" Jack roared.

"Yeah, imagine that," Jim replied, punching his brother on the shoulder. "Cops held me as a possible accomplice, then put out the word to be on the lookout for someone fittin' my description—red hair, about the same height as me. A couple'a hours later they nabbed Joe in the next town over. They had both of us. The newspaper printed this big headline. I'll never forget it. It said *Teacher Trips Up Twin Thieves From Tamaqua*. Damn, I hate school teachers!"

The table was howling.

"Anyways," Malloy said, raising his hand to stifle the laughter, "in this bunch there ain't no wife beaters, no rapists, no child molesters... or perverts," he added, gesturing toward Duffy and his group. "That you can take to the bank."

Heavy footsteps on the tile caused everyone to turn.

"Sounds like you's all havin' a party here."

A huge Black man dropped a tray heaped with food onto the table and drew back a chair.

"And this," Malloy smiled, nodding toward the big man. "This here's Cheesesteak. One a' us. He works the kitchen and gets to eat whatever he wants after everyone else been through the line. Lord knows, Cheesesteak needs the nourishment.

"Cheesesteak," Malloy said, nodding toward Jack, "Meet Jack Dugan. I finally convinced him to join us."

The big man and Jack eyed each other up.

"How's come they call you Cheesesteak?" Jack asked.

"'Cause he's from Philly," Malloy replied before the big guy could answer.

Jack stared blankly at Malloy then at the big man.

"Philadelphia—home a' the cheesesteak," the big man said, staring at Jack over a forkful of food. "Ain't you never heard a' Philly cheesesteaks?"

Jack shook his head.

"Where you from, bumpkin?" the big man asked, and the men at the table erupted in laughter.

"I still don't get it," Jack said.

"A cheesesteak's a big ole' sandwich they make special in Philly," Malloy explained. "So we call him Cheesesteak 'cause he's big...an' 'cause he's from Philly. Philly Cheesesteak. Get it?"

Jack rolled his eyes.

"You know," Malloy said, slapping Cheesesteak on the shoulder, "we could call you Tastykake, seein' as how they come outta' Philly, too. But Tastykake? Sounds kinda' fag-like."

The big man shot Malloy a hard look.

"If I liked boys better'n women, maybe you would be callin' me Tastykake. But then I'd hav'ta be sittin' over there," nodding toward Duffy's table.

Again the table roared.

"That ain't funny," Jack said.

"Damn straight it ain't funny," Cheesesteak replied. "Glad you decided to join us. What's you in for anyways?"

"Attempted murder, assault with a deadly weapon," Malloy replied before Jack could respond.

"How'd you know that?" Jack asked, staring at Malloy.

"Ain't many secrets in here," Malloy laughed. "But I wanna' hear the details sometime."

The crackling speakers came to life.

"But it's gunna' hafta' wait for later. Meal time's over," Malloy said, picking up his tray.

Chapter 4

In the exercise yard Duffy and his gang from C grouped together and Rabbit entertained them. Sometimes with a skip rope moving at lightning speed, other times with a show of shadow boxing. Rabbit would lay out a series of fast jabs followed by what would certainly be a deadly uppercut if there was a person on the receiving end. "Knockout!" his cronies would yell as Rabbit danced around with his fists overhead, proclaiming an imagined victory.

Rabbit, Jack learned, had been a lightweight contender working his way to a title fight. But boxing was Rabbit's second line of income; selling drugs brought him real money. One night Rabbit killed a dealer who was trying to muscle in on his turf. With one punch Rabbit drove the man's splintered nose bones deep into his brain, killing him instantly. Ruling his hands were lethal weapons, a jury gave Rabbit ten years for involuntary manslaughter.

Malloy, Jack, and the men from B reigned over the east end of the yard. For their entertainment Cheesesteak did bench presses with a barbell that took two men to lift onto the rack. At Cheesesteak's urging, Jack began working out with him.

The yard routines were more for show than for exercise. Everyone knew to avoid Rabbit. And at the other end of the yard Cheesesteak—and his new exercise partner, Jack—telegraphed a similar message: Don't mess with anyone from B, unless you want these two as your enemy.

"So, how's 'bout those details? What got you sent here?" Malloy asked after Jack finished a set of curls and slid onto a seat next to him, taking a break.

"They said I attacked a guy an' tried to kill him. Said I busted his head with a porch railin'," Jack replied.

"So that's what *they* said. What do *you* say?" Malloy asked.

"I know I didn't do it. All I did was bust a window."

"Big difference between bustin' a man's head and bustin' a window," Malloy laughed. "You got some 'splainin' to do."

"Here's what happened," Jack began. "My dad died when I was eight. He was killed in a coal mine."

"Hold on a minute. Your dad was a miner? Where you from?" Malloy asked.

"A little place, Creedonton."

"Creedonton!" Malloy exclaimed.

"You know it?"

"Never been there, but everybody in the coal region knows about old man Creedon an' his family," Malloy said, as he unbuttoned his shirt cuffs and began rolling up the sleeves. He held his forearms out toward Jack.

"Them's little pieces of coal," Malloy said, nodding at the dark specks under his skin. "I hit a leftover blastin' cap with a pick. It went off like a shotgun an' sent coal flyin' every which way. Lucky I had my head turned, or I wouldn't have no eyes."

"You were a miner?"

"Started when I was fifteen in a small mine in Gilberton," Malloy replied. "Lied about my age to get the job. The owner was a nice guy. He was fair, an' he treated us like we was part of a team. He respected us. Then one day he gets all us miners together. The man was close to tears when he said, 'It's over, boys. Not for you, but for me. A man named Jimmy Creedon bought me out. I didn't wanna' do it, but Creedon would'a kept lowerin' the price of coal till he pushed me into bankruptcy. I had to sell out to him. I wish you the best. Good luck to 'ya'." Malloy laughed. "Good luck. I sure wish that man did have some luck to give us. God knows we needed it after Creedon took over."

"So you know Jimmy Creedon?"

"Yeah, I know the bastard," Malloy replied, buttoning his sleeves. "But that's my story. We can talk about it some other time. Go on, tell me about your dad. What happened?"

"When I was a little kid, they told my mom and me that my dad died in a cave-in. But a couple a' months ago I learned he was killed robbin' a pillar. I heard it from the town drunk. He was laughin' about it too, sayin' my dad was crushed..." Jack paused and stared off, wrestling with the image.

"Don't say no more. I don't need no details, Jack. I seen men die that way, and I know it ain't pretty," Malloy said.

"Anyway, the drunk kept on laughin' and wouldn't shut up, so I whacked him with a rock."

"That was the assault that got you sent here?" Malloy asked.

"No, I just beaned him. I hit him with a rock 'bout this size," Jack said, holding up his clenched fist. "An' I said I'd kill him if he didn't shut the hell up."

"Good for you, boy," Malloy said.

"Then later that night I busted a window—a real expensive one—at Creedon's place. I wanted to make him pay for sendin' my dad in for that pillar."

"So you went after Jimmy Creedon," Malloy laughed. "Damn, I wish I coulda' been there. You say you busted a window at his place."

"A real expensive one," Jack repeated. "And the next day somebody whacked the drunk with a porch railin' an' almost killed him. Somehow my ballcap— with my name inside—ended up in the drunk's place. The cops heard about my threat to kill him, found my cap in his house, and put two and two together and came up with five...or maybe ten."

"Whatta' ya' mean?"

"Five to ten years they gave me for attempted murder," Jack laughed. "Since I was eighteen when it happened, they sent me here instead a' some place for kids."

"So it wasn't you that whacked the drunk with the railin'?" Malloy asked.

"No, I didn't do it. I swear."

"So how'd your cap end up in his place?"

"I honestly don't know," Jack replied. "The night it happened I was at home waitin' to talk to a college scout about playin' ball for his school. Maybe get a scholarship to pay my way."

"Scholarship?"

"Yeah. I was pretty good ball player. Some said I mighta' been good enough to play college. But I guess we'll never know."

"How 'bout the scout? Couldn't he vouch for you, for where you was that night."

"The man never showed."

"Son of a bitch," Malloy said as he crossed his arms and leaned back against the fence. "Sounds to me like you mighta' been set up, son. By Jimmy Creedon, maybe? Maybe he found out you was the one 'at busted his window?"

"I guess we'll never know," Jack replied, shaking his head. "So what's your story, Malloy?"

"They say I killed a man."

"That's what *they* say. What do *you* say?" Jack laughed, asking the question the way Malloy had done.

"I *know* I was set up," Malloy replied.

"So, how 'bout the details?"

"Tomorrow," Malloy said, rising from his seat. "Exercise time's about over."

Seconds later the crackling speakers confirmed it.

Chapter 5

The next day in the yard Jack slid onto a bench next to Malloy. "Your turn. You gunna' give me them details?"

"My wife an' me, we had a little boy," Malloy began. "Cutest little fella' you ever saw. Looked just like his mother. His name was Joey."

Malloy stared away and swallowed hard.

"He died when he was jus' two years old. In the end it was a blessin' God took him. He was sick an' was just wastin' away." Malloy stared off again before continuing.

"We didn't have no money for no doctor, no medicine. We nursed him as best we could, but we was in one a' the shacks Creedon called 'company housing.' The bastard made us rent from him; you couldn't live nowhere else and work his mine. That place was friggin' nightmare. So cold and drafty you'd be better off bein' outside. Hell, sometimes water would freeze in the coffee pot overnight. Our baby didn't stand a chance a' ever gettin' better in that place. And when Joey died, we had 'ta bury him in a dynamite crate. We didn't even have the money for a proper casket. No marker on his grave.

"I swore no man's child would ever die that way. So I began tryin' to bring in the union, hopin' to get us better wages, decent houses, maybe even a doctor. But Jimmy Creedon didn't want no part a' that. It woulda' meant less money in his pocket.

"One night one a' Creedon's foremen got shot in an alley, an' the next day the cops show up and find a gun in my back shed. I swear, I never owned a gun in my life. So I go on trial for murder. Outta' the blue comes a guy named Robert Lufkin. He was flashin' a gold badge, sayin' he was a Philly cop just passin' through town. In court he swore that he saw me mixin' it up with the foreman in the alley. Claims he heard me say somethin' like 'I'll bring the union in here if I have to do it over your dead body.'

"Hell's bells, I never talked like that!" Malloy shouted. "It'd be just plain stupid. I kept my union talk hush-hush an' just between me and the guys I worked with. You'd be an idiot, talkin' that way to a foreman.

"But I didn't have nobody to vouch for where I was the night the foreman got killed. The only one I was with was my wife. And you can imagine what her testimony would'a been worth...squat."

"You think that guy, the Philly cop, had somethin' to do with it?" Jack asked.

"I don't think it," Malloy replied. "I know it! Nobody ever saw the man in town before. But he had that gold badge, nice suit. Had all right answers when the lawyers questioned him. And when they asked him to identify who he saw in the alley that night, he comes outta' the witness stand and walks up to me, points his finger in my face, and says, 'This is the man I saw.' I'll remember that bastard till the day they put me in the ground. Premeditated murder is what they charged me with, and I'm in here for life."

"You think Creedon set it up?" Jack asked, "On account'a the union thing."

"I don't think it. I know it. But there ain't no way I can ever prove it," Malloy replied. "Not sittin'in here for the rest a' my days."

"Your wife. Is she..." Jack began.

"Helen. That's her name. Yeah, she's still alive. Creedon kicked her outta' his place and she moved in with her aunt. The aunt died a couple 'a years ago, and Helen got the house. She'll never leave Gilberton. Never leave where our little Joey's buried.

"Anyways," Malloy said, "it looks like you and me got more in common than the Coal Region. Could be we was both set up by Jimmy Creedon."

"Only difference is you seen the man that did it to you—that cop, Lufkin. Me, I didn't see nobody," Jack said.

"But at least you had the pleasure of bustin' Creedon's expensive window," Malloy replied, laughing.

"Yeah," Jack laughed. "Yeah, I did."

Chapter 6

Jack, Malloy, Cheesesteak and the others were in the yard when the siren wailed and the loudspeaker crackled. Malloy cupped his hand over his eyes and looked toward the gate. "Bus's comin' in."

The bus with wire mesh in the windows ambled up the road and ground to a halt at the gate. Guards in the towers gave the signal and the gate slid back slowly. The old bus lurched through and the gate clanged shut.

"You see Duffy?" Malloy asked, rising on his toes, scanning the yard.

"In front, on the left," Jack replied.

"Watch him," Malloy said, "He's still on the lookout for a replacement for the fat...for Larry," he said, catching himself. "He'll be watchin' for a weakling, a loner."

The bettors were huddled around four-eyes with his notebook, watching as men stepped from the bus and lined up against its side.

"No returnees," Malloy said to Jack as the last man walked toward the end of the line.

Four-eyes pocketed his notebook and the crowd around him drifted away.

"Wait, we got one more," Malloy shouted.

A gangly kid jumped from the bus and swaggered out into the yard in front of the lineup. He did a half circle, eying up the place and grinning like he was in an amusement park.

"That idiot was never here before, that's for sure," Malloy said as a guard ran toward the kid. "He's gunna' get hisself in a heap a' trouble comin' here with attitude like that."

"Look at Duffy," Jack whispered. Malloy turned.

"That kid's just what he wants," Malloy said. "A misfit. The guards'll give him to Duffy just to get him off their hands."

"He looks young," Jack replied. "Probably doesn't know any better."

"Sorta' like you," Malloy laughed.

"So whatta' you gunna' do?" Jack asked.

"Hell if I know," Malloy replied, shaking his head.

A guard pushed the kid into line, and the new inmates started toward the door in the limestone building. Jack saw Duffy snaking his way through the crowd.

"You know him?" Jack asked Malloy, nodding toward the guard trailing the line.

"Sanders," Malloy replied.

"One 'a Duffy's friends?"

"No. He's a decent guy—for a guard. Why?"

"I got an idea."

Jack waited till the line was queued up outside the door, then he squatted down forcefully. He smiled as his pants ripped at the back seam. Jumping to his feet he moved toward the line. Sanders, his rifle up, stepped in front of him.

"Where you goin'?"

"Need new pants!" Jack said, turning and bending over. "Can't have my ass hangin' out. Not in this place."

"Go on in, see the quartermaster," Sanders replied, laughing. "But wait till the new guys go through first."

"Thanks," Jack said, running toward the door. He followed the last man through the doorway seconds before Duffy got there.

Sanders stopped Duffy at the threshold.

"Let me in," Duffy demanded.

"You got no business in there," Sanders replied. "Move away."

Jack waited in the hallway as the new men were processed before the grey metal desk. When the kid with the swagger walked up to the desk, Jack yelled, "Hey!"

"What?" the guard at the desk said, looking up. He saw Jack's blue denim shirt with the number stenciled over the pocket. "You ain't new! What're you doin' here?"

"Gotta get new pants," Jack said, bending over, aiming his split trousers toward the guard. "Sanders said to come in and get 'em. But you know," he added quickly, "I don't have no cellmate. How 'bout givin' me someone to talk to? He'll do," Jack said, motioning toward the kid.

"What's your name?" the guard barked.

"Dugan, Jack. B block, one-twenty-eight."

The guard at the desk looked toward a fellow guard slouched in the corner. "Know anything about this guy? Dugan. B, one-twenty-eight. Any problems with him?"

"Nope," the guard replied, totally disinterested.

"Ok, kid, looks like you're gunna' join Dugan there."

Glancing at his list the guard gave a shot at pronouncing the new kid's name. "You're Shi...Shi...Shit," and laughed.

"Shicatanno," the kid replied. "Lou Shick-a-tan-o."

"What the hell kinda' name's that?"

"It's Polish," the kid replied.

"Like hell," the guard laughed. His name badge read Kaminsky.

Back in the tiers the inmates watched as the new men marched to their cells. Outside his cell door, Jack stepped back to let the kid go in first. Jack turned, took a slight bow, and smiled at his friends in B. Malloy shook his head, smiling back.

Chapter 7

News of what Jack did traveled quickly through the prison grapevine, and Jack knew the implications of it the first evening in the dining hall. Duffy stared at him with an intensity that would burn a hole through steel.

"You both stick real close," Malloy cautioned Jack and Leo, who sat staring around the room. "You're Duffy's new worst enemy, Jack. And you," poking Leo with a fork to get his attention, "I'd say you're probably second on the list."

"I can take care 'a myself," Leo said with a smirk.

"Not in here you can't," Jack replied, seconds before Malloy had a chance to say it.

Leo ignored the remark and began rambling off his life story. He bragged about his crimes, most of which were minor compared to what had put his tablemates in prison, and he seemed to relish the fact that he had finally made it to the big time. He was serving three-to-five years for his second robbery conviction.

Malloy sat back in his chair, quiet as the kid rambled on. Finally he looked up and smiled as Cheesesteak approached the table with his heap of food.

"And this little fella's Cheesesteak," Malloy said, interrupting the kid as the big man plopped into a chair and hoisted a fork above his overloaded tray.

"Cheesesteak! You from Philly?" Leo asked excitedly.

"Who's askin' and why?" Cheesesteak mumbled.

"I'm Leo, Leo Shicatanno, an' I'm from Philly," the kid said, extending his hand across the table.

Cheesesteak growled and Leo drew his hand back.

"I just guessed you might be from Philly 'cause a' your nickname. Philly, home a' the Cheesesteak. Right?"

"If it'll get you to shut up so's I can eat in peace," Cheesesteak replied, looking up over his tray, "you're right. I'm from Philly. Probably not your neighborhood," he laughed. "You look a little pale to me."

"I know some Black folks!" Leo shot back.

"Yeah. I bet they be the cleanin' lady or da'shoeshine boy," Cheesesteak replied laughing. "Yes sir, Mr. Leo. Whas' you wan' me to do, boss. Any 'ting you want dere boss. Jus' don't beat me no mo'!"

Everyone howled as Cheesteak dug into his tray. Leo just stared at the big guy, for the first time lost for words.

Malloy stared at Cheesesteak. "What you got there?" he asked, pointing at Cheesesteak's shirt pocket.

"Almost forgot about it wit' all dis Philly talk goin' on. It's a pitcher," Cheesesteak replied, digging in his pocket.

"Picture a' what?"

"A' me," Cheesteak said, turning a postcard face down on the table. In the spot where an address would go was a pencil sketch.

"Damn that's good!" Malloy said, eying the drawing. "Looks just like you!"

"Yeah," the twin named Jim said, leaning across the table, staring at the picture. "Uglier'n hell."

Cheesesteak glared at him as the table roared at the twin's remark.

"Who drew it?" Malloy asked, waiving his hand to quiet the laughter.

"Guy who works the kitchen wit' me. Name's Bob some'n or other. Just goes by Bob," Cheesesteak replied.

"Tell me about him!" Malloy said.

"He's on E. Quiet guy. Works the kitchen to be away from the rest. Jus' wants ta' keep to hisself."

"He drew this?" Malloy asked, picking the card up to study it close.

"Yeah. I didn't ast' him to. He jus' come up to me and says, 'Here, Cheesesteak, I want you to have dis.' And he give me the pitcher."

"I wanna' meet this guy," Malloy said, handing Cheesesteak the drawing.

"Sure. I'll set it up," Cheesesteak said, pocketing the card. "Give me a couple'a days. In the yard, OK?"

Malloy nodded.

"Rumor in the kitchen is that Jack here saved you," Cheesesteak said, turning toward Leo.

"Whatta' you mean 'saved me'?" Leo asked, shooting quick stares at Cheesteak, Malloy, and Jack.

"Tonight, in your cell, ask Jack about the fat man...I mean about Larry," Malloy said. "And listen up good. You tell him, Jack. About Duffy and C block."

"Why not now?" Leo pressed as the speakers began to crackle.

"That's why," Malloy said, rising from the table with his tray. "Mealtime's over. No more talkin'."

Chapter 8

That night in their cell Jack told Leo about Duffy and the guards he controlled and the favors he offered them. He warned Leo about staying clear of Rabbit, and told him how C and B kept to their own spots in the yard. He cautioned him about the danger of ever being caught alone or being viewed as a loner or misfit.

"Malloy said to tell me about...Larry, I think," Leo said.

"Larry Toomy," Jack replied. And he told Leo about how Duffy finagled Larry's assignment to C. He told him about the beatings and the bruises and how Larry ended his life with a dirty pencil stuck in his arm.

"Good Lord," Leo replied softly.

"That's what it's like in here," Jack said. "That's why B sticks together."

"I heard you ask the guard at the desk to put me in as your cellmate. Why'd you do it?" Leo asked.

"Larry died 'cause he didn't have protection. I don't want anyone to go through what he did," Jack replied. "You came off the bus actin' like you were king of the world. But in here, you ain't worth nothin' alone. You gotta' have others watchin' out for you. And in B we watch out for each other. That's why."

"Thank you," Leo replied. "Maybe someday I can pay you back."

"Just stick with us."

"What about you?" Leo asked as the lights went out. "Why are you here?"

"No talkin' after lights out," Jack replied, rolling over in his bunk.

Chapter 9

Two days later Cheesesteak walked toward Malloy in the yard. A short man with horn-rimmed glasses trailed behind him.

"This here's Bob, the one that drew the pitcher," Cheesesteak said, motioning over his shoulder.

"Good to meet you, Bob," Malloy said. "Thanks for comin'." Malloy walked to a bench and patted the spot next to him. Bob sat down.

"I saw the drawin' you did a' Cheesesteak. It's good. Very good."

Bob smiled.

"If I was to describe someone to you, you think you could draw him? A good picture, like you did a' Cheesesteak." Malloy asked.

"Doin' it that way ain't real easy," Bob replied. "When I drew Cheesesteak, I was puttin' down what I saw with my own eyes. But when you'd be describin' what someone looked like, I'd be tryin' to put down what you saw. It's hard tryin' to get it right. Could take a lotta' time."

"Time," Malloy laughed. "I got a lotta' that. A lifetime, in fact. I ain't going nowhere anytime soon."

"Whatta' you want me to draw? I don't do no naked ladies or..." Bob began.

"No! Nothin' like that," Malloy shot back.

"Just had to ask," Bob said. "You'd be surprised at what some of them ask me to draw," nodding toward Duffy's group at the end of the yard.

"No, I wouldn't be surprised at all," Malloy said.

"I got morals," Bob said.

"What're you in for?" Malloy asked.

"Murder," Bob replied mater-of-factly.

Malloy look at him with an upraised eye. "A moralistic killer, eh?"

"Hear me out," Bob replied quickly. "A drunk driver killed my wife and baby girl. Son of a bitch barreled through a red light and hit us broadside. But the cops wrote somethin' down wrong. The guy got himself a slick lawyer and got off. A technicality, they called it. So's he off, free as a bird. He's walkin' around like nothin' happened, and I lost my wife and baby.

"I vowed to get the bastard. I found out where he lived, where he worked, and for two months I followed him, just biding my time, waitin', watchin'. Then one day I saw him on the street and I followed him to a barroom. I went into the place and walked right up to him. 'You destroyed my life,' I said. And before he said a word, I put two bullets in his head in front of a roomful a' people. Premeditated murder is what they called it. Damn straight I planned it out, and I'd do it again in a heartbeat. Son of a bitch deserved to die."

"I can't deny you that, Bob," Malloy said. "Not at all."

"So, who do you want me ta' draw?" Bob asked.

"The man who got me sent here. Just like your drunk driver, this guy wrecked my life, and I never wanna' forget what he looked like. You'll make the drawing?"

"Like you said, we got the all the time in the world to work on it," Bob said, extending his hand.

Chapter 10

Kate just wasn't the same after Jack was sent away. She never smiled and she even quit chiding me about my smoking when we saw each other on the back porch. It was like something inside her died.

During Jack's fourth year in prison Kate took ill. It amazes me that workin' alongside doctors every day she never caught the attention of anyone. It was like she didn't exist, or wasn't worth worrying over.

When she finally collapsed in the hospital hallway one day, I guess they couldn't ignore her anymore. They admitted her on the spot.

Father O'Malley banged on my door. Seeing as how I never owned a car, the old priest drove us to see her.

"Haggerty," she said when I stood by her bedside, "tell Jack I love him."

"You'll tell him yourself," I replied. But I knew that would never happen. I sat at Kate's side the entire night. Early in the morning she reached out to me. Her hand grew cold in mine, and her last words were, "You gotta' tell him, Haggerty."

Father O'Malley and I went to Rockville to deliver the news. A guard took us to the warden's office, and the minute Jack entered the room and saw us, he somehow knew.

"Jack," Father O'Malley began.

"My mother's dead," Jack said before O'Malley could finish the sentence. The old priest nodded.

We took chairs around the table.

"You can be released to go the funeral, Jack," the warden said.

"No," Jack replied, "I don't wanna' go."

We all stared at him, but before we said anything, Jack continued.

"I want her funeral to be proper. Respectful. I don't want people gawkin' at me and whisperin' while they should be payin' their respects to her. I want her remembered for the fine woman she was... not the mother of a convict with a guard standin' by his side."

"The guard won't be in uniform," the warden offered quickly.

"Won't make no difference," Jack said, holding his hand up to stifle any more debate. "She loved roses, Haggerty," Jack said. "You'll see there'll be roses?"

"Of course, Jack," I uttered. "But what about her things? The house?"

"I'm never comin' back to Creedonton," Jack replied. "Give her things to charity. The house, you sell it Haggerty, and keep the money."

"But..." I stammered.

"Listen!" Jack said, staring into my eyes. "I know about you—after my dad died."

The priest spun in his seat and stared at me.

"Comin' to our house, sayin' you needed an egg or a cup a' sugar or wantin' to borrow a can a' soup. All the time you'd be watchin'."

Father O'Malley's stare turned into a glare.

"And what you really wanted was to peek in the refrigerator or the cupboard. Then the next day there'd be a box of groceries on the porch."

The priest's expression changed to a smile. Jack continued.

"You'd get a load a' coal for your house and have 'em dump half in our coal bin, sayin' they overloaded the truck an' had some left over.

"Haggerty," Jack laughed, "Jimmy Creedon don't send a man down a worked-out mine to rob a pillar and then somehow send out extra coal on a truck."

"Jack," I began.

He held up his hand again.

"And there were the Christmas and birthday presents I knew Mom could never afford. Yes, Haggerty," he said, smiling at me. "I knew it was you that got 'em. Mom never said anything about it;

I guess she was too proud. But I figured it out a long time ago, and I thank you for all you did. So I'm tellin' you now, sell the house. Keep the money. Consider it payback."

Jack rose from his chair, and the guard moved quickly to his side.

"Is there anything you need?" I babbled.

Jack turned in the doorway.

"I got everything I need here. Three—I guess you'd call them 'meals'—a day, and real friends.

"You know," Jack said after pausing, "I met some really good men in here. Yeah, some of them are killers. But I truly believe some folks deserve to die for what they did. You might not consider these guys decent in your view of the world, but the way I see it, they're a heck of a lot better than some on the outside who really should be behind bars.

"Don't forget the roses," he added as he walked from the room.

Chapter 11

Nine months of prison routine passed.

"Well, you made it kid," Malloy said as Jack walked to B's table with his tray. "We're gunna' miss ya'."

Everyone at the table nodded in agreement as Jack sat down.

"I'm gunna' miss you, too, all 'a you guys," Jack said. "But I ain't gunna' miss this slop," he laughed, nodding at his tray. "First thing I'm gunna' do when I get out is get me a steak."

"First thing!" the twin, Joe, shouted. "Hell, Dugan, maybe you shoulda' been over there with Duffy's pals if the first thing you're gunna' do is getcha' a steak!"

Everyone at table roared at the remark.

"Leave him be," Malloy said sternly. "Not everyone got his mind in the gutter."

"So where you headed, Jack?" the other twin asked.

"He's goin' to Philly," Leo replied before Jack could answer.

"Philly?" Malloy asked, staring at Jack.

Again Leo spoke up.

"My grandfather lives there. He has a restaurant, and I told Jack to look him up. If nothin' else," he said, turning toward Jack, "it'll at least give you time to get your feet on the ground. After that, who knows? But for now, you're goin' to Philly, right?"

"Probably. I don't got no place else to go," Jack replied. "I sure as hell ain't goin' back to Creedonton."

"Philly?" Malloy repeated, staring at Jack. "Well I'll be damned."

"What?" Jack asked, staring back at him. "What's the big deal?"

"Here," Malloy said, fishing a folded piece of paper from his pocket and opening it on the table. Jack and the others stared at it.

"It's a drawin' Cheesteak's buddy, Bob, did," Malloy said, "Can you believe it."

"Looks like 'a frickin' snapshot," Leo said, leaning over the table. "Who is it?"

Jack smiled at Malloy, then spoke.

"It's the guy that set you up, isn't it? Lufkin, right? It took me a minute to figure out why you were so whizzed up about me goin' to Philly, but then I remembered. You said the guy at your trial claimed he was a Philly cop."

"That's what the man said," Malloy replied. "Here, you to take it," he said, pushing the sketch toward Jack.

"Whatta' want me to do with it?" Jack asked.

"Hell, Jack, I don't know. Maybe just show it around. See if you can find out who the son of a bitch really is. If you learn anything, anything that might set the record straight, I'd appreciate you lookin' into it. And if you got the time, maybe you could look up my wife."

"Wow!" Jim said.

"Get your head outta' the gutter!" Malloy said, staring at the twin. "What I mean is, if Jack finds out this guy was a sham, I want her to know about it."

"What if it don't come to nothin'?" Jack asked.

"Then so be it," Malloy replied. "All I know is I ain't never gettin' outta' here, and you're the only one I know's headin' off to Philly. So if you're willing to take the drawin' along and ask around a bit, I'd appreciate it. That's all."

Jack stared at the drawing. "And what's that?" he asked, pointing to a small sketch in the corner of the page.

"It's a ring the guy was wearin'," Malloy said. "When he came up and pointed to me at my trial, he had it right in my face. I think it's pretty close to what I remember—the crest and the colors on it. But I don't know what it means."

"That dere's a police ring."

Jack and Malloy turned and saw Cheesesteak standing behind them with his heaping tray.

"Whatta' you mean 'police ring'?" Malloy asked.

"It's 'a Philly police academy ring," Cheesesteak replied, taking a seat.

"What the hell!" Malloy exclaimed.

"Sure is. My sister's husband had one jus' like it," Cheesesteak said. "The no good bum would backhand her across the face with it. He liked hurtin' her, till I put a stop to it. For good," Cheesesteak chuckled.

"Your sister's husband was a cop! The guy you killed was a cop!" Malloy exclaimed. "You never told me that!"

"You never asked," Cheesesteak replied. "Yeah, he was a cop. He had my sister so scairt to death she'd lie about the beatins he give her. Say she fell or somethin'. Then one day I stopped by their place and saw him standin' over her laughin'. She was bleedin' with her face all busted up. I grabbed the son of a bitch and strangled the life outta' him. And he had a ring just like that one there. I yanked it off his finger and gave it to my sister to pawn."

"Holy hell," Malloy whispered.

"I say old Cheesesteak just upped the ante. So the guy at your trial was a cop," Jack said, as he folded the drawing and slipped it into his pocket. "I'll see what I can find out," Jack said, extending his hand toward Malloy. "I owe it to you."

"I appreciate it," Malloy replied, taking Jack's hand.

Part III -- COMEUPPANCE

Chapter 1

Jack ducked into an arched entryway and pulled the collar up on his thin jacket. Clutching the lapels at his neck with his left hand he huffed his breath into his right fist trying to warm his aching fingers. The cheap suit they gave him before he was released was no match for the weather and he shivered from head to toe.

Swirling icy mist had been falling all day and the early November darkness brought on a strong brisk wind that drove the sleet into his face and hands like hot needles. He was soaked, and his clothes were plastered to his skin.

Three hours earlier he had left the comfort of the Girard Street bus terminal.

Shivering in the alcove he questioned his sanity for having ventured out, and he cursed himself for not spending a half buck for a city map at the bus station. His rationale was that he had the directions Leo had given him.

Jack fished the sodden scrap of paper from his pocket and read the directions again. They had been good for eight blocks, but after that either Leo was dead wrong or he had made a bad turn somewhere along the line. Now he was hopelessly lost.

Moving on, walking down long city blocks in the stinging sleet and darkness, Jack began to wonder if there really was an Aspsley Street.

"Never heard of it," was the response he got several times from folks who took the time to respond to his inquiry. As he walked away he cursed Leo under his breath for not providing better directions, and he cursed himself for even beginning this godforsaken venture.

Four more blocks, he said to himself. With the icy wind blowing in his face he decided to go just that far before giving up. After that, he hoped some kind soul might direct him back to the bus station.

There was no one on the streets and his heart sunk as he stumbled through the darkness. On the fourth and final block he spied a lump balled up on a stoop wrapped in a moth-eaten blanket. With nothing to lose, Jack shook the lump's shoulder.

"Ashphsley?" the old man slurred in response to Jack's question, looking at him with a vacant bloodshot stare. Jack turned and began to walk away.

"Sheven blocks up."

"What'd you say?" Jack said, turning.

"Sheven blocks 'at way," the vagrant replied, motioning with his head. "Got a buck?"

"Here," Jack said, pulling some coins from his pocket. "It's all I can spare."

"Ummm," the pile of rags mumbled as Jack dropped the coins into his hand.

Jack counted off the cross streets. When he got to seven he saw the street sign. Apsley. *Thank God!*

Halfway down the block he saw a red and white checkerboard curtain at a window in what looked like just another row house in the lineup. But above the curtain, in neat block letters stenciled on the glass: Angelo's.

Jack dashed across the street. Stepping in a pool of slush at the curb he winced as his thin shoes sucked up the icy water like a sponge.

On the porch he reached out with a hand numb from cold, pulled the door open and almost fainted as he was enveloped by the warmth that flowed out.

"Get in or get out!" a voice barked.

The shout brought him to his senses and Jack slipped inside, pulling the door closed behind him. Immediately he felt that every eye in the place was on him as he moved back against the wall.

The place was crowded. Every stool at the bar was taken and a cluster of men stood at the far end.

Beyond the bar was a back room. Booths around the perimeter were filled, and in the center of the room tables and chairs had been pushed together in a large rectangle. Around it was a rowdy crowd wearing gaudy shirts with 'K of C Bowling Champs 1962' embroidered on the back.

The table held mugs, pitchers of beer, and plates with cigarette butts stubbed out in the remnants of food.

From his spot against the wall, his arms folded across his chest, certain that people were staring at him, Jack fought off the urge to bolt. He had come too far to let fear get the best of him.

On the wall behind the bar above a silver cash register, shelves were stocked with liquor bottles. As he watched, the bottles were rarely touched, but the beer taps at the bar were worked non-stop. It was definitely a working man's bar.

The place had dark paneled walls, and the ceiling was stained light brown from years of smoke. The booths in the back were intimate alcoves with red and white checkered tablecloths, dimly lit by candles in wax-encrusted wine bottles.

Waitresses scurried from the bar to the back room delivering pitchers of beer to the bowlers and an occasional glass of wine to the booths. Scribbling furiously on their pads they would disappear through swinging doors in the back and emerge later with big trays laden with food and baskets of bread. As he watched them with their heaped trays, Jack felt a wrench in his stomach. His last meal was prison slop, yesterday.

More than anything, Jack was trying to see around the patrons on the bar stools, hoping to get a look at whoever was working behind the bar. A stool finally came open and Jack summoned up the courage and slid onto it.

No wonder I couldn't see him, Jack thought, looking down at a small old man behind the bar.

Angelo, Jack recalled Leo saying, was tiny. And this man certainly was.

Grey curly hair, a walrus mustache, Leo said. Round wire-rimmed glasses. And always a white shirt, sleeves turned up. But it was the vest and watch fob that clinched it. A navy-blue pin-striped vest with a golf watch fob draped into the left pocket.

Just as Leo had described.

When the old man stood before him, Jack pulled out his last two soggy dollar bills and laid them down.

"Draught," Jack said. It wasn't a fraction of what he wanted to say, but it was all he could get out. "Whatever you got on tap."

The old man began to turn away, and Jack's voice somehow outraced his fear. "Leo told me to see you."

The old man showed no reaction to the remark, he just ambled away.

A jumble of thoughts flashed through Jack's mind.

Was this the right place? But how many places named Angelo's could there be on Apsley Street? Maybe the old man wasn't Angelo. But how do you account for the wire-rimmed glasses, the walrus mustache, the white shirt, the vest and the watch fob?

And then there was the sinking fear that Leo's claim that Angelo was his grandfather was just some bullshit story. Jack's stomach was in a knot.

"Who are you?" the old man asked when he returned, sliding a mug of beer across the bar.

"I'm Jack. Jack Dugan."

The old man eyed him up slowly, taking what seemed like an eternity.

"Are you Angelo? I really need to talk with you, sir. Please!" Jack pleaded.

The old man turned. Over his shoulder he said, "We'll talk later."

Thank God, Jack mumbled to himself.

Jack took a sip of his beer. He hadn't drunk anything in years, not since that night so long ago in Neely's back yard. He drank slowly, uneasily. This wasn't the kind of place where you nursed a beer.

Jack glanced frequently at the mirror above the bar trying to catch a glimpse of the people around him. Real or not, he felt that they were watching him. But a chance to talk to the old man was all he had going for him. He watched the clock next to the mirror slowly tick off minutes—minutes that seemed like hours.

At midnight the old man announced last call and worked tirelessly filling the onslaught of final orders. A half hour later the waitresses began blowing out candles as the booths were vacated. After stacking freshly washed glasses in a pyramid behind the bar, the old man closed out the cash register and held steadfast in his refusal to pull any more pitchers for the bowlers in the back room. After a few rounds of friendly yet unsuccessful banter with the waitresses, they finally gave up and filed through the door casting glances at Jack, who sat at the bar with his mug still half full.

"Best you leave, too, so no one wonders why they must go but you can stay," the old man said, reaching for Jack's mug. "Walk around a while, then knock on the door. We'll talk."

The icy mist was still falling, and Jack clutched his thin coat against the cold. After two trips around the block and certain that no one was following him, he mounted the steps and rapped on the door.

The old man pulled aside the green shade he had drawn over the door and nodded. A deadbolt clicked and he opened the door letting Jack slip inside.

Flicking a lighter, the old man touched the flame to a candle in a wine bottle. He lit a cigar off the candle and blew out a plume of grey smoke, motioning for Jack to follow him into the back room. He carried the candle to a table and pointed for Jack to sit. Taking a seat opposite him, the old man studied Jack's face in the yellow glow.

"Are you Angelo?" Jack asked.

The old man puffed his cigar. "Are you Jack Dugan?"

"Whatta' you mean?" Jack replied, surprised at the question.

The old man laughed.

"Prison is full of liars," the old man replied. "Men who listen to stories about someone's life on the outside. They hear about a pretty wife, a nice house, and maybe someone named Angelo.

"And once they're let free, they use that information to their own advantage. They steal, rob, rape. So how do I know you're not one of them? Someone who heard Leo talking about a man named Angelo, or this place? And now you're here trying to convince me that Leo was your friend. So convince me," he said, drawing on his cigar.

Jack inhaled and smiled, remembering what Leo had told him.

"Leo's mother was Teresa, your—or Angelo's— only child," Jack began.

The old man just stared.

"Leo never knew his father. And his mother died hours after he was born. Some kind of complication," Jack added.

Again there was no reaction from the old man.

"They weren't married," Jack said, and he thought he heard the old man sigh.

"Angelo wanted nothin' to do with him. In fact, he thought the guy got Teresa pregnant so he would someday get this," Jack replied, motioning into the room.

"All you say," the old man said, "is common knowledge around here. You could have heard it on the street."

"Maybe," Jack replied softly. "But I doubt they know what Angelo did about it."

"What? What did Angelo do?" the old man asked, leaning into the candlelight.

"According to Leo, Angelo carries a pouch," Jack said.

The old man shifted on his seat and pulled a leather drawstring bag from his pocket and set it between them. "Lots of people carry pouches."

"I'm sure that's true," Jack replied. "But Leo said that Angelo's pouch is a little bit different. He told me that Angelo gave two men a hundred dollars as down payment to beat the man who got Teresa pregnant. And he paid them another five hundred dollars when they brought him proof of their work."

Jack upended the old man's coin pouch and spread the contents out with his palm. Then, from the pile, he flicked two yellowed teeth across the table. "The proof that they beat him good. And no one knows about it but Leo. Am I right?"

The old man stared into Jack's eyes.

"No one but Leo knows this," the old man said softly, scooping up the teeth and coins and placing them back in the bag. "For Leo to tell you this, it means only one thing: He trusts you. Otherwise he wouldn't have shared this secret.

"Jack Dugan," the old man said, extending his hand across the table, "I'm Angelo, Leo's grandfather. Welcome, my friend. "

Jack grasped the old man's hand and smiled.

"Maria!"

The old man's shout sent Jack skidding back against the chair.

"Maria!" Angelo shouted again, and a stout woman in a sauce-splattered apron burst through the far door.

"Angelo! What?"

"This man," Angelo said, pointing at Jack. "This is Jack. Jack Dugan. The one Leo wrote us about. The one who kept him safe."

"You're sure!"

"Yes, woman, I'm sure."

The old woman wiped her hands across her apron as she flitted to Jack's side. Bending down, she grasped Jack's head like a melon and began kissing his cheeks. "Jack", she squealed. "Jack Dugan. Jack Dugan." Kiss, kiss, kiss and a massive choking hug before she let him go. "Tell me about my Leo," she asked.

"Talk to him later!" Angelo said gruffly. "He's hungry. Bring him some food, and anisette and wine. The good wine. Go, woman. Go."

"How'd you know I'm hungry?" Jack asked.

"I watch people's eyes," Angelo laughed. "You stared at the waitresses all night. Not at the women, but at the food."

Jack laughed.

Maria returned with a bottle of clear liquor and two small glasses.

"Anisette," Angelo said, pouring into the glasses. "Good for when you're wet and cold. Or when you just want some," he laughed.

Angelo picked up his glass, tilted his head back, and poured the drink down his throat. He nodded for Jack to do the same.

Jack's eyes welled up as the licorice-flavored liquor made his mouth, his throat, and his chest feel as though they were on fire. A wonderful warm fire.

Angelo poured them each a second then a third shot. Jack put his hand over his glass as the old man raised the bottle to pour a fourth. Fortunately, Maria came through the kitchen door with a tray bearing a heaping plate of spaghetti, a basket of steaming bread and bottle of red wine.

"Eat," Angelo said, but the command was unnecessary as Jack plunged into the food. Angelo sat back puffing his cigar, smiling as he watched Jack devour the food.

"Oh, that was good," Jack said as he wiped up the last drop of sauce with a wad of bread.

"Good?" Angelo bellowed as he poured them each a glass of wine. "Only good?"

"No. No," Jack replied. "It was fantastic!"

"Ah. That's what I want to hear," Angelo said leaning back, sipping his wine, puffing his cigar.

"So, what do you want from me, Jack Dugan?" the old man asked.

Jack stared at him.

"You come here for what? Money?"

Jack angrily pushed back from the table.

"I don't want your money. Nothin' like that," he replied. "All I want is a fresh start. That's all. I don't have no family and no place to go. What I need is a job. Any job."

"A job, eh," Angelo smiled. "So tell me, Jack Dugan, what can you do?"

"I worked in the prison laundry."

"Laundry," Angelo laughed. "Maria does the laundry."

Jack hung his head at the remark. "I'll do anything," he whispered toward the floor.

"If you truly mean that," Angelo replied, reaching across the table to touch Jack's shoulder, "we'll come up with something. You trust me, and I'll give you a chance...for helping my Leo."

Jack looked up and said nothing.

"Now, what I think you need," Angelo said, "is sleep. We'll talk more tomorrow."

Jack rose, shook the old man's hand and started toward the door.

"Where you goin'?" Angelo shouted.

"I don't know. Bus station, I guess," Jack replied.

"No!" Angelo said, smiling. "You sleep in Leo's room. He won't be using it," he added, laughing. "Come."

Jack followed the old man up a narrow staircase and blinked as Angelo snapped a pull chain on the landing, illuminating a tiny bedroom. "Bathroom is over there," Angelo said, nodding his head toward a door. "You sleep now, and we'll talk in the morning."

"Thank you," Jack called as the old man descended the staircase.

"No, thank you, Jack Dugan," Angelo replied.

Chapter 2

Sunlight blazed through the dormer window. Jack sat up and glanced around the room, his mind wrestling with the thought that he must have been dreaming. But there was no speaker, no crackling voice. Slowly recollection of the previous night came back to him.

He squinted at the clock on the night stand. Nine o'clock. He had never slept this late. He rose slowly off the bed and stretched, inhaling deeply. *Oh, my God, bacon.*

Jack finger-combed his hair at the mirror in the small bathroom and swabbed a finger across his teeth. His shirt was a wrinkled mess. As he tried smoothing it with his hands he smiled; there was no number over the pocket.

Jack scampered down the stairs and found Angelo at the table they had shared the night before. The old man pointed and Jack slid into a chair opposite him.

"You sleep good?"

"Like a baby," Jack replied.

"Maria, he's up!" Angelo shouted.

Moments later the old woman pushed though the kitchen door with a plate heaped with scrambled eggs, toast and bacon.

"Eat!" Angelo barked.

As Jack dug into the food, Angelo lit the stub of a cigar.

"Maria and I talked. And here's what we offer," Angelo said, blowing a cloud of smoke into the air.

Jack looked up from his plate.

"You work in the restaurant. Wash pots and pans, bus the tables, sweep the floors, stock the coolers, clean the toilets."

Jack nodded.

"And in return, you stay in Leo's room, eat all your meals here, and earn fifty dollars a week. You share any tips with the kitchen help and waitresses."

"You're kiddin' me," Jack replied.

"Not enough?" Angelo questioned.

"Oh, no. It's...it's...fantastic!" Jack shouted.

The old man smiled.

"Now listen. If you work hard...in time...maybe... just maybe," Angelo cautioned, shaking his index finger, "I teach you how to work the bar. Deal?"

"Yes. Yes! Oh, yes!" Jack said, reaching out to shake Angelo's hand.

"Finish your breakfast. Then get to work," Angelo said gruffly, puffing his cigar to life.

Chapter 3

Angelo watched Jack. Wrestling a hundred-and-sixty-pound keg of beer into the cooler under the bar on a sweltering July day, Jack bantered with the patrons who chided him for time it took to connect the taps.

"Good things come to them that wait!" Jack yelled from the confines of the cooler as he attached the tubing. Emerging dripping in sweat, he drew the first beer from the new barrel and offered it free to the guy who had been protesting the loudest. Laughing, the loudmouth threw a ten dollar bill on the bar buying rounds for the house.

Good. Very good, Angelo thought to himself.

A few weeks later Jack substituted for a waitress who called in sick. Jack's charm with a group of young factory women who frequented the place also caught the old man's attention.

"Listen," Jack explained as he pointed to items on a menu he had opened up on the table. "You each buy a small chef's salad—keep you lookin' real pretty. And you split a large pizza and a carafe' or two of house wine. It's the best deal, believe me."

Angelo did the math in his head and smiled as Jack took the order.

But it was the regulars' acceptance of Jack that clinched it.

Over the years Angelo had hired countless young men hoping to find one that would relieve him of spending hours on his feet behind the bar. But it was the relentless harassment from the regulars that caused all of them to walk away.

Most of the regulars were veterans. Europe, the Pacific, Korea, and a few young ones just back from Vietnam. Army, Navy, Air Force, Marines, it didn't make any difference which branch they served. At the bar they were a brotherhood.

When the long-hairs began showing up, Angelo would cringe when they walked through the door.

They'd come in asking for a job, with a mop of hair down to their shoulders, wearing beads and tee shirts all colors of the rainbow with peace medallions hanging around their necks.

"You lookin' for a job, cutie-pie? You are a girl, aren't 'ya...with that long pretty hair," one of the regulars would bellow. "What's your name, sweetheart?" another would add. "You a girlfriend a' that Fonda bitch? This here's America. Love it or leave it, you freekin' queer!"

"And get yourself a haircut!" someone would yell as the long-haired youth bolted to the door.

The regulars were a force to be reconed with, yet Jack took it upon himself to confront them about his own situation on day one. He stood behind the bar and stared each of them in the eye.

"I respect what you guys did, fightin' for the rest a' us," he said. "I thank you for it. Some a' you," he said, staring at the Nam vets, "got the short end a' the stick. It ain't right the way folks treated you. You did your duty, plain and simple.

"I want you guys to know I wasn't in the service. I didn't run away; I just won't ever be allowed in, since I did time. They don't take convicts. You understand that?"

Every one of them respected Jack for being up front about it. And while they didn't tease him about not being in the service, everything else was fair game. Any chance they got, they harassed him no end. But Jack rose to the challenge and gave it right back to them, always with a smile and a laugh. And the regulars loved it.

Angelo watched Jack water down drinks for patrons on the verge of overindulging and jokingly cut off those who had had too much. "Hey, pal" Angelo heard Jack say one day as he stared into the eyes of a man who was demanding another drink. "I heard about your wife. If I let you go home with another one under your belt, I swear she'd beat the snot outta' you and then she'd come after me. My mug is ugly enough already, so give me a break. Have a coffee, on me."

With both of them laughing, Jack poured the man and himself a coffee and leaned across the bar, patiently listening to the man's woes.

Before long Jack left dish-washing behind and became a permanent fixture behind the bar. Angelo began to play pinochle in the back room in the morning with a group of his cronies. After lunch he'd leave for long nap, and in the evening he'd return to take a stool at the bar, sip a glass of wine, smoke a cigar, and hold court with the regulars arguing baseball in the summer, football in the fall and the ponies year round.

As Angelo watched Jack, Jack likewise noticed Angelo's routines. During the first week each month Angelo would leave with a pouch tucked under his arm. Returning, he would slip behind the bar and stash the zippered envelope in the safe under the cash register. Jack watched but never asked about it.

Jack watched Angelo open the mail at his table in the back room. Angelo would bellow "Maria" and the old woman would scramble from the kitchen. "From Leo," Angelo would say, holding a letter aloft.

Maria would stare blankly over his shoulder as Angelo paraphrased the letter. "Leo says he's fine. The food is okay, but nothing like you make. He's anxious to come home. Love, Leo."

Jack came to realize that Maria couldn't read.

"When he come home?" she would ask.

"He don't say," Angelo would reply.

The old couple never mentioned the possibility of visiting Leo. Angelo owned a car—a glistening black Buick that he drove every Sunday from the garage behind the restaurant to Mass at St. Ann's and directly back. Jack rode with them to church, just once. After that ride he was glad that a road trip to see Leo was never broached.

Angelo spent more time focusing on his cigar than on keeping the car headed in the right direction. He ran red lights, clipped curbs, and took his half out of the middle of the road. When they finally arrived at the church, Jack prayed only that they would make it back home alive.

Angelo did make an attempt to teach Jack to drive. Barking orders, swearing in Italian, flailing his cigar around, whacking out the hot ashes that fell on his pants. The one-and-only driving lesson ended with both of them out of the car yelling at each other in the street.

Jack eventually got a neighbor to teach him how to drive, and when Jack proudly laid his driver's license on the bar, Angelo beamed with pride. "See, I taught you good!" the old man said.

Chapter 4

Jack was bent over the sinks swirling dirty glasses over a cone-shaped brush with his left hand then plunging them into the cool rinse with his right before setting them downside on the drainboard. It was mindless crapwork—the non-glamorous side of being a bartender—the kind of work that made countless college kids quit after a few days, if they lasted that long.

The most recent one walked out the night before, and Jack once again found himself doing glasses.

The screendoor squeaked and he looked up.

"Leo! Holy hell! Leo!" Jack yelled.

"Hello, Jack," Leo replied softly.

"Hello my ass!" Jack shouted as he dropped a glass into the sink and bounded to the open end of the bar. "Leo! I can't believe it. You're out!" reaching his arms out to embrace him.

Leo shot his hands up and backed away. "Don't!"

"Don't what?'

"Don't touch me."

"What's wrong, Leo?" Jack said incredulously.

"I just don't want no one touchin' me is all."

Leo stepped back, and Jack stared at him.

"You didn't call or nothin'," Jack said. "We didn't know you were gettin' out or we woulda'..."

Leo waived his hand and Jack stopped. They stared at each other in an awkward silence.

"You're still here," Leo finally said. "How long's it been, Jack?"

"Twenty-eight months," Jack replied.

Leo stared at him as he dug a cigarette pack from his pocket, clawed out the last smoke and aimlessly tossed the crumpled pack behind the bar. It took him three attempts with shaking hands to fire up a match.

"Over two years," Leo said, blowing smoke into the air. "More'n two years and you're still here," sucking again on his smoke. "I never thought you'd stay this long."

Leo stepped around Jack cautiously and moved into the back room. Jack followed, keeping his distance.

"I'm here on account a' you, Leo," Jack said. "Remember, you told me to look up Angelo. Said he might give me a job."

"Yeah, I remember," Leo replied, half sitting on a table, dragging on his cigarette. "But I never thought you'd stay...this long," letting the words linger.

"Angelo and Maria's been good to me," Jack said.

"I see that," Leo said, taking another deep drag. He coughed as he let out the smoke. "You put on some weight. Happy as a hog in shit. Seems like you settled in for good."

"I like it here. Angelo and Maria..." Jack began.

"Yeah, I know, they been good to you," Leo replied nastily, cutting him off. "In fact, it looks like you got it so good now you just left the past behind."

"What're you sayin', Leo?"

"It just ain't like I thought it would be," Leo said as he stood up and paced the room slowly, keeping his eyes on Jack. "Somehow I thought puttin' you in touch with Angelo would give ya' a start. Make a few bucks, get your feet on the ground. And then you'd be off to settle your score with that guy back home. Creedon, right?"

"Jimmy Creedon," Jack replied.

"Yeah, the one you say probably set ya' up. Put you in prison for some bogus shit for breakin' his frickin' window. But it looks like you just forgot about it, now that you're all cozy here."

Leo walked behind the bar and grabbed a bottle from the top shelf. He poured sloppily into a glass and downed the drink in a gulp.

"So you just let it go," Leo said, slamming the glass onto the bar. "Let it slide," he said, laughing, motioning 'safe' like an umpire, sweeping his outstretched hands across the bar.

He poured again and downed another drink. "And how 'bout Malloy an' that drawin' and the favor he asked you to do? You ever do anything about it?"

"I'm workin' on it," Jack replied.

"Two years, Jack! Two freakin' years and you're still workin' on it! Sure you are!"

"I am!" Jack shouted.

"Did you ever see Malloy's wife? Ever look her up?"

"I will when the time's right," Jack replied.

"When the time's right! For God's sake, Jack, Malloy kept you alive at Rockville. An' now you're too damned busy to even see his wife! What are you doin', waitin' till you win the Irish Sweepsteaks? You wanna' walk up and hand her a bundle a' money? Truth is you just forgot what Malloy did for you. Like it was nothin'!"

"I'm workin' on it! I swear!" Jack shouted. "Malloy'll understand!"

"Malloy's dead!" Leo yelled.

"What!"

"He's dead. Cheesesteak too!"

"Wha....what happened?"

"Duffy."

"Oh, no. No," Jack sighed, dropping into a chair. "What happened?"

"Like you really care," Leo hissed.

"Tell me, Leo, dammit!" Jack shouted, jumping up with his fists clenched.

"Sit down. Just sit the hell down!" Leo yelled.

Jack slumped back into his seat. Leo stared at him a long while before speaking.

"Malloy and the rest of us got sick an' were laid up. I think Duffy got somebody to put somethin' in our food. Cheesesteak was the only one didn't get it 'cause he got his grub direct from the kitchen, remember?"

Jack nodded.

"Cheesesteak went out in the yard alone, hell-bent to do his weights. It happened real fast; Duffy had it planned out good.

"Cheesesteak was lyin' on his back doin' bench presses when two a' Duffy's guys showed up with Rabbit. Rabbit chased everyone away with his boxin' moves while the other two guys stood behind Cheesesteak. They wouldn't let him put the barbell back on the rack. They were laughin' as they just kept pushin' it out, not lettin' him set it down.

"Finally Cheesesteak's arms wore out and the bastards guided that big bar fulla' weights down on his neck. They just stood there laughin', watchin' it strangle him."

"Oh, for the love of God." Jack sobbed.

"After Cheesesteak was gone it got real bad. They got Malloy a couple days later when he was workin' in the laundry. They snuck up and stabbed him in the neck with a sharpened spoon. He was dead before he hit the floor.

"And after that, they came after the rest a' us," Leo added softly.

"Whatta' you mean?"

Leo stared back silently.

"Who'd they go after?" Jack pressed.

"Everyone. Everyone in B," Leo whispered.

"Oh, God, I'm sorry, Leo."

"Nothin' you coulda' done about it. What's done is done."

Jack hung his head and stared at the floor. Neither of them said a word for a while.

"I gotta' go now," Leo finally said.

"Why? Where? Aren't you gunna' wait and see Angelo and Maria? They'll be comin'..."

"I'll be back," Leo interrupted. "There's somethin' I gotta' do."

"Can't it wait?"

"No. It can't."

"What? Where you goin'?"

"Old man Bronstein still got his store on the corner?" Leo asked.

"Yeah, he's still there."

"Then I'm goin' to see him."

"Why? Why now?" Jack blurted.

"One thing I learned in that place," Leo said, "if there's somethin' you feel you gotta' do, you best do it while you can. You never know when your time's up. And now I wanna' apologize to Bronstein for robbin' him when I was a stupid-ass kid. I wanna' make my peace with the man.

"And, hey," Leo laughed, "if nothin' else, I'll get some more smokes, a Coke, and some Tastykakes. I haven't had them suckers in years. I'll be back shortly. And don't say nothin' to Angelo and Maria about my bein' here, I wanna' surprise 'em."

"I'm sure you'll do that, Leo," Jack replied. *I'm sure you will,* he said to himself as Leo pushed through the door.

Chapter 5

This was Sammy's big day. The thought of what it would be like kept him up most of the night, like when he was a little kid waiting for the magic of Christmas. But this would be even better.

Christmas for Sammy had always been a bust. He would go to bed hyped up by department store Santas and television shows of happy families sharing presents under glistening trees. But when morning came Sammy would find his mother passed out on the floor, the living room barren as ever.

Today would beat any old Christmas hands down. Sammy had gone to bed dreaming about it, knowing that today he would make the magic happen.

For two years—since he was twelve—he prepared for it. Two long years that started with the worst beating of his life. The initiation.

There were eight of them—senior members of The Warriors. When Sammy told them he wanted to join the gang, he had to fight each of them to prove it.

Standing bare-chested before the mirror he stared at his reflection and slowly ran a finger over the ragged red scar on his chin. He moved his hand down to his chest, fingering the round knotted scars from cigarette burns. Permanent reminders of the ordeal he had endured on his first step to becoming a Warrior.

Turning his head and lifting his elbow, he could see the crude black "W" they tattooed on his arm with a needle and India ink after he took the beating without shedding a tear. *Warrior,* he whispered to himself.

Sammy had made it through countless other tests. Rolling drunks, snatching purses, serving as lookout while senior members of the gang hustled weed, hotwired cars, and pulled off heists. Time and again Sammy had proved his worth.

Smiling into the mirror, he mouthed *My day.* The council had voted. He was one step away. One final test. If he passed, there was a Warriors jacket waiting for him.

Sammy pulled on an Eagles sweatshirt and bunched the teal-colored fabric under his chin. He reached down for the sawed-off shotgun on his bed. Working the pump, he watched the sleek red 12-gauge cartridge slide into the chamber. Then he punched three more rounds into the magazine.

Tugging the waistband of his jeans, he slid the weapon down his leg, jerking as the cold metal barrel touched his skin. Cinching his belt to hold the weapon in place, he lifted his chin and the shirt fell down. He checked his profile in the mirror and smiled. *Perfect.*

Flea was Sammy's ass man. It was his job to watch his friend's back and let him know if anything bad was coming from behind.

Fourteen years old, Flea was a shade under five feet tall—hence the nickname. The nickname stuck, too, because he hung around the Warrior chieftains like a bothersome bug that wouldn't go away. Like Sammy, Flea had endured an initiation beating. Today he would move up a notch by serving as lookout while Sammy earned his colors.

Sammy stepped awkwardly from his porch, the gun nestled in his jeans giving him a stiff-legged gait. On the sidewalk he nodded at Flea, who rose from the stoop and followed him down the street watching behind them for anything suspicious. At the corner Sammy stopped and nodded. Flea walked into the store.

Sammy leaned against the door frame and smiled as he heard Flea's exchange with the grocer. "You want cigarettes?" the old man laughed. "For your mamma—a likely story. Tell your mamma to come buy her own cigarettes. Go on. Get out!"

Flea stormed from the store in mock indignation.

"What'd you see?" Sammy asked.

"Nobody," Flea replied smiling. "Ain't nobody in there but the old man."

Sammy motioned with his head and Flea backed up against the wall near the door. "You done good, Flea," Sammy said. "You know what to do now?" Flea nodded and whispered, "Good luck."

Sammy took a final glance around then pulled out the shotgun and stepped through the doorway.

The old man was behind the counter.

Sammy let the screen door bang shut, and the old man turned his way. Sammy held the gun waist high and aimed in grocer's direction. The old man gasped and threw his hands up.

"I don't want no trouble. You want the money, take it," the old man said, nodding toward the register.

"Open it," Sammy replied, the shotgun beginning to quiver in his hands.

Flea cupped his hands against the screendoor, anxious to see his friend in action.

"Put the money in a bag," Sammy demanded, "and throw in four packs—no, make it a carton—a' Kools."

Leo stopped in his tracks midway down the aisle when he saw the grocer glance at him when the old man turned to get the cigarettes from the shelf behind him. The grocer's jaw dropped.

Leo had put a Coke in his jacket pocket when he was checking out the magazines in the back of the store. He dug into his pocket for the bottle and continued down the aisle toward the counter.

Gripping the hourglass Coke bottle at its midsection, Leo thrust it forward. "I ain't stealin...," he began to explain.

Flea saw Leo step into the front aisle, pointing something.

"Sammy! A man's comin' at you, an' he got a gun!" Flea yelled at the top of his lungs.

Sammy turned and took a step closer to the counter. He saw Leo with the dark object in his outstretched hand.

For a split second Leo's eyes locked on the black hole at the end Sammy's shotgun. Then a spurt of fire roared toward him and he felt outrageous pain as buckshot ripped into his chest. The blast lifted him off the floor and bashed him into a shelf. The Coke bottle shattered, tearing his hand to shreds.

Sammy stared at what he had done. His shotgun was pointing toward the floor.

Bronstein reached under the counter and brought up a pistol. Holding it in both hands, he aimed at Sammy and squeezed the trigger. The automatic emptied itself in seconds, booming nine times. Three of Bronstein's bullets tore into Sammy's chest. The other six shots, thrown off by the recoil, annihilated a shelf of soda bottles.

Flea watched Sammy spin from the impact then fall to the floor, his Eagles' shirt turning scarlet. Then Flea ran as he never ran before.

Chapter 6

Jack dismissed the first muffled boom thinking it was a truck backfiring or kids setting of a cherry bomb. It happened all the time.

Then the nine sharp cracks from Bronstein's pistol reverberated up the block. Jack dropped the glass he was washing and peered over the half curtain at the front window. People were running down the street.

"What's goin'on?" Jack shouted as he ran onto the porch. A kid from the neighborhood slowed and spun to face him, running backwards.

"They's been shootin' at Bronstein's!" the boy yelled. Then he turned and continued down the street.

Jack leaped from the porch and passed the kid mid block. At the corner Jack began elbowing his way through the gathering crowd. "What the hell!" a man barked when Jack shoved him aside. Jack glared at him and pushed his way into the store.

Bronstein was bent over, his head in his hands. The silver pistol was on the counter.

Sammy was on the floor, blood pooling around him, the shotgun at his side.

Then Jack saw Leo.

His back against the shelves, legs splayed out, head drooped on his chest, Leo looked like a huge ragdoll someone had tossed to the floor.

"Leo!" Jack cried, dropping to his knees. "Leo!" he screamed, clutching the lifeless body in his arms.

Chapter 7

Jack laid a rose on Leo's coffin and walked slowly behind Angelo and Maria to the undertaker's limo.

Despite Jack's objection, Angelo had the staff change into their work clothes after the funeral and open the restaurant. Angelo stood inside the door and greeted the throng that filed into the place to pay their respects. *Wierd*, Jack thought, as he watched them bring casseroles, cakes, bread, and other food *into* the restaurant.

All of the regulars came, and they were on their best behavior. There was no banter or chiding, just polite nods and handshakes. Some of them introduced Jack to their wives, and the mismatch between their barroom banter about the women and the real thing left Jack smiling.

There were others Jack had never seen before. Families with kids, their faces scrubbed, hair combed. They embraced Anglo and went over to whisper kind words to Maria, who sat a table staring as if in a trance. Before long every seat in the place was taken and the soft buzz of conversation filled the room.

When the last of the mourners filed into the restaurant, Angelo walked behind the bar and rang a spoon against a wine glass. The crowd fell silent.

"Thank you. Thank you all. Maria and I, we thank you for being with us on this sad, sad day," he said. "And now, a toast!" The crowd held their glasses high. "To Leo!" Angelo bellowed. "May God rest his soul!"

The room buzzed to life again, and in short order all of the food that had been brought in was devoured.

Shortly thereafter the crowd began leave, pausing to pat Maria's shoulder and shake Angelo's hand. Jack and the staff began clearing the tables.

When they finished cleaning up and the last of the workers filed out, Jack latched the door, drew the shade and started toward the stairs.

"Jack, come. Sit with us," Angelo said. Jack stopped and turned. "Yes, come. We need to talk," Angelo said, acknowledging Jack's hesitation.

Jack took a seat at the table next to Maria. Angelo pulled a cigar from his pocket and pondered it a second, then laid it down, unlit.

"We have news, Jack. Bad news," Angelo said.

Jack stared at the old man.

"Maria has the cancer," Angelo said softly.

"Oh, my God!" Jack replied, stunned. "Maria. Oh, Maria," he said shaking his head, reaching out, grasping her hand.

"We found out two weeks ago. The doctor said it's bad," Angelo whispered.

"How bad? What's that mean?" Jack demanded, staring at the old man.

"Three months."

"What!"

"Three months," Angelo repeated, dropping his head.

Jack turned back to Maria. She looked into his eyes and squeezed his hand.

"We're going home, Jack," she whispered.

"Whatta' you mean?"

"I want to go home," was all she replied.

"We're going back to Italy, Jack," Angelo said, "to be with her family when..." and he choked on the words, tears welling in his eyes..."when it happens."

They sat at the table in silence for a long while.

"Tomorrow we'll talk, Jack," Angelo finally said, rising from the table. He helped Maria to her feet. "Tomorrow."

Chapter 8

I was sitting on the back porch enjoying a mid-morning smoke when I saw a shiny car roll up the alley and stop. *Oh, my God.* I couldn't believe my eyes.

"Haggerty!" Jack yelled as he vaulted the fence, ran up the stairs and wrapped his arms around me.

"Seven years ago you came slinkin' up that alley," I said.

"Like the devil's on my tail," Jack replied, laughing, releasing his grip.

"Look at you," I said stepping back. "All gussied up, lookin' real important-like."

Jack was wearing a crisp white shirt, a silk tie loosened at the knot, the trousers of a fine wool suit.

"I just took a chance you'd still be here," Jack said.

"You mean upright, on the green side a' the grass," I said, laughing.

"Something like that I guess. Boy, Haggerty, it's good to see you," Jack replied.

"It's good seein' you, too," I said.

Jack leaned against the porch railing and pulled a fat cigar from his pocket.

"What brings you back?" I asked.

Jack was rolling the cigar over a lit match and he winked me over the flame and lifted a finger, a signal asking me to hang on for just a minute.

Then he let it all spill out. He talked non-stop for a good half hour telling me about Malloy, Cheesesteak and the others. He gave me all the details about Duffy, Rabbit, the guards on the take, and about Larry Toomy—the one they called Fat Man.

We laughed ourselves to tears when he told how he split his pants in the yard as part of his ploy to keep Leo away from Duffy. Then he told me what

---

happened to Malloy and Cheesesteak, and how Leo was killed.

He finished by telling me about Angelo and Maria and how they gave him a job and then, after Leo was killed, how they left everything to him when they went back to Italy. The restaurant, the shiny car in the alley and two apartment buildings.

"They just gave it all to you?" I said.

"All of it. But more than that, they left me a trust fund they set up for Leo."

"What's that mean?" I asked.

"It means a heck of a lotta' money. More than you or me ever dreamed about, ever," Jack replied. "Angelo and Maria started it with the money they got from a life insurance policy when Leo's mother died. Any extra money they got went into it, and they planned on giving it all to Leo one day," Jack said. "But when he was killed..."

"They gave it to you," I said, finishing Jack's sentence. "So you're a rich man now...an' a landlord, too, just like Jimmy Creedon," I laughed.

Jack reflected on the comment.

"You know," he said, "I don't think of myself as a landlord. It's more like I'm a caretaker."

I guess my dumb expression told him I didn't know what he meant.

"You see," Jack said, "Angelo and Maria came over here with nothin'. They worked like dogs—both of them—savin' every penny they could. Over time they bought up a dozen old apartments and fixed them up nice and rented them out at a fare rate to folks just tryin' to make a go of it. They weren't in it to make a killin', and they didn't care what color or religion the renters were. It was just their way of givin' back some of what they were blessed with."

"Sound like real decent folks," I said.

"Real decent," Jack replied. "And they never made a show of it. In fact, I'm a little bit ashamed of what I thought was goin' on at first."

"Whatta' you mean?"

"The first week each month Angelo would head out with a zipper pouch under his arm and come back later and put it in the safe," Jack said. "I would'a bet dollars to doughnuts that old Italian was into the numbers or some kinda' payola thing. But now I know he was just out collecting his rents."

"Taught you not to judge people, eh?"

"For sure," Jack laughed. "And when they decided to give me the properties, Angelo took me around and introduced me to every one he rented to. Standin' in their doorways, lookin' straight into their eyes, he made me promise them that nothing would change. No uppin' the rents for no good reason. As long as they paid on time they'd have a place to live. I swear, Haggerty, those folks loved that man. And when Leo was killed, every one of 'em showed up to pay their respects."

"Funny what life teaches you."

"Ain't that the truth," Jack said as he leaned back, puffin' his cigar.

"So what brings you back?" I asked.

"Just passin' through."

"Headin' where?"

"Gilberton."

"Gilberton? What the hell's in Gilberton?"

"Malloy's wife," Jack replied. "I hope."

"You don't know if she's still there? Why didn't you just call her?"

"And say what?" Jack laughed. "'Hi, Mrs. Malloy. You don't know me from Adam, but your husband asked me to look you up. Two years passed, so I'm just callin' to see if you're still alive, wonderin' if I have to follow through on it.' No, I believe it's best if I see her in person, see if she's still around. I owe it to Malloy."

"So what're you gunna' say to her?"

"I'll tell her what a good man her husband was. Tell her how he was killed for keepin' me an' the others away from Duffy."

"That's what Malloy wanted you to do, tell his wife he was a good guy?"

"No. It's a lot more than that, and I'm still workin'on it," Jack replied.

"What? What'cha workin' on?"

"It's complicated. Pieces are comin' together, but I don't have it all figured out yet. But when I do, you'll be among the first to know, I promise," Jack replied.

I sensed Jack didn't want to talk about it any more, so I didn't press him on it.

He puffed his cigar and I lit another smoke.

Chapter 9

A boom rattled the windows.

"I thought the mines were shut down," Jack said, watching a plume of smoke and dust rising from the ridge north of town.

"The mines are kaput. That's work on the new highway. They're blasting up the valley for it. Two lanes each direction, it's gunna' be part 'a the interstate system," I replied.

"It's about time," Jack laughed. "The roads around here are miserable."

"So they're buildin' a new one—jus' for you," I replied, laughing. "From up the ridge there," I said, pointing with my finger, "it'll come down onta' the flat land in the valley and go right around town. No red lights, nothin' to slow the traffic. A clean shot from New York all the way to Tennessee, I believe. Plans call for a turn-off—an exit, they call it—down the valley west a' town for folks wantin' to turn off for gas or food or a place ta' stay."

"Sounds like it'll be good for business," Jack said. "I bet folks around here are happy about it."

"Some are, some aren't, and some are just takin' a 'we'll see' attitude," I replied. "But I know one guy who ain't thrilled about it. Ever hear me talk about Anna's uncle Albert?"

"No, I don't recall," Jack said, shaking his head.

"Albert must be pushin' ninety now, if he ain't already there," I laughed. "He was farmin' a piece 'a land his daddy had for years. In fact, the family was here even before old man Creedon showed up. Albert's daddy was 'bout the only one that didn't sell out to Creedon. I suspect he knew that wiley bastard was up to somethin'.

"Their place never was much—a couple hundred acres or so. They ran some cows and pigs and managed to raise enough corn to feed 'em. Albert had just about enough land to scratch out a livin'.

That was until they started pushin' the new highway down the valley."

"What's the highway have to do with it?" Jack asked.

"The highway folks tried to buy his place for the exit, but Albert turned 'em down," I replied. "They wrangled back and forth a bit, but when Albert wouldn't budge, they got a court order and took the land they needed. Imminent domain they call it. Fancy word for stealin'."

"They took his land?"

"Oh, they paid him for it, but the worst part is they only took a piece 'a the place—the cropland. All Albert has left is an old meadow that's 'bout worthless. You can't go more'n a foot down till you hit solid rock. Can't hardly grow nothin' on it."

"They can do that? Just take whatever they want?"

"They can and they did."

"Damn," Jack said. "It don't seem right."

"Is what it is," I replied. "Without land to grow feed, Albert sold off the livestock. I suspect he'll have to give up everything sooner or later. The old coot will probably end up livin' with me."

"I just don't seem right," Jack said again, leaning on the railing, puffing his cigar.

"So, ain't you gunna' ask me?" I asked, changing the subject.

"About what?"

"Creedon."

"I guess we'd finally get around to it," Jack laughed. "He's still alive?"

"Still alive. Still meaner 'an a cornered cat. You got somethin' in mind for him?"

"No," Jack said, shaking his head. "Last time I mixed it up with him, he won. Remember?"

"Yeah, but you did bust his fancy window," I laughed.

"Yeah, I did," Jack laughed back. "But I paid dearly for it. I'm not about to tangle with him again."

There was another boom on the ridgeline. Another cloud of dust rose into the sky.

"Well, Haggerty, I better get goin'," Jack said, glancing at his watch. "Whatta' you figure it is to Gilberton? Half hour?"

"Best part of that."

"Then I better be on my way," Jack said, flicking the nub of his cigar into the yard.

"Been real good seein' you, Jack," I said as he moved toward the stairs. "Your mom and dad would be mighty proud of how you turned out. You come back anytime you want!" I yelled as he walked toward the shiny old Buick in the alley.

Chapter 10

The road to Gilberton turned quickly from poor to downright miserable.

Outside of Pottsville the pavement narrowed to barely two lanes of potholes with a couple of smooth spots in between. With tight turns, narrow shoulders and steep drop offs, there was little room for mistakes.

The land on both sides of the road bore the scars of years of mining. Gray shale covered the mountainsides, and the narrow valleys below were filled with black coal dirt carved by lifeless streams, the water tinted yellow from the iron oxide that leached from the coal waste.

Jack crested a hill and saw a cluster of buildings in the valley below. On the side of the road he eyed a weather beaten sign: *Welcome to Gilberton, A Great Place To....* Someone had painted out word *Live* and scrawled *Die* over it.

Jack slowed to a crawl as he entered the town and rolled down what he learned from a corner street sign was Main Street. He drifted slowly, reading the signs. Miner's First Bank, Hake's Hardware, Gartenberg Jewelry, Rineharts—For Well-Dressed Gents. Change the names, he thought, and this could be Creedonton, Kulpmont, Shamokin —any one of the small towns he remembered from his boyhood.

There were only a handful of cars parked along the street and he didn't see more than a dozen people on the sidewalks. He recalled the scrawl on the sign: *A Good Place to Die,* and smiled.

Stopping for the one and only red light at the main intersection, he saw a place that caught his attention. Fay's. The restaurant looked presentable, probably as good a place as any to try to find what he was looking for.

Jack drifted to the curb and punched a nickel into a parking meter. A half hour. More than enough, he thought, to get a cup of coffee and rehearse what he would say to Mrs. Malloy, provided he'd find her.

Jack scanned the place quickly and settled on a squat chrome stool at the counter.

"What'll it be, hon?"

Jack looked up into a pair of piercing green eyes belonging to a buxom waitress in a frilly yellow apron. She was holding a carafe'.

"Coffee, black."

The waitress reached under the counter and plopped a heavy mug in front him. She titled the pot then flicked her wrist to stop the flow.

"Cream?"

"Just black," Jack replied.

"Black it is," she said, adding a touch more to his mug. "Don't get no black'r 'en that."

Picking up the mug, Jack swiveled on the stool and nodded to the folks staring at him from the booths lining the walls. They quickly turned their heads away.

"Got good pies," the waitress said.

"Fresh?" Jack asked, swiveling back to face her.

"So fresh you gotta' slap em'," she replied quickly, a well-rehearsed line. "Baked 'em myself this mornin'."

"She did like hell! They're store bought." The sarcastic comment came from one of the booths.

"They're still good, Walter!" the waitress yelled back.

"What kind you got?" Jack asked, smiling.

"Coconut cream, apple, peach, an' huckleberry."

"Huckleberry? I haven't had huckleberry pie in ages."

"Bakery up the street makes em'," the woman said truthfully. "They buy the berries from kids who pick em' to earn a few dollars."

"Takes a lot of work to pick a bucket of huckleberries as I recall. How 'bout some vanilla ice cream on the side?" Jack asked.

"Cost ya' a quarter more."

"A whole quarter? I think I can stand it," Jack replied, laughing.

"You must be from 'round here, mister," the waitress said as she scooped a wide wedge of pie from a deep dish. "Seein' as how you know 'bout huckleberries an' all."

"I grew up a couple a' miles from here," Jack replied, watching as she plopped a scoop of ice cream on the plate before sliding it across the counter.

"Scranton? Wilkes Barre?" she asked.

"South of that. A small place, you probably never heard of it."

"Flo! Need a refill here!" one of the booth patrons called out, hoisting his empty cup in the air.

"Hold your pants on!" the waitress wailed. "I only got two hands and I'm busy now waitin' on this here fella. What's your name anyway, hon?"

"Name's Jack," Jack replied, picking up his fork. "The sign outside says this is Fay's, but the guy back there called you Flo. You're not the owner?"

"Dammit, Flo. I ain't got all day!" came the impatient voice from the booth.

"Hold your pants on!" she yelled again.

"Damn man buys a cup a' coffee and thinks I'm indebted to him for life," she said, rolling her eyes as she picked up a fresh carafe' from a warmer. After making her rounds of the booths topping off cups, she put the pot back on the warmer and turned to Jack.

"Fay's the ex 'a Joe, the guy who runs this place," she explained. "'Bout a year ago she took off with some salesman, and Joe figures there's no sense changin' the name. Signs cost money, an' nobody cares what he calls the place. Fay's, Flo's, Joe's, nobody cares long as the food don't kill ya'," she laughed. "So, you just passin' through?"

"Just stopped by to visit an old friend. You know a Mrs. Malloy?"

"Can't say that I do. Where's she live?"

"I really don't know. I was hopin' to check a phonebook and see if she's listed. You got a book I can use?"

"Sure, hon," she said, pulling a coffee-stained phonebook from under the counter.

Jack flipped through the pages and found H. Malloy. *Helen.* Jack smiled, remembering the name Malloy had told her. One-o-five West Pear.

"You find her, hon?"

"Maybe," Jack replied. "There's a listing that might be her. On West Pear Street."

"Oh," the waitress said wistfully.

"Somethin' wrong with West Pear?" Jack asked.

"Not the best part of town is all. Might say that end of town seen its better days."

"Whole damn town seen its better days!" The outburst came from a man who had walked quietly from the back room.

Jack turned on his stool as the guy walked past him, tossed a dollar on the counter and barged through the door.

"What's that about?" Jack asked as the door slammed with a bang.

"Leroy's mad at the world," the waitress said, stuffing the bill into her apron. "He's about to go belly up. Goin' outta' business. You see the sign for Rinehart's up the block?" she asked, motioning with her head.

"For Well-Dressed Gents."

"That's the one. The store's been in Leroy's family some sixty years or so, and now it's goin' down the tubes."

"Why's that?" Jack asked, draining his cup and waiving the waitress off as she moved to pour a refill.

"Look outside," she said, nodding toward the front window. "Whatta' ya' see?"

Jack swiveled on his seat.

"Not much," swinging back to face her.

"It's what, mid-afternoon on a Saturday and you don't see nothin'. Hardly no people, no cars, nothin'. And this here's the so-called business district. Only there ain't no business. Nothin'," she repeated, slapping a tea towel over her shoulder.

The waitress did a quick take around the restaurant to see if anyone was listening. Leaning her elbows on the counter, her face close to Jack, her voice low, "The mall did it.

"You see," she continued in a whisper, "some out 'a towners came in about six months ago and put up a strip mall on the edge 'a town. New fancy stores. They stay open late, got plenty 'a free parkin' and cheap prices. The highway skirtin' town makes it easy to get there. They got 'bout everything you ever need lined up in a row. Air conditioned, too," she added, waving her hand in front of her face.

"Little guys like Leroy, they don't stand a chance. That little mall's got clothes, housewares, books. They even got a hamburger place, an' the kids love it. Yes, sir, that mall's hurtin' all the downtown stores. I'd bet my next paycheck this place won't last long. All we get is the local trade," she said, jerking her head toward the short-sleeved patrons in the booths. "And when their places go down the toilet, this place'll be gone too. That, mister," she said, "is the truth.

"And that one over there," motioning toward an elderly man in a booth against the far wall who was staring blankly into a cup cradled in his hands, "he's feelin' it the worst."

"Why?" Jack whispered.

"Henry Johnson," she whispered back. "He owns most 'a the downtown —includin' this place—and he lives on the rents. There was a time he was a *very* rich man. Now every place that shuts down whacks him good. In time they say he'll go flat broke. Some folks are even layin' odds on if he'll bite the bullet when it happens."

"Suicide?"

"Yes sir," she whispered. "Henry grew up here with a silver spoon in his mouth. He inherited everything from his papa, an' all his life he lived high on the hog an' never knew what it's like bein' poor. Folks think when he finally goes bust it's gunna' drive him over the edge."

"He'd kill himself?"

"Won't know how to handle it. Henry'd think he'd be better off dead than bein' poor is what some folks figure. More coffee?" she asked, smoothing the wrinkles on her apron.

"No, I don't think so," Jack replied rising from his stool. "That's one hell of a story you have there."

"You come back here a month from now and see if I'm right," she said, smiling as she watched Jack tuck a two dollar tip under his saucer.

"About West Pear Street?" Jack asked.

"Eight, maybe ten blocks goin' South down *Main Street*," she replied, rolling her eyes.

Chapter 11

The storefronts on Main grew more desperate with each passing block. Neon signs petered out giving way to soft drink sponsored ones, and a few blocks later there were only hand-scrawled posters propped in the grimy windows of second-hand stores and pawn shops.

Jack counted the blocks and eyed the street signs at each intersection. He finally made a slow turn onto West Pear which had, indeed, seen better days.

At the house numbered 105 he mounted a set of splintered stairs that hadn't seen a coat of paint in years, nor did the porch and the house they led to. But the place was clean. There was a braided rag mat in front of the door and white lace curtains at the single small window next to it. Jack pushed the doorbell button. Hearing nothing, he rapped.

"She ain't home! An' she prob'ly don't want whatever you're sellin'!"

"Excuse me?" Jack said, turning toward the door of the adjoining duplex. A gnarled grey-haired woman in a flowered housecoat stared back at him through the screen.

"Ain't nobody home there, and I don't want what you're sellin' neither," the woman said brusquely.

"I'm not selling anything. I'm looking for Mrs. Malloy. Helen Malloy," Jack said.

"What fur?"

"I'm an old friend and I just stopped by to visit. This is Helen's house, isn't it?"

"An 'old friend' would know that," the woman replied suspiciously.

"Look," Jack said, trying hard to contain his frustration. He had no option than to lie. "It's been a long time since I saw her. Last time I did, she lived here. Okay? "

Raising his hands palm up, Jack said, "See, I don't have a case or samples. I'm not tryin' to sell her—or you—anything."

"She ain't home," the old lady barked.

Oh , God. Jack rolled his eyes. "Maam, I came a long way to see her. Do you know where I mind find her. I just want to say 'hello.' Please?"

"She works at the mall."

"Do you know where?"

"Food place. Burger somethin'."

"Thank..." Jack started, but didn't get the words out before the old witch slammed her door.

*****

A kid on the corner gave Jack directions to the mall. The lot was packed, and when he finally found a parking spot Jack sat in his car for a while watching a steady stream of people going from their cars to the stores and from store to store. Others came across the lot pushing carts or carrying bags.

The Burger Palace was jammed with screaming little kids demanding Prince and Princess meals. At the tables, happy little kids toyed with strands of cheap plastic bauble beads, ignoring their half-eaten burgers.

Jack stared around the place. Fries on the floor, sticky puddles of spilled soda, and much to his amazement people were clearing their tables before they left. *Wish I could get my customers do that,* Jack thought.

Jack asked a girl at the counter for the manager and did a double-take when a fuzzy-faced kid came out from the back room.

"Are you the manager?" Jack asked.

"No, I'm president of the United States," the kid shot back.

Idiot, Jack thought.

Jack bit his tongue and politely asked if he could speak with Mrs. Malloy. "Helen Malloy," he added.

"She ain't here," the kid mumbled.

"Does she work here?"

"Sometimes."

"Is she expected?" Jack asked, frustration creeping into his voice.

"She ain't here now!" the kid spat back.

"I got that!" Jack replied tersely. "But is she done for the day or is she on break or…"

"I told you she's gone. Bye bye, jus' like I'm goin'," the kid replied, flapping his hand in Jack's face before he pushed through the swinging door heading to the kitchen.

Freekin' idiot wouldn't last ten minutes in my place. The regulars would eat him alive.

Jack fumed about it as he drove back to West Pear and waited in his car in front of Helen's house, hoping she'd return soon. There were no lights on, and after a few minutes he caught sight of the neighbor witch staring at him from her window.

Probably gunna' call the cops, Jack thought.

"Leo, Leo, Leo," Jack whispered into the air. "Helen's gunna' have to wait a little while longer. But not real long, I promise," he said to himself as he pulled away.

Jack drove slowly on the twisting rutted roads heading back home, preoccupied with the myriad of thoughts rolling through his head. *Yeah. Yeah, that'll work*, he reassured himself as the plan came together.

Chapter 12

Bob Savage walked into Angelo's and caught Jack's eye. He motioned for Jack to join him the back room and walked to the furthest booth on the far wall.

"Looks like you lost your best friend," Jack said, sliding into the seat opposite him.

"Worse than that."

"What?"

"Creedon learned about AKD."

"So, it's just a corporation so far as he knows. No names attached to it, right?" Jack asked.

"That's right. All he knows is AKD is involved, and he doesn't have any names. But he knows about the plans."

"How?" Jack demanded.

"We bought the land without raising any suspicion," Savage replied. "The transfer of deed was recorded and published along with a bunch of others in the local paper. I don't think anybody reads that 'legal notice' crap anyway."

"But," Jack said. "There's a 'but' coming, I know it."

"But when we filed the site development plans, Creedon got wind of it," Savage replied. "Apparently he has friends on the Planning Commission."

"So he knows."

"It's more than that, Jack. All we get is a run-around and a bunch of lame excuses when we inquire about the status of the permits. My guess is Creedon has someone putting up roadblocks to buy him time."

"Time for what?" Jack asked.

"For this," Savage said, pulling a set of blueprints from his briefcase.

Jack spread the documents on the table and glared at them. "Damn it! Where's this goin'?"

"Where do you think?" Savage asked.

"Shit!" Jack said, slamming his fist on the table.

"Creedon owns the land. It's part of his grandfather's holdings," Savage explained.

"But what about financing? This thing's gotta' cost a bundle," Jack said, jabbing his finger on the drawings.

"Word on the street is Creedon mortgaged everything he owns—his house, the downtown stores, everything."

"I don't get it," Jack replied. "If he pulls this off, his properties in town won't be worth squat."

"That's true. But once this begins making money," Savage said, hammering his finger on the blueprints, "he can buy back the mortgaged properties. He'd have them reassessed so he could get them for a song. The bank'll be anxious to unload them before they deteriorate and lose even more value. Creedon'll end up owning everything again if he wants to."

"But he's a major shareholder in the bank. He'll be cuttin' his own throat," Jack replied.

"To a degree. He may lose a few bucks initially, but he'll make up for it in write-offs. In the long run he'll make out like a bandit. It's a shell game, Jack, and the man is very good at it.

"But back to you. You're not dead in the water; not if you can pull off your plan first," Savage said.

"I can't make a move without the permits!" Jack shouted.

Jack and Savage stared silently at the blueprints.

"I'm not just gunna' up and quit," Jack said. "Not yet."

"You have an idea?" Savage asked.

"How about this," Jack said. "Find a local contractor up there with connections to the planning folks. Promise him an exclusive contract to build the whole shebang, provided he gets the permits through the system. Whatta' ya' think?"

"It might work," Savage said. "We'll give it our best shot. And I have one more piece of news."

"I'll venture it's bad," Jack said.

Savage shook his head. "My law school buddy—the local attorney I'm working with up there—went by Creedon's site yesterday. It's all staked out and there's construction equipment on the ground. Apparently Creedon has his permits in and he's ready to get started. And these plans," he added, tapping on the blueprints, "there's nothing fancy about them. My guess is he'll have this thing underway in two, maybe three weeks."

"Damn!" Jack shouted, slamming the table again. "Two or three weeks only gives us to early July to get goin'!"

"I know. I know," Savage said, shaking his head. "We'll jump on the contractor idea immediately, and I'll set up a meeting with my attorney friend to pick his brain."

"You got your work cut out for you," Jack said, rising from his seat. "Good luck. You're gunna' need it."

Jack walked to the bar and poured himself a Jameson's. He hoisted the glass in Savage's direction as the attorney made his way toward the door. "I'm countin' on you, Bob."

Chapter 13

"Good God, Jack," I said when I answered the knock at the door. "What are you doin' out in this? Come on in."

"I can't believe this rain," Jack said as he followed me to the kitchen, dripping water.

"Coffee?"

"Sure, I'd love some," Jack said as I went to fetch him a towel.

"Help yourself. Pot's on the counter. Pour me a cup, too," I called.

I came back and threw Jack a towel then reached under the sink.

"Irish?"

"You're a good man, Haggerty," Jack laughed, nodding at the Jameson's bottle in my hand.

"In the coffee?"

"No. Straight. I never did like mixin' good whiskey with anything," Jack replied.

We took our drinks and our coffees to the kitchen table and clinked the glasses in a toast.

"What's with this weather?" Jack asked. "The radio in the car was actin' up. Probably on account a' the lightning. Just lots a' static and fadin' in and out, so I shut it off and didn't get to hear any report."

"I just caught a piece a' the weather before the TV went off the air," I said, settling back in my seat. "They said somethin' 'bout a tropical storm movin' up the coast. Leftover from Hurricane Agnes. Said we're gunna' get a shit load 'a rain."

"They said that on TV? A 'shit load 'a rain'," Jack laughed.

"Well, not exactly," I laughed back.

"Well there, mister weather man," Jack said, raising his glass in a mock toast, "your forecast's right for once. We're already gettin a' shit load 'a rain. I know, 'cause I just drove in it."

I lit a smoke—the first one ever inside the house, I believe—and aimed the pack at Jack. He waived it off and got up and helped himself to another Jameson's.

"You know, Jack," I said as he came back to his chair, "for someone who said he'd never come back here you sure been showin' up a lot. Somethin' goin' on you wanna' tell me about. You got a lady friend here or somethin'?"

"No," Jack laughed. "Purely business."

"Business?"

Jack settled back in his chair.

"I want you to hear this directly from me, so you know the truth about what's goin' on. First off, I suspect you already heard that an outfit named AKD bought Albert's farm."

"Yeah, I heard he sold the place. I couldn't hardly believe it. Who'd want that old place anyway?"

"Me," Jack replied.

"Whatta' you talkin' about?"

"AKD's a shell corporation I put together," Jack said.

"What's that mean?"

"AKD: Andrew, Kate Dugan," Jack replied. "It's a company I formed, and I used just their initials to keep my involvement in it a secret."

"So that was you—or your AKD thing—that bought what's left 'a Albert's farm," I said.

Jack smiled and nodded.

"Why in the world would you want that rocky old field?" I asked.

"Because that rocky old field happens to be next to the exit they're putting in on the new interstate, remember?" Jack replied. "And if you haven't heard, I paid Albert a fair price. I figure he didn't deserve to get the short end a' the stick like he did when the highway folks took his good land. I can afford to make it right by him."

Jack paused then stared at me.

"Albert didn't end up movin' in here with you, did he?" Jack asked cautiously, recalling our earlier conversation about the old farmer.

"Hell, no!" I laughed. "With the money he made, the old coot moved to some retirement place in Florida. So, thank you for that!" I said, toasting Jack with my glass.

"Anyway," Jack continued, "remember when I stopped by. Then I went on over to Gilberton?"

"Yeah, what about it?"

"Darned if I didn't come across a way to bring Creedon to his knees," Jack laughed.

"In Giberton? Whatta' you mean, Jack?"

"A waitress in a little restaurant there told me how a new strip mall is killing the downtown, bit by bit. It's especially painful for an old rich guy who owns most of the storefronts—he's like the Creedon of Gilberton," Jack laughed.

"So I bought Albert's farm and was planning on puttin' up my own mall. Build a couple 'a nice stores, a restaurant, gas station, maybe even a motel. In time, they'd suck the life out of Creedon's rental places downtown. Remember, he inherited them; he owns 'em outright, and rents are what he's livin' on. I know that for sure; I had it checked out real good before I bought Albert's place."

"Well ain't that a hoot!" I said, laughing. "You're takin' on Creedon after all."

"It's not a done deal yet," Jack said. "Creedon caught wind of what I was planning when we applied for the permits, and now he's makin' a move to build the exact same thing on his land on the other side of the exit.

"The problem is, the marketing folks I talked to say there's probably only gunna' be enough business to support one of us. If you have places on both sides, they'll cannibalize each other and neither one would make a go of it. I have about a week left to get approvals, get building, and beat Creedon to the punch."

"Can you do it?"

"I'm tryin' like hell," Jack replied. "We tried to get a local contractor to push on my behalf, but Creedon got to him. Creedon told the man he'd blackball him so bad he'd never get another construction job anywhere in the state, and the guy backed out."

"Creedon's got pull," I replied.

"Yeah, tell me about it. So now we're tryin' the legal route. I have a meeting tomorrow with a lawyer up here—a local guy my Philly attorney knows from law school. Hopefully we can figure out a way to get my permits through the roadblocks Creedon's puttin' in my way. There's gotta' be something I can do to get this thing movin'."

"So you plan to go head-to-head with Jimmy Creedon on his own turf," I laughed.

"I certainly hope so," Jack smiled back, sipping his drink.

"I sure do admire you, Jack. But I'm sure you know it ain't gunna' be easy. Creedon's king here."

"Uneasy lies the head that wears the crown," Jack replied.

"What's that mean?"

"Shakespeare wrote it," Jack said, chuckling. "It means a man so high up on the ladder musta' stepped on a lot of little folks to get there, and they'd like nothin' better than to see him fall on his ass. Knowin' they're just waitin' to see it happen keeps him up most of the night."

"Shakespeare said that, 'bout him 'falling on his ass'."

"Somethin' like that," Jack laughed as he retrieved the Jameson's from the counter.

We talked into the wee hours with the Irish whiskey fueling our discussion. Much too late into both the bottle and the evening, Jack insisted on driving to a motel, but I wouldn't hear of it. Fortunately I won the argument and steered him to the living room couch.

Chapter 14

Jack was at the kitchen table when I came down.

"I brewed some coffee," he said, nodding to the percolator on the counter. "It's still rainin' like hell," he added as I poured a cup of what smelled like very strong brew; perfect for my throbbing hangover.

"I wanna' see what Creedon's up to," Jack said. "I have a couple hours before I meet with the attorney. Let's go for a ride."

We were soaked to the skin before we were in his car.

The road out of town paralleled a tiny creek that used to meander along as a small trickle. In the 30's a WPA crew channelized the stream, made it straight as an arrow and built two-foot-thick, three-foot-high stone walls down both sides of it. The Depression era boys also cobble-stoned the streets. Now, every drop of rain that falls goes right into the stream.

Jack stopped alongside the creek wall, and we got out to take a look at how the stream was faring. The muddy surge roaring by was less than two feet from the top of the wall.

"Good God," we said in unison and laughed at the coincidence.

A half mile later the road turned onto a bridge. Jack stopped the car.

"With all that water, you think the bridge'll be okay?" Jack asked.

"Better have a look-see," I said, opening my door. Jack was ahead of me and he reached the railing first.

"That don't make sense!" Jack shouted.

I looked over the railing to see what he was talking about.

The stream below was just a trickle.

Jack turned to me. "What happened? Where's all the water?"

"Oh, shit," I replied.

"What? Whatta' ya' mean, 'oh, shit'?" Jack shouted.

"My guess is the stream cut its way into an old mine shaft somewhere up the line. Now all the water's goin' underground."

"Whatta' you mean it cut into a mine shaft. How could that happen? The mines are deep down! You're not makin' sense!"

"Let's get outta' the rain. I'll tell you 'bout it in the car," I shouted.

"What? Whatta' 'ya think's happening?" Jack asked the minute I closed the door.

"First, let me tell you about coal veins. You ever hear 'bout Necho Allen?"

Jack looked at me with a blank stare. "Who?"

"You musta' been sleepin' in civics class," I laughed. "Necho Allen's the one they say discovered coal the next county over. Story goes he built a campfire on a hilltop somewhere 'round Pottsville. He woke up the next mornin' an' it was still burnin'. Seems he caught fire ta' a' seam a' coal on the surface."

"I thought the coal was deep underground; that's why you got the mines," Jack said, questioningly.

"You musta' slept through science class, too," I laughed. "Anthracite was formed deep underground a long time ago—we're talkin' caveman time. Later, when the earth heaved and the mountains shot up, the coal seams went along for the ride. Now them coal veins go up, down, sideways, every which way. Some's a mile underground, an' others show up at the surface, like the one Necho Allen caught on fire. Remember, old man Creedon hit the Mammoth Vein just a couple 'a feet under a tree stump. Back in the days the mines were goin' strong, there were some houses 'round here where you could go down the cellar and hear the miners hammerin' away. That's how shallow some 'a them veins are."

"Damn, Haggerty, you're a walkin' encyclopedia," Jack said, laughing. "So you think the stream found its way into a mine shaft."

"I do," I said. "And if I'm right, there's gunna' be hell to pay somewhere 'round here."

"Whatta' ya' mean?"

"Water's a powerful force," I said, "especially when it gets bottled up in a small space, like in a mine tunnel. A cousin 'a mine—Simon—was workin' in a shaft up 'round Scranton, an' one day his crew poked inta' an old flooded mine. Water shot outta' the wall like a garden hose, and the guys close by scrambled out. But Simon an' four others were a good way below 'em.

"In seconds the little spurt got bigger and 'afore you know it, it was shootin' out like a fire hose, eatin' away the sides a' the tunnel. The guys who got to high ground heard the tunnel cave in when the water finally washed away the support timbers."

"Damn," Jack said. "What about Simon and the others?" he asked.

"Never did find 'em," I said. "The company tried pumpin' out the tunnel but gave up after two days. Anyway, Simon an' the the others could'a been washed a mile underground. The owners just sealed up that section and put up a marker. Was all they could do."

"Damn, Haggerty, you suspect that can happen here. The water'll wash out the supports and the old tunnels'll collapse?" Jack asked.

"Either that or the water'll find its way to the surface someplace."

"Where?"

"Your guess is as good as any," I replied.

"Aren't there maps of the tunnels?"

"There'd be records 'a the big ones. But after Creedon shut down, you had a lotta' men outta' work, and minin' coal's all they know. A lotta' 'em started their own shafts. Bootleggers they call 'em.

Two or three guys workin' on their own. There's no way 'a knowin' where they dug tunnels.

"Let's go," I said. "No use worryin' 'bout somethin' you can't control. You wanna' see what's Creedon up to, drive on."

Rain was falling in buckets as we crossed the bridge and followed the old highway out of town and into the valley. Jack was hunched over the steering wheel doing all he could to keep the car on the road. We could barely see the white center line when the wipers swabbed across the windshield.

"You just watch the road," I said. "I'll tell you when the turn's comin' up."

It took us ten minutes to go about three miles in the thundering rain.

"Turn's coming up soon," I said when I finally caught sight of the whitewashed fence that circled Albert's old farm.

"Turn right," I said, catching sight of a break in the fence.

Jack drove onto a gravel lane the highway folks carved across what had been Albert's best cornfield. We had to stop a short distance ahead so Jack could move orange barrels that blocked access to a newly paved section of the interstate.

"That rain's unbelievable," Jack said, shaking water off his head like a drenched dog. He eased the car ahead and angled it across the new southbound lanes.

"There it is, Creedon's land," I said, straining to peer out the windshield. "You wanted to see it, now's your chance. Ain't nobody around to stop ya'. Ain't nobody dumb enough to be out here in this rain, 'cept you and me," I added, laughing. "You comin'?"

We walked to the edge of the new highway, our clothes plastered to our skin by the pouring rain. Off to the side was a lineup of machines. Bulldozers half the size of a house, huge dumptrucks, construction trailers up on cinderblocks.

"Creedon ain't waitin' for no permits," I said as I eyed the site.

Trees were heaped in piles and topsoil was plowed to the side in huge mounds. Surveyor stakes poked up everywhere.

"Son of a bitch!" Jack yelled. "Creedon beat me to it. The bastard got me again."

Chapter 15

"I guess he…" I began, but my words were cut off by a roar.

Fifty yards away a plume of water shot from the ground. We watched in amazement as the column of water grew and the earth around it began collapsing as the roaring water gnawed out a widening circle.

In seconds a bulldozer closest to the geyser was undermined. The huge machine rolled onto its side like a dying dinosaur then slowly sank into a sea of mud.

"What the hell!" Jack shouted to me above the roar. "What's goin'on?"

"It's the water from the stream," I shouted, "just like I told ya'. It backed up in a shaft an' built up pressure. Then it found a weak spot and pushed its way to the surface. Right there!" I yelled, pointing to the giant fountain of muddy water mushrooming from the ground.

We watched wide-eyed as the water surged out, turning the acres of plowed-up land into a gigantic pool of mud that slowly engulfed everything in sight. Bulldozers, trucks, the trailers—all of them were slowly sinking into the muck.

We stood in the rain staring dumbstruck at the destruction, hardly believing our eyes.

"Un-be-lievable," Jack whispered.

"Lakefront property," I said laughing.

"What?"

"Creedon got hisself a freekin' muddy lake. An' he aint' never gunna' build nothin' on that mess," I said.

Jack turned and began running. When I reached him, he was on the far side of the new road, staring at Albert's old meadow.

"It's okay," Jack shouted, spinning to face me. "It's okay!" he cried.

"'Cause of the rock!" I shouted. "Your old meadow ain't nothin' but solid rock. It ain't undermined; it's safe. You lucky Irishman! You still got your land! You won, Jack! You won!"

We danced in the pouring rain like kids in a summer storm. Jack's fine suit was ruined for sure, and back in the car I was mighty perturbed to find the pack of smokes in my pocket was nothing but a soggy wad.

That night at my place we finished off the Jameson's.

Jack left early the next morning. "I'll be in touch," was all he said.

* * * *

Tropical Storm Agnes battered Pennsylvania for four days in late June, 1972. Before it was over, nineteen inches of rain fell. In the mid-state, the Susquehanna River, its tributaries, and every stream feeding them rose to record heights.

The devastation in river-side cities like Wilkes Barre and Harrisburg was mind-boggling. Homes inundated by the water burned to the waterline, the flames fed by ruptured gas pipes while fire trucks sat stranded.

Miles of train track and roads were washed away. Bridges collapsed. Sixty-eight thousand homes were destroyed, and three thousand businesses were wiped out. One-hundred-and-fifty people drowned.

Chapter 16

A week later Jack called and asked me to join him. "Just dress up," was all he replied when I asked where we were going and why.

I put on the only suit I own and choked myself into a tie. Jack picked me up mid-morning in the old Buick.

A secretary led Jack, his attorney Savage and me to a room on the second floor of the bank building. Five men in suits were seated in red leather chairs around a huge polished table. One of them was Jimmy Creedon. He was at the far end of the table and he just glared as we walked in.

"Gentlemen," Jack began, nodding to the men around the table. "For those of you who don't know me, my name is Jack Dugan. On my left is my attorney Mr. Savage, to my right is Mr. Haggert, a good friend. I want to thank you for convening this meeting."

The response from the men at the table was just slight nods of acknowledgment; none of them said anything.

"I'll cut to the chase," Jack said after we took our seats. "Gentlemen, I want to pay off the mortgages you hold on Mr. Creedon's properties."

"Excuse me?" one of the men said, looking at Jack over his half glasses. The others at the table exchanged quick glances then stared at Jack. Jimmy Creedon just glared.

"I want Mr. Creedon's properties," Jack repeated. "I want to pay off the mortgages on all of them, including the house."

"Not my house!" Creedon shouted.

"All or none," Jack said, turning to stare into Creedon's eyes.

"NO!" Creedon shouted.

"All or none," Jack said again, softly but emphatically.

"If it was up to me, gentlemen," Jack continued, "the decision would be pretty simple. You see, when I finish building my shopping plaza at the exit on the interstate, Mr. Creedon's downtown properties that you hold mortgages on will be worthless.

"Balk at my offer now and *maybe* I'll come back later and offer you half of what's on the table today. But that's a big 'maybe'. Maybe I won't. I'll just leave you holding mortgages on a bunch of vacant deteriorating storefronts. So, all or none," he repeated. "I'm prepared to pay in full. Right now. Are you interested?"

"You want to buy them all?" the man with the half glasses asked, incredulously.

"Yes. Provided it's all or none. Every one of them. We brought a check." Jack nodded to Savage who slid a blank note onto the table.

"We...we need time to consider your offer," the man in the glasses stammered.

"Of course," Jack replied, smiling. "Mr. Savage, Mr. Haggerty, and I will leave now and give you some time. I think two minutes should be sufficient."

"That's preposterous!" the man in the glasses shouted.

Jack rose and motioned for Savage and me to follow him. Jack turned in the doorway. "Two minutes, and the offer expires. We'll wait in the hallway."

We had a hard time keeping from laughing at the sound of the argument going on behind the closed door. Jack glanced at his watch a couple of times and finally rapped on the door. If looks could actually kill, the one Jimmy Creedon shot us as we walked in would have had us all dead on the spot.

"Gentlemen, please vote by a show of hands," Savage said.

Jimmy Creedon was the only one who didn't raise his hand.

"Four in favor, one against," Savage said.

"Gentlemen," Jack said, "it's been a pleasure. Mr. Savage will see to the legal details."

"I won't stand for this!" Creedon bellowed from his seat.

"You're not standing," Jack said, staring at him coldly. "In fact, you're exactly where I want you to be, groveling on your ass."

"Uneasy lies the head," I whispered, and Jack laughed.

In the parking lot a quick "I'll be in touch" was all Jack said before he drove off. Savage gave me a ride home.

Chapter 17

The phone rang. It was Jack, asking if I was going to attend a public meeting he had set up at the town hall. "You gunna' be there?" he asked.

"Be there? Hell, the whole town's gunna' be there! It's all everyone's talkin' about!" I replied. "The paper says you're gunna' show your plans for your land at the exit. You got everbody wonderin' about it. When you gunna' tell me more?"

"In due time, friend, in due time," Jack replied. "I'll see you at the meeting."

By six-thirty the town hall was packed. Chief Myers, Garver and Mains were standing in the back in case there was trouble.

Bobby from *The Creedonton Call* got in early to get a seat at the front and had his notebook and pen ready. I got there early, too, and sat next to him. It sounded like we were in a beehive from all the buzzing going on.

At seven o'clock Jack came in and walked to the podium. The chatter in the room died quickly; every eye was on him.

"My name is Jack Dugan," he began. "For those who don't know me, I grew up here. I played baseball on the high school team," nodding to his old coach in the back row.

"I've been away a while. Actually put away," he said smiling, catching Chief Myers's eye. "But that's water over the dam. I'm sorry," he added quickly. "Talking about water probably isn't what you folks want to hear, considering what Agnes dealt you a couple'a weeks ago."

Jack held up his hand and the laughter in the room died.

"As you probably know, as a result of the Agnes storm, Mr. Creedon's property west of the new highway was destroyed. In fact, nothing can ever be built on it according to the civil and geotechnical engineers who examined the site.

"But my property—on the other side of the highway—is fine, I'm happy to say. My land is practically solid rock and was never undermined. The engineers checked it out thoroughly; it's perfectly safe."

Everyone was on the edge of their seats, leaning forward, as if it might give them a half-second advantage to hear Jack was going to say next. Jack glanced toward the doorway.

Savage walked into the room with a draped poster board and an easel. It took him a minute to put up the easel, and the room was deathly silent the whole time. Finished, Savage stepped back.

"I think that most of you heard about my plan to build a strip mall at the new exit," Jack said.

The room buzzed to life. Jack raised his hand and the chatter died.

"Listen carefully," he said. The seconds seemed like hours till he continued.

"Here's the plan for my land."

The entire room inhaled as Jack reached for the drape covering the poster board. He flipped it back.

"The Andrew and Kate Dugan Community Park!" Jack shouted.

Jack had to raise his voice to be heard over the gasps. "Paid for entirely by me! My gift to you, in memory of my parents!

" This...this, "Jack said, raising his hand again in a feeble attempt to silence the crowd. "This is a preliminary sketch, subject to change. But it's the best we could come up with on short notice.

"We envision tennis courts," he said, pointing with his finger, raising his voice over the cheers and clapping. "A baseball field," nodding again to his high school coach. "An amphitheater, picnic pavilions. You get the picture. This is what I'm going to build on my land. That is, of course," and the crowd hushed, "the local authorities will grant the permits!"

The applause was deafening. Shopkeepers jumped from their seats and hugged each other. There was no containing the crowd. People stormed the podium, hands outstretched toward Jack.

Jack declined my offer to stay at my place. "You and your Jameson's are a bad influence," he said, laughing. "Actually," he added quickly, "I just want some time alone."

He checked into The Pines Motel, and the owner refused to let him pay for the room.

Chapter 18

The next morning Jack called and asked me to accompany him again. I didn't bother asking where or why; by now I knew Jack liked surprises.

We drove downtown in the Buick.

"My name's Jack Dugan and I own this store now," Jack said to old man Delaney, in his denim apron, perched on his stool behind the counter of the hardware store.

Jack's acquisition of Creedon's downtown properties wasn't news. Everyone in town had heard about his two-minute offer to the bankers.

"So what's it mean?" old man Delaney asked. "Do I gotta' get out?"

"What it means," Jack said, "is that you can rent the store from me for as long as you like. Or, if you want to buy the place—own it outright—we can make arrangements for that, too. It's up to you."

I thought old man Delaney would just tumble off his stool and drop over dead in shock.

As we made our way up and down the street, Jack made the same offer to stunned shopkeepers in every downtown property.

Later that afternoon I rode with Jack to Gilberton.

"What're you gunna' do in Gilberton?" I asked as he negotiated the curvy potholed road.

"You'll see soon enough," he replied. "It'll be worth the wait, believe me."

Chapter 19

I followed Jack into The Burger Palace, where he politely asked for the manager. When a young fellow came to the counter, Jack asked if Mrs. Malloy was working.

"Yeah, but she ain't scheduled for a break yet," the insolent twerp said with a smirk.

"Actually she doesn't need a break," Jack replied. "In fact, I think she's going to quit. Now. Right now."

As the kid stumbled for a reply, Jack cupped his hands and shouted. "Mrs. Malloy. Helen Malloy, come to the counter please."

Jack smiled as an old woman shuffled dumfounded from the kitchen.

"Helen Malloy?"

"Yes?" She stared at Jack blankly.

"You don't know me. My name is Jack Dugan, and I knew your husband. I knew him very well and, in fact, your husband saved my life."

"He what?"

"He did. He protected me, and he kept a lot of other men out of harm's way in Rockville Prison. I'm here now to repay that debt," Jack said.

"What do you mean?"

"You don't have to work here any more."

"But I need this job," she replied.

"No, you don't," Jack said, sliding a check across the counter.

"Oh, my God," she gasped as she studied it.

"In fact, that amount will come to you quarterly," Jack said, smiling. "And this is for the hell you've been through," he said, handing her a manilla envelope.

Helen fumbled with the clasp then stared at the two papers that were inside. Jack gently took one of the sheets from her hand. "We'll talk about this one later," he said, "in private."

"That one," he said, nodding at the sheet she was left holding, "is a deed. It's for a fine house in Creedonton, and now it's yours. You can keep it and live there if you like, or you can sell it. Do whatever you want to with it. Come on, let's go," Jack said, reaching for her arm.

"As for you, kid," Jack said, turning toward the young manager who stood cross-armed at the counter, "you might wanna' start thinkin' about findin' another job."

"Wha...whatta' ya' mean!" the kid shot back, arrogant as ever.

"My local attorney is a good friend of Stanley Walker—you know—the man who owns this place," Jack said. "Mr. Walker and I had a nice long chat, and he wasn't happy hearing what I told him about you. I told him I'd be here today around four, and he said he'd stop by to meet me...and then have a talk with you. I thought it'd be a nice going-away present for Mrs. Malloy. Havin' the pleasure of watchin' you squirm."

The kid stared, his mouth open. But his time he didn't have a comeback.

Jack glanced at his watch. "How 'bout that, it's four-o-two."

A man in a tailored suit walked in and Jack turned to him. "Mr. Walker?"

The man nodded, and Jack extended his hand. "I'm Jack Dugan. It's nice to meet you." Turning to the kid, "I believe this gentleman's here to see you."

Helen laughed as the kid's face turned white as the inside of a hamburger bun.

On the ride back to West Pear Street, Jack told Helen about how her husband kept him out of Duffy's clutches and about how he protected the rest of the men in B block.

When we got to Helen's house, Jack asked me to wait in the car so he could talk with her in private. They sat on her porch, and I saw Jack show her the paper he had taken from her earlier. When they were done talking, it seemed like Helen was never going to let Jack go. She was cryin' like all get-out as she hugged onto him. Before he left, he handed her a small envelope.

Later, heading back to my house, I asked Jack what it was all about.

"The paper was authorization I got from the state to move two bodies from the potter's field at Rockville and have them buried in Gilberton," Jack said. "You see, when Malloy was killed, Helen couldn't afford to have him brought home, so they buried him in the prison graveyard. I got approval to move him and have him buried next to their son.

"But you said you got the okay to move two bodies," I said.

"Cheesesteak's the other," Jack replied. "Nobody knows where his folks are buried. They couldn't find his sister or any other kin, so he was buried at the prison, too. So I bought plots in the Gilberton cemetery for him and Malloy. I figured those two should rest beside each other. Just seems right.

"You know," Jack added with a laugh, "I'd bet some a' those old miners would be jumpin' from their graves if they knew a Black man was layin' next to them."

"From what you told me about Cheesesteak, bein' Black shouldn't make no difference. That Cheeseteak sounds like he was a good man," I said.

"That he was," Jack replied, nodding.

"You mind me askin' what was in the little envelope you gave Malloy's wife before you left?" I asked.

"A check for three tombstones," Jack replied.

"Three?"

"One for Malloy, one for Cheeseteak, and one the for Malloys' baby boy," Jack explained. "Like I said, it just seems like the right thing to do."

Chapter 20

I didn't hear from Jack in over a month, then one Saturday morning he called. He asked me to go with him to one more meeting. "The last one, I promise," he said.

"Do I haf'ta wear a tie?" I asked.

"No. Just come as you are...but you gotta' have clothes on," he added, laughing. "I'll pick you up on Monday 'bout ten."

*****

Jimmy Creedon and his attorney were sitting at the conference table in Harry's office in the police station. Opposite them were Jack's attorney and the local lawyer who had worked with him on Jack's land deal. Those two just sat back and said nothing, despite Creedon's relentless questioning about why they were there.

The truth is, they didn't know. Chief Myers had just called and asked them to show up. "We need to tie up some loose ends involving Jack Dugan," was all Harry had said.

"Myers! What's this about?" Creedon demanded when Harry entered the room.

The Police Chief took a seat and didn't reply. Since Jimmy Creedon had lost almost everything, the Chief and a lot of other folks didn't fear him like they did before.

"What are you doing here?" Creedon bellowed when Jack and I walked into the room. "I have nothing to say to you!"

Jack didn't respond. He took a seat, and I sat down next to him.

"Mister Creedon has the right to know what this meeting's about," Creedon's attorney insisted.

Harry spoke up. "I asked you here so that we might get answers to some questions Mr. Dugan has. This isn't a trial; we'd just like to get at the truth."

"The truth about what?" Creedon barked.

Harry didn't reply; he just nodded to Jack.

Jack pulled a crinkled sheet of paper from a file folder and laid it on the table.

"The truth about this man," Jack said, pointing to the sheet. "An artist in prison made this sketch. He drew it based on another inmate's description of the man," Jack explained.

"Down here," he continued, pointing to a corner of the page, "is a sketch of a police department ring that the man in the drawing was wearing. My question is: Do you know who this is, Mr. Creedon?"

I glanced at the drawing and couldn't believe my eyes. "Jack," I whispered.

"Not now, Tom," Jack whispered back.

"Mr. Creedon, do you..."Jack began.

"No, I don't know who it is!" Creedon yelled. "Who's it supposed to be?"

"He said his name was Lufkin," Jack replied. "That's how he identified himself when he testified at the trial of an inmate named Malloy. And, by the way, Mr. Creedon, do you remember Malloy?"

"No! I don't know any damned convicts! I don't know anyone named Malloy!" Creedon shouted.

"You might not *want* to remember him," Jack said.

"You're calling me a liar?" Creedon yelled.

"Not a liar. Maybe a 'convenient forgetter'," Jack said, smiling. "Malloy worked for you at your Gilberton mine."

"I don't recall," Creedon hissed.

"Then let me refresh your memory," Jack said. "Malloy was a miner who was trying to bring in the union."

Creedon went 'patoo', pretending to spit on the table.

"Your reaction indeed," Jack continued. "And one night, one of your foremen was found shot dead in an alley. The next day, acting on an anonymous tip, the police found a pistol in Malloy's shed, and he was charged with murder."

"So your convict 'friend' killed my foreman," Creedon chuckled.

"That's what the jury was led to believe by Mr. Lufkin, here," Jack said, tapping the drawing. "When he testified at Malloy's trial, Lufkin identified himself as a Philadelphia police officer, and he said he was passing through Gilberton on the night your foreman was killed. He told the jury that he saw Malloy and your foreman arguing in the alley where your foreman was later found dead."

Creedon laughed. "It sounds pretty cut and dried. Your 'friend' Malloy ended up killing the guy. The cops find his gun. Case closed. Where the hell's this going?"

"It just seems to me," Jack said, "that there are a lot of coincidences in Lufkin's story. He said he was a Philadelphia policeman and just happened to be in Gilberton, which is pretty far off the beaten path. He just happened to witness an argument between your foreman and a miner—one who was trying to unionize your mine. The foreman ends up dead, and the next day the police happen to get a tip and find a gun in Malloy's shed. Like I said, there seems to be a whole lot of things 'just happenin'."

"Now hold on, Dugan!" Creedon's attorney protested. "You said the man in the drawing was wearing a police ring. He saw an altercation in the alley, and he testified about it. What difference does it make why he was in Gilberton? He could have been there for a hundred different reasons. I don't see any great mystery here."

"You know, counselor," Jack replied, "I can understand your position, but I don't accept it."

"Why? Why ignore the obvious facts?" Creedon shouted.

"Because commiting murder is totally out of character for Malloy," Jack replied. "None of you have any idea what Rockville Prison is like. I can tell you it's a hellhole. Guards on the take, powerful inmates with special privileges. Murder, rape, extortion is rampant.

"And in that godforsaken place, Malloy made it his mission to protect other inmates—including me. He eventually was murdered for doing it. Stabbed in the neck with a sharpened spoon.

"So when Malloy told me he didn't have anything to do with the foreman's murder and that he was suspicious about the cop who testified against him, I believed him."

"He was a convicted killer! A criminal, just like you! He conned you!" Creedon roared.

Jack gritted his teeth and shot Creedon a stare like I never saw before. Then he continued.

"I spent countless Sunday afternoons in the Philadelphia Public Library poring over photographs of graduating classes from the city police academy trying to find Lufkin. Trying to find out if he was a cop like he claimed. And in the end, I never did find him, but I did find this," Jack said, pulling a sheet from the folder.

"It's a photo of an academy class. You see the man circled? Third row, fourth from left. His name is Lufkowsky. Notice his resemblance to the man in the drawing. Very close, wouldn't you say?"

"Slight," Creedon mumbled after casting a halfhearted glance at the documents.

Harry and the attorneys stood up and hunched over the table. They looked back and forth at the academy photo and the drawing.

"I'd say there's a big resemblance," Harry said. "They're very close."

"So maybe Lufkowsky shortened his name to Lufkin after he graduated. There's no crime in that, a lot of people do it," Creedon's attorney chuckled, plopping back into his seat. "And if Lufkowsky and

Lufkin are the same man, the academy picture confirms that the guy in your drawing was a Philly cop. So where are we headed now, Mr. Dugan?"

"We're trying to find out two things about about Lufkowsky," Jack replied. "One: did he shorten his name to Lufkin? And, two, did he ever go by a nickname?"

"What are you talking about...a nickname?" Creedon's attorney barked.

Jack pulled out another sheet and laid it down. It was an enlargement of the academy picture—a blow-up of the section where the officers' names were listed. Jack pointed to a name he had underlined as he explained, "Lufkowsky's first name was Joseph. But Malloy said that the man who testified against him was named Robert.

"Just to make sure Malloy wasn't mistaken, I checked the court transcrips of Malloy's trial. Sure enough, the man who testified against him had identified himself as Robert Lufkin. But maybe Robert was a nickname. I needed to check that out.

"A couple'a cops come into my restaurant regularly, and I asked them if they knew Lufkowsky. They didn't, but they put me in touch with a retired cop they thought might help me.

"Turns out the old cop knew Lufkowsky very well. In fact, they were in the academy together. They were both in the Army during the war and went into the academy right after. They graduated the same year—nineteen forty-seven. The guy was certain that Lufkowsky hadn't shortened his name to Lufkin, and he never heard him go by anything but Joseph.

"He told me Lufkowsky was a real fine cop, and even went on to make detective in just two years. He also told me that Lufkowsky was killed in a shootout with a bank robber. I checked it out.

"Here's the writeup that was in the paper," Jack said, pulling a copy of a newspaper clipping from his folder. "Lufkowsky was killed on January the tenth, nineteen-forty-nine. January the tenth of forty-nine—fourteen months *before* Malloy's trial. Joseph Lufkowsky couldn't have testified against Malloy; he was dead."

"So you had nothing!" Creedon laughed. "After all that searching, all you ended up with was that damned convict drawing you started out with. So what if the cop who testified against your 'friend' wasn't Lufkowsky. The bottom line is, the man had a badge, he was a cop, and he swore to what he saw.

"Myers," Creedon barked, turning toward Harry, "I did what you asked me to do. I came in and I listened to Dugan's questions and I looked at his drawing. I don't know who the guy is, and apparently neither does Mr. Dugan. So I say we're done here," he added as he started to rise from his chair.

"And I say 'not quite yet'," Jack replied. "Mr. Creedon, please sit down."

Creedon glared at Jack. "Do I have to put up with more of this crap?" Creedon barked at his attorney.

Before the lawyer could answer, Jack replied. "I think both you *and* your attorney should hear what I have to say."

I thought I saw Creedon's attorney twitch a bit. Creedon sat down and glared. Jack continued.

"About five weeks ago, when I left here to drive back to Philadelphia after the Agnes storm, the trip was a nightmare. Roads and bridges were washed out everywhere, and you couldn't go more than a couple miles without hitting detour after detour.

"Half the time I had no idea where I was headed, and it seemed like I was driving through every little town between here and Philly. Dozens of little places with names like Beaverdale, Quentin, and Tamaqua. Tamaqua. Good old Tamaqua."

"This is ridiculous," Creedon sighed, shaking his head.

"Can you believe it," Jack said, dismissing Creedon's remark. "As soon as I made it to Philly, I was back in the library again.

"I began searching through high school yearbooks from the early nineteen-forties—around the time Joseph Lufkowsky would have graduated from high school before joining the Army. It was quite a job. Did you know there are sixty-two high schools in Philly?"

"Dammit, Dugan, you're a pain!" Creedon shouted.

Jack laughed off the comment.

"It took a couple weeks' of searching, but I finally found this," Jack said, as he pulled another sheet out and laid it down.

"It's a copy of a page from a yearbook from Philly's Northside High School. Joseph Lufkowsky is on the left, and next to him is his twin brother, Richard, nicknamed 'Bo'.

"Imagine that," Jack said, laughing. "Twins. Just like the two jewelry thieves I met in prison. 'Twin Thieves from Tamaqua' the newspaper called them. Funny, isn't it, how you remember things about a place with an unusual name like Tamaqua. When the detour took me through Tamaqua and I saw the sign for the town, I remembered the twins like that," Jack said, snapping his fingers.

Jack took a few seconds to arrange the papers on the table, putting the police academy photo, the yearbook picture, and the pencil sketch side-by-side.

"They all look alike," Jack said. "A bit younger in the high school pictures, of course, but there's no denying that Joseph and Richard Lufkowsky and the man in the sketch are almost identical. So what does it mean?" Jack asked rhetorically. "Here's what I found when I began digging deeper.

"As I mentioned earlier, Joseph became a cop and was killed fourteen months before Malloy's trial, so he's totally out of the equation.

"But knowing now about his twin, I went back to the retired cop who knew Lufkowsky to see if he could tell me anything about his brother Richard, and boy, could he ever. Richard was downright bad, ever since he was a kid. He ended up making collections for loan sharks who preyed on guys working on the Philly docks. You have to be one tough cookie to do that job," Jack laughed. "And I did more research on Richard, checking the police reports that are public record. Like I said, the man was downright bad.

"At the time Joseph was killed, Richard was finishing up a term in the Philadelphia County Prison for almost killing a guy with his bare hands. Lucky for him the guy lived, or it would have been murder. Richard got out of jail a month after his brother was killed in the shootout.

"After that, there were no more police reports about Richard. It was like he fell off the face of the earth, or he changed his ways.

"But here's what I think happened. There were no more police reports about Richard Lufkowsky, because *he* ceased to exist. His brother's death gave him a golden opportunity to disappear. Golden— literally—in the shape of a detective's badge.

"My theory is that Richard Lufkowsky changed his name to Robert Lufkin and moved up in the world of crime. No more doing the dirty work for others. With a new identity, he went on his own and big time. And with his brother's badge and police academy ring, he found a niche, as they say in business.

"When it suited his needs, he could pose as a cop. The ruse gave him the ability to intimidate people and get information. It gave him credibility with inexperienced small town police officers, and his big-city-cop persona enabled him to steer their investigations in the direction he wanted. It would also allow him to come across as a very credible witness. To anyone who didn't know better, he was a bonafide officer of the law. It was a perfect cover for him.

"I strongly suspect that Robert Lufkin was not witness to, but was responsible for the murder of Mr. Creedon's mine foreman, and he framed Malloy for the crime.

"Why?" Jack added quickly. "Because Malloy wanted to unionize your mine, Mr. Creedon."

"You're trying to tie me into your crazy 'theory'?" Creedon bellowed.

"Mr. Creedon," Jack replied, "do you deny your family's hatred of the union—or any group that attempted to better the lives of your miners, going back to the Molly Maguires?"

"They were a bunch of Irish hooligans! My grandfather..." Creedon began.

"They were miners, Mr. Creedon!" Jack shouted. "Men who made your grandfather and your family a fortune! And a lot of them died doing it—including my dad!"

"So that's what this is about!" Creedon shouted. "Revenge for your old man's death. It's not going to work, Dugan. You can't link me to Lufkin!"

"That's not my job," Jack replied. "All I'm doing is laying out the information I found. If the police," nodding to Harry, "want to pursue it further and tell their counterparts in Gilberton that Lufkin wasn't a real cop, that's their decision. Seeing as how Malloy was sent to prison on the testimony of someone who may have been both an impostor and the perpetrator of the crime, I'd think the police would want to get at the truth. And now they have some information to go on.

"And there's still one more thing we need to explore," Jack said as he turned to me.

"Tom, when I brought out the drawing of Lufkin, you reacted to it. Why?" Jack asked.

"'Cause I seen him!" I replied. "He was at your house the day Levansky was attacked."

"What!" Jack and Harry exclaimed together.

"I swear. He said he was a college scout. He said his name was Johnson an' he wanted to talk to you 'bout playin' ball for him."

Jack stared at me, dumbfounded.

"Oh, yes. The mysterious Mr. Johnson," Creedon laughed. "You're pulling out all the stops, aren't you, Dugan? First you try to make me out like a bad guy; now you're trying to clear yourself by having your friend lie for you."

"I ain't lyin'!" I shouted. "It's the truth, Jack. Neither you or your mom was home when Johnson —that Lufkin guy in the drawin'—showed up. He said he'd wait for you, and I left him sittin' on your glider, twirlin' your ball cap 'round on his finger. When I left my house later that night, he was gone."

"The last time you saw him he was holding my ball cap?" Jack said incredulously. "You never said anything about it at my trial!"

"I tried, Jack, honest," I shouted. "I even talked to your lawyer about it. But the attorney workin' against you said it wouldn't do you no good."

"Do you remember his name?" Jack shouted. "What about you?" he asked, turning toward Harry. "Do you remember the prosecutor's name?"

Harry shook his head. "Sorry, I don't. But I'm surprised you don't remember him, Jack."

"Hell, I was eighteen years old and on trial for attempted murder. I was so scared I'm surprised I remembered my own name!" Jack shot back.

"We could look it up in the records," Harry offered.

"No! I want to get to it now! Come on, Tom, think!" Jack yelled.

"Oh, man," I said, shaking my head trying to recall. "Michael. That was his first name. I remember that 'cause he had a little beard, jus' like Mickey Donnley. The guy's name was Michael, Michael, Michael...Vernon!" I shouted as the name finally came to me.

Jack turned toward Savage, who leaned over and whispered back and forth with his attorney friend. Then Savage turned in his seat to face Creedon's lawyer.

"My colleague here tells me that Michael Vernon is now a partner in your firm, counselor. Is that right?" Savage asked.

Creedon's attorney didn't reply.

"Looks like there's a lot of explainin' to do around here," Jack said, smiling.

The room was deadly silent. Then Jack spoke.

"You know, I run a restaurant, not a police force. But if I was a cop, I might have the drawing of Lufkin put in the local paper, asking if folks might have seen him around town the day Levansky was attacked. And I'd probably make a point of showing the drawing to some folks, like Mr. Creedon's former butler. But again, that's not my job.

"I'm not a lawyer either," Jack continued, "but I think if I was, I might want to check into why Mr. Vernon wanted to suppress Mr. Haggerty's testimony about seeing Johnson— Lufkin—on my porch holding my ball cap, which was a very important piece of evidence at my trial. That, and the fact that Vernon is now a partner in the firm that does all your legal work, Mr. Creedon. It's a very interesting relationship, in my opinion. I think the Bar Association might find it worth looking into.

"So, Chief Myers, I'll leave it in your hands. Here," Jack said, sliding the papers across the table to Harry.

"I'm going to leave you folks now. I have a restaurant to run, a park to build, and some rental properties to look after," Jack said.

As he stood to leave, Jack winked at Creedon.

Chapter 21

Harry, Garver and Mains met with the Gilberton Police Chief.

"Call me George," the Gilberton Chief said as they made their introductions.

"Looks like we we got our work cut out for us, George," Harry said as they took chairs around a table. "Here's what we have so far," he said, spreading out the contents of Jack's folder. "Plus these," he said, pulling out a thick file of signed affidavits from a satchel.

"Creedon's former butler was a goldmine of information," Harry began. "He swore that Creedon met with Lufkin at least twice around the time of the Dugan incident. I pity that old butler," Harry added. "After Creedon went bust, he just tossed the guy out like a piece 'a trash after thirty-some years. The old guy was more than happy to tell us all he could about Creedon's shenanigans."

"So Creedon does have a link to Lufkin," George said as he studied the pencil drawing of the man.

"It certainly appears that way," Harry replied. "I wondered how a guy like Creedon could get hooked up with a Philly thug like Lufkin, and I asked the old butler if he had any idea. He told me that Creedon's grandfather had connections with iron and railroad barons in Philly in the old days and that Jimmy maintained contact with their kids and grandkids. My guess is that they helped him find Lufkin. The rich helpin' the rich stay rich."

Everyone around the table laughed.

"That was pretty gutsy of Lufkin to go around posing as a cop," George said. "He certainly had everyone around here convinced he was legitimate."

"He did the same thing in Creedonton," Harry laughed. "After we put the pencil sketch of Lufkin in the paper and asked folks to tell us if they ever saw him, more'n a half dozen came in.

"A couple of them said he was flashin' a gold badge, makin' like he was a cop—just like he did at Malloy's trial," Harry said. "He even had Dewey—one of my own guys—believin' he was on the force in Philly."

"That was a real good idea puttin' the drawin' in the paper," George said. "Real smart. You nailed down that Lufkin was in your town that day. It also backs up what the butler said and eliminates any notion about sour grapes on his part, seein' as how Creedon kicked him out like a mangy old dog."

"And folks seeing him in town gives credence to Dugan's neighbor's claim that he saw Lufkin at Dugan's house, posing as a college scout," Harry added.

"It's a real shame Malloy isn't around to see how this thing turns out," George said.

"Yeah, I know what you mean; it's a damn shame. But according to Jack Dugan, Malloy's wife will be one happy woman if we can clear her husband's name," Harry replied.

"What do you think our chances are of finding Lufkin?" George asked. "He's the key to both cases."

"Our chances might be slim, but heck, who even thought we'd be sittin' at this table even talking about it?" Harry replied. "All we can do is try. I got us a meeting on Thursday with a detective in Philly—a legitimate one," Harry added, laughing.

"We lay out what we know and take it from there. If nothing else, I know a great restaurant that will make the trip well worthwhile—a place called Angelo's. So, George, did you dig out the Malloy file?"

"Sure did," the Gilberton Chief said, hoisting a file from the table.

"Then let's get on with it. We got a lot to do to try and clear up this mess," Harry said.

"These messes," George countered, laughing.

Chapter 22

I went to the corner store early one morning to get some smokes. When I asked for them, I swear people were lookin' at me like I was some kinda' drug addict. At the counter, I heard folks mummerin' something about Jimmy Creedon.

"What about Creedon?" I asked, turning to the woman behind me.

"He killed hisself last night," she replied.

*****

There was a lotta' speculation 'round town 'bout what caused Creedon to do it. Some say the police were gettin' close to finding the truth about what he did to Jack and Malloy. Others say Jimmy Creedon just couldn't stand the thought a' bein' poor.